# A
# Cold Case
of
# Killing

Also by Glenn Ickler:

*A Carnival of Killing*

*Murder on the St. Croix*

*A Killing Fair*

*Fishing for a Killer*

# A Cold Case of Killing

Glenn Ickler

NORTH STAR PRESS OF ST. CLOUD, INC.
St. Cloud, Minnesota

ISBN: 978-1-68201-033-4

First edition: May 2016

Printed in the United States of America.

Published by
North Star Press of St. Cloud, Inc.
P.O. Box 451
St. Cloud, MN 56302

www.northstarpress.com

*To my four sons:*
*Warren, Mitchell, Alan, and Jeffrey*

# Chapter One

## Blockade

TWO YELLOW SAWHORSES supporting a weathered wooden sign that said ROAD CLOSED – POLICE in black stenciled letters stood across the middle of the street, stopping us half a block from our destination. Looking down the block beyond the barrier, we could see so many flashing blue and red lights that it looked like Christmas in July.

Al parked the blue Ford Focus with the *St. Paul Daily Dispatch* logo at the curb, with the bumper almost touching the end of the sawhorse on the right. We got out and started walking toward the flashing lights, Al with his camera slung over his shoulder and me with my reporter's notebook in my left hand.

Al is Alan Jeffrey, the *Daily Dispatch*'s best photographer. I am Warren Mitchell, better known as Mitch, and I think of myself as the paper's best investigative reporter, whether anyone else does or not. We had been sent to East Geranium Street on St. Paul's East Side by our city editor, Don O'Rourke, when a subscriber called to report a flurry of police activity at the house next door to hers.

"The place is swarming with cops," the caller had said. We found her description to be accurate when we reached the scene and encountered more yellow, this time in the form of a ribbon of plastic tape encircling the property line of a modest two-story frame house. On the street, I counted six marked squad cars and two unmarked black sedans, all with lights flashing. I expected to see an ambulance, but instead I saw a hearse parked on the opposite side of the street. Okay, that meant they expected to be bringing out a body, not a patient.

I was pleased to see that no television crews or other reporters were on the scene as yet. It's always an advantage to be first. As we approached, a uniformed officer who looked like he spent all his breaks in a doughnut shop moved toward the yellow tape and held up his right hand like a stop sign. "You don't come no further," he said as we arrived at the tape.

"What's going on, officer?" I asked as Al raised his camera and began shooting photos of the vehicles and the house.

"I ain't authorized to say nothin' to the press," the officer said. "You'll have to wait 'til one of the detectives comes out to ask any questions." Behind him, two uniformed officers came out the front door. Each carried a large cardboard box.

"Who all is in there? Can you ask one of them to come out?"

"I ain't authorized to say who's in there and my job is to stay out here and make sure nobody crashes the tape." The two uniforms loaded their boxes into the trunk of the nearest squad car.

"I know most of the detectives. Couldn't you just duck in for a minute and tell somebody that Mitch from the *Daily Dispatch* is here?" The two uniforms returned to the house.

"My job is to stay right here," the cop said. "You're just gonna have to wait 'til one of those detectives that you say you know comes out on his own." He backed away from the tape and took a more relaxed position with his back against the trunk of a large oak tree at the front corner of the lawn.

As I watched the door for a familiar face, I heard the roar of an engine behind the house. Al heard it, too, and we both started walking just outside the tape line toward the backyard.

"Funny time to be mowing the lawn," Al said.

"I'm betting it's an excavation, not a clip job," I said.

"I dig that."

The cop stepped away from the tree. "Hey!" he yelled. "You guys are trespassin' on that neighbor's lawn. Get outta there."

"We're outside the tape," Al said. "We'll get off the grass if the neighbor complains." The dividing line between the two lots was a four-foot-high white picket fence on which the yellow tape was strung. On our side was grass; the other side was lined with a multi-colored patchwork of flowering plants.

The cop's face turned as red as some of the blossoms in the flowerbed as he walked toward us with his hand on the butt of his nightstick. By the time he caught up to us, we had gone far enough to see a small backhoe lower its scoop into a rose garden that stretched across the entire width of the backyard about thirty feet from the house. The chrome yellow of the backhoe stood out in stark contrast to the red, white, pink, and salmon-colored blossoms covering the plants about to be torn out by the roots. Two men wearing hardhats and holding shovels were watching the backhoe, along with two more uniformed policemen.

Al shot a series of photos as the backhoe driver raised the scoop, ripping up a cluster of rose bushes, and backed away, leaving a shallow furrow about three feet deep. The machine sat with the engine idling while the men with shovels moved in and began probing the scraped area.

"Are they digging up a body?" I asked our red-faced pursuer.

"I ain't authorized to tell you nothin'," he said. "Now get offa that guy's lawn."

"It's all right, officer," said a female voice behind us. "I'm the one that called the press to come here."

I turned and saw a woman wearing a blue St. Paul Saints T-shirt and baggy knee-length red shorts walking toward us. She looked to be in her fifties, with curly salt-and-pepper hair and a few extra pounds on her breasts and belly. Although it was mid-July, her skin was mid-March white. If she was truly a Saints fan, she apparently only attended night games.

"Hi, I'm Donna," she said, grabbing my right hand and shaking it until I thought it would rattle. "Donna Waldner. I called your Tipster Line." The *Daily Dispatch* rewards Tipster Line callers whose tips turn into stories with fifty-dollar checks.

"Thanks for calling," I said. "I'm Mitch and this is Al."

"Nice to meet you," Donna said. She reached for Al's hand but it was holding a camera so she settled for a pat on his wrist.

"Do you know what's going on here?" I asked Donna.

"Not a clue. Just all of a sudden a whole bunch of cop cars show up and some of them go into the house and the others go out to the backyard. And then a truck with a Bobcat pulls in and the Bobcat goes back and starts diggin' up the Andersons' beautiful rose garden. It's a shame what they're doin'."

We had walked past a flatbed trailer hitched to a parked pickup truck on our way in, but I hadn't connected it to the police action.

"You said 'Andersons' house.' Is that the name of people who live here?"

"Yah," Donna said. "Jack and Jill, would you believe. Nice people. You'd never expect the cops to be tearin' up their place like this."

"You've known them a long time?" I asked.

"Yah. We've lived here ten years now and Andersons were here when we moved in. Jill brought over a hot dish the first night we slept here. I think they've been livin' in that house for a real long time."

"They're an older couple?"

"Yah, they're somewhere in their sixties. Jack just retired this spring, so he's got to be at least sixty-five."

"And you say they've been good neighbors?"

"Oh, yah, very good. Nice and quiet. They pretty much keep to themselves but they're friendly enough when you see them. Jill spends most of her summer workin' on all those gardens." She pointed toward the Andersons' backyard, where several smaller patches of flowers augmented the space where the

Bobcat was churning up buckets of soil and rosebushes. I couldn't help wondering what their water bill must be.

"Do you socialize with them at all? Cookouts or card games or anything like that?"

"No, not really," Donna said. "They don't seem to be into that kind of thing. I mean, we said they should come over for dinner some time when she brought the hot dish, and she said okay, but when we'd try to set a time they could never make it. They never seemed to go anywhere else, either, so after a while we kind of got the message. Like I said, she spends all her time putterin' in her gardens, which is a lot more ambition than I've got. I don't know what Jack does with himself now that he's retired."

"What kind of work did Jack do?" I asked.

"He worked at the Mall of America out in Bloomington but I don't really know what he did there. Fred might know. I could ask him when he comes home and call you."

"Fred is your husband?"

"Yah. He works at the 3M office on the Hudson Road. Security guard."

I handed her my card. "Okay, you ask Fred and give me a call. If I'm not there, you can leave a message."

Donna took the card, pulled down the neckline of her T-shirt, and tucked the card into the top of her bra. "Anything else I can tell you?" she asked.

"Do the Andersons have any children?"

"Not that I've ever seen visit them or heard them talk about."

"I guess that's it, then, unless you have some idea of what the cops are looking for," I said.

"Like I said, not a clue. This is the last place in the world I expected to see this kind of thing goin' on."

"Thanks for your help," I said. "And I'll see that you get your fifty dollars."

"Yah, that would be nice," Donna said. "Nice talkin' to you guys. Hope you find out what the heck this mess is all about." She turned, walked to her house, and went in the back door.

While we'd been talking to Donna, our red-faced police shadow had returned to the shade of the oak tree. We watched the backhoe rip out another bucketful of roses, then walked back to the street to wait for somebody in plain clothes to come out of the house.

"Oh, look at that," Al said. "We've got company."

# Chapter Two

## Growing Interest

O H, DAMN," I SAID. Our company was a crew from Channel Four, led by flaxen-haired Trish Valentine, the possessor of the finest set of boobs on Twin Cities television. She was in mid-July form, wearing a pale blue scoop-neck blouse with the top three buttons open to display an evenly-tanned expanse of cleavage.

"Hi, guys. What's going on?" Trish asked.

"Don't know," I said. I pointed to the cop leaning against the tree. "The guardian of the perimeter says he's not authorized to tell 'nobody nothin'.' What brings you here?"

"A woman called the station and said the place next door to her was swarming with cops. What's that noise behind the house?"

Damn that Donna. Why couldn't she have been satisfied with calling just the *Daily Dispatch*? "It's a Bobcat," I said. "They've started fall plowing in the family's flower garden a few months early."

"Whoa," Trish said. "We've got to get a shot of that. Come on, Tony." She beckoned to her camera man and trotted toward the backyard with Tony at her four-inch heels. The cop took two steps away from the supporting tree and started to raise his hand, then did a "what-the-hell" shrug and went back to leaning against the trunk, all the while keeping his eyes focused on Trish's blouse.

I hauled out my cell phone and punched in Don O'Rourke's number. I told him what little I knew and mentioned that Trish Valentine was on the scene.

"We need to get something into the online edition," Don said. "I'm going to switch you to Corinne Ramey. You can give her your notes and she can whip up a quick bulletin."

Don made the transfer and Corinne, a young reporter whose desk was next to mine, said she was ready to copy. *To hell with notes,* I thought, and I gave her a five-graf story, complete with commas and periods, describing the scene and quoting Donna Waldner.

"Good job," Corinne said when I'd finished.

I gritted my teeth and swallowed a nasty response. "Good job" is one of my most hated clichés. First of all, it's been run into the ground by overuse. Second, it's grammatically incorrect. I have a good job. I keep my good job by doing good work.

"Thanks," I said after a brief pause.

"No problem," Corinne said. Aargh! Another of my pet peeves. What ever happened to good old "you're welcome"? I broke the connection without another word.

"Looks like moving day at the Andersons' house," Al said as two more large cardboard boxes were carried out and deposited in the squad car's trunk.

"Our tax dollars at work," I said.

"I wonder what's in those boxes."

"Too bad you don't have a camera with X-ray vision."

"I'm saving that for Trish," he said.

Speak of the devil and she returned, with Tony, who stood at least a foot taller than Trish even in her four-inch heels, following in lockstep.

"They're really ripping the crap out of that flowerbed," Trish said. "I broke into whatever network drivel we're showing at this hour and reported breaking news live with the Bobcat yanking up rosebushes behind me. The garden clubbers are already tweeting about what a terrible thing the police are doing to that flowerbed. Do you know whose body they're looking for?"

"I don't even have confirmation that it is a body that they're looking for," I said. "Granted, all the visual evidence points that way."

"Do you know the name of the people who live in the house? Are they home?"

"The cops haven't identified the homeowners and I haven't seen anybody who looks like a resident," I said, dodging the name question without telling a lie. I've learned this technique by covering politicians' press conferences.

"God, I'd like to know what's going on," Trish said. "I'll bet that cop couldn't stop us if all four of us crashed the tape at once."

"He has a lot of backup," Al said, waving toward the convoy of squad cars in the street. "I'm not interested in getting clubbed or handcuffed."

"Why not wait it out?" I said. "We've got no competition and it's still early." It was, in fact, only a few minutes past nine on a Monday morning.

My cell phone played the opening bars of "The William Tell Overture." It was Don O'Rourke wondering if I had anything new.

"Only thing new is Trish Valentine reporting live," I said. She was, in fact, moving into position to do a live shot in front of the house. Don told me to stay on the scene and report any new developments immediately. Our conversation ended in time for me to hear the sign-off: "Trish Valentine, reporting live."

"Always better than reporting dead," Al muttered. "I assume Don wants us to stick to this story."

"Like bubblegum to the bottom of your shoe," I said.

"So this is our sole assignment?"

Before I could answer, a male voice in the street behind me shouted, "Hey, guys, what's happening?" I turned to see Barry Ziebart of Channel Five and his cameraman hustling toward us. If this trend continued, we'd soon have as many reporters and photographers as police officers on the scene.

The cop under the tree walked toward us, pointing to the yellow tape. Barry stopped and we went through the ritual of telling him that none of us knew anything other than what our eyes were seeing. Barry and his cameraman went to the backyard to get the obligatory live shot of the Bobcat at work, and the rest of us watched more cops carry more boxes out of the house and put them into squad car trunks. When the Channel Five duo returned, the beginning of a path was visible in the grass on Donna Waldner's side of the fence. A few more trips by media observers and Donna would have to invest some of her fifty Tipster Line bucks in grass seed.

"I'd give my right boob to know what's in those boxes," Trish said.

"You'd fall over onto your left side and wouldn't be able to get up," Al said. Tony laughed so hard at this that Trish finally stopped him with a look that would have frozen hot coffee on the Fourth of July.

I used the waiting time to study the house. It was a run-of-the-mill two-story wooden structure, probably built in the pre-Depression nineteen-hundreds like everything else on the block. A shallow screen porch ran halfway across the front and a bay window with a lamp in the center took up most of the other half. The white clapboards should have been repainted a couple of years earlier, the green trim around the windows was chipped and peeling, and the red brick chimney looked like it could use some tuck pointing. Whatever Jack's vocation was, his hobby was not home maintenance.

It was almost ten thirty when a man in plain clothes stepped out the front door and looked around. "Jeez, the whole damn press corps is here," he said.

"Not quite all of it, just the elite part," I said. "Tell us what's going on."

"Give us a sound bite," yelled Barry.

"I can put you on live," Trish shouted.

"I'm not authorized," the officer said. "I'll see if my boss will come out." He zipped back into the house.

Another five minutes passed. Another uniformed officer emerged with still another box and carried it to yet another squad car. As he returned to the front door, the uniform stepped aside to let a man in a dark gray, pin-striped suit come out. Could this be the boss?

"My God, it's Brownie," Al said. "This is a big deal."

Indeed, it was Detective Lieutenant Curtis Brown, the head of the Homicide Division, otherwise known (but not to his face) as Brownie. He stopped on the middle of the three front steps and looked us over. We all started shouting questions and Brownie walked to the tape with his hands high above his head as a signal to shut up.

When silence was achieved, Brownie said, "Good morning, everybody. What brings you out on this hot July day?"

"That's what we want to know," Barry said.

"I can put you on live right now," Trish said.

"What are you looking for?" I asked.

"We're looking for evidence," Brownie said. "But you'll be disappointed to learn that there's no blood. It's a cold case."

"How cold?" Trish asked.

"Twenty-five years. You were probably in diapers when the victim disappeared."

"Ooh, thanks for the compliment," Trish said. I was guessing that she'd have been starting junior high.

"Who was the victim?" I asked.

"The daughter of the couple that lives here," Brownie said. "She was fifteen years old when she vanished. It was a Saturday morning. The parents gave her some money and sent her to the little convenience store on the corner three blocks away for a loaf of bread, and nobody has seen her since. Her parents said she never came home and the clerk at the store said she never came in."

"Are you here because you've got some fresh information?" Barry asked.

"We have, and we're looking for more," Brownie said. "As I said, the case is twenty-five years old but we've never closed it."

Trish moved up to the tape so she was face-to-face with Brownie across the tape and asked, "What are the parents' names?" She stuck her microphone in Brownie's face as he answered.

"Anderson," he said. "Jack and Jill Anderson, would you believe?"

Seizing the moment, Barry Ziebart jumped to the other side of Brownie as Trish was asking, "And what is the victim's name?" Barry's microphone joined Trish's in front of the detective's face.

"Marilee," Brownie said. "Marilee Anderson."

"Do you think she's buried in the backyard?" Trish asked.

"I can't comment on that," Brownie said. "All I can say is that we're trying to cover every possible angle. We'll be here for as long as it takes to go through everything in the house and the yard."

"Do you think her parents killed her?" Trish asked.

"I can't comment on that at this time," Brownie said.

"Thank you, Detective Brown. Trish Valentine, reporting live from St. Paul's East Side." Trish moved away and Barry Ziebart asked a couple of questions that brought non-committal replies before he, too, signed off with, "Barry Ziebart, reporting live."

Brownie backed away a couple of steps and said, "Okay, that's it; no more questions—live, dead, or wounded. Looks like we're going to be working here all day, and you're free to stand outside the tape and watch but I doubt that you'll see much. I'll be giving a general briefing on the case at sixteen-hundred at the station. See you there."

"Just one more quick question," I said. "Are the Andersons in the house while all this is going on?"

"They're not," he said. "At our request, they're staying with some relatives."

"Who? Where?" we all asked in unison.

"I'll tell you that at the briefing if they say they're willing to talk to the press. If not, you'll have to wait until they come back home to try to get an interview."

"Thanks," I said. "Call me if the Bobcat uncovers anything but grub worms." Brownie waved and went back into the house.

"I've had about enough of standing out here in this heat," Al said.

"How hot is it?" Trish asked.

"It's so hot my anti-perspirant stick is sweating," Al said.

"Mine, too," I said. "Let's see if our boss will let us go back to our air-conditioned office." I called Don O'Rourke and told him the police were working on a cold case and that there would be nothing more to report until Brownie's four o'clock briefing at the station. "It involves a fifteen-year-old girl who disappeared twenty-five years ago," I said.

"Oh, my God," Don said. "Marilee Anderson."

"You remember it?"

"Don't you?"

"Twenty-five years ago I was seventeen, living on a farm in southeastern Minnesota and not giving a damn about missing teeny-boppers in St. Paul," I said.

"Well, it was a very big story. And I was working the week-end police beat when it broke on a Saturday. Come on in and go through the clips in the library. You can do a background piece while you wait for your four o'clock briefing. God, I can't believe it. After all these years. Marilee Anderson."

"What did Don say?" Al asked when I put away my phone.

"He said I'm going to be very busy for the next few days."

"What about me?"

"Every good story needs good pix to back it up."

As we neared our car, we met a reporter and photographer from the Minneapolis paper trotting toward the Andersons' house. Both were sweating from the effort. "What did we miss?" the reporter asked.

"Everything," I said. "Briefing downtown at the PD at four."

"Just in time for the five o'clock TV news," he said.

"Don't think I haven't thought about that," I replied. My only hope was to combat immediacy with comprehensive reporting.

# Chapter Three

## Background Check

B ACK AT THE *DAILY DISPATCH*, I immediately went to the paper's library—for some reason they don't call it the "morgue" anymore—looking for twenty-five-year-old stories about Marilee Anderson's disappearance. I was rewarded with a deluge.

The first story was from the Sunday morning edition, under Don O'Rourke's byline. Marilee Anderson, fifteen, had been reported missing by her parents, Jack and Jill Anderson, at about eleven thirty Saturday morning. They had told police that they'd sent Marilee to the corner store to buy a loaf of bread at about nine o'clock, and when she hadn't returned within an hour, Jack went looking for her. James Bjornquist, the nineteen-year-old clerk who'd been on duty at the store that morning, had told Jack that the girl had never appeared in the store.

Jack told police that he'd spent the next hour walking all around the neighborhood looking for Marilee and calling her name. He'd stopped at a couple of houses with young people her age and zigzagged through a small park where she sometimes went to "be by herself." Finally, fearing that Marilee had been kidnapped, he'd gone home and called police.

This was before the era of ubiquitous surveillance cameras, so there was no photographic record of activity nearby or inside the store. Police searched the area and put out an APB. They questioned the parents and learned that Marilee, their only child, was moody and sometimes rebellious, but otherwise a normal teenage girl. Nearby neighbors told police they'd occasionally heard loud voices, including Marilee's, quarreling at the Andersons' house.

The parents went on TV and made the usual tearful pleas: "Marilee please come home if you're free"; "kidnapper, if you have our daughter, please release her or contact us."

After three days of no response, police stopped searching for a missing person and began looking for a body. The case officially became a suspected homicide and a young detective named Curtis Brown was assigned to the investigation. There was a photo of Brownie, proving that he'd once had hair on his head. However, even a full head of hair could not hide his ears, which stuck out like the side mirrors on an eighteen-wheeler, just as they do to this day.

Staff writer Don O'Rourke had interviewed many of the potential murder suspects. Chief among them were the young store clerk, James Bjornquist, who'd been alone behind the counter; Marilee's Uncle Eddie, Jack Anderson's brother, who lived next door in the house now occupied by Fred and Donna Waldner; Patrick O'Brian, described by Don as looking dark and malevolent, who lived two houses east of the Andersons; and, of course, Jack and Jill Anderson.

Young Bjornquist had sworn he'd never seen Marilee in the store that morning. In addition, several people who had shopped there that morning had told police that they had seen no one matching Marilee's description.

Uncle Eddie, who lived alone, had been extremely upset by what he viewed as an accusation and claimed to have slept in late that day. The only co-occupant of Uncle Eddie's house who could provide an alibi was his poodle, Bruno, but police eventually stopped questioning him for lack of evidence.

All O'Brian would say to Don was that he was not at home the morning of Marilee's disappearance and knew nothing about her except that she acted like "a snotty little brat" whenever they met on the street. Don's description of O'Brian as dark and malevolent-looking intrigued me, so I cross-referenced him on the computer. I found stories about him being arrested, charged, tried, and convicted of raping and strangling a fourteen-year-old girl three years after Marilee vanished. I made a note to check if he was still serving his life sentence in the federal prison at Sandstone in northern Minnesota.

Jack and Jill Anderson had expressed their deepest affection for their daughter and had no objections to a thorough search of the house and grounds. I noticed in the accompanying photos that there had been no flower gardens in the backyard at that time. The search had produced no evidence of any extraordinary activity either inside or outside the Anderson residence.

The most interesting non-suspect questioned by Detective Brown and reporter Don O'Rourke was Eleanor Miller, a sixty-six-year-old widow who lived next door. She had a lot to say about the Andersons, none of which was complimentary. She described Jack and Jill as loud, controlling parents and Marilee as a rebellious brat—there was that word again—whose main line of defense was high-volume screaming fits that sent shivers up Mrs. Miller's spine. "Her voice was like broken glass on a blackboard," she said to Don.

Now this was a person I wanted to talk to. I wondered if she was still in the neighborhood. Possibly she'd be living (if she was still living) in some sort of senior facility, because she'd be ninety-one now. I'd have to try to track her down.

By the time Al and I left for Brownie's four o'clock follies I had put together a cogent, compassionate, and comprehensive background story on the Marilee Anderson case. I'd included a description of the girl—basically five-foot-two, eyes of blue, with blonde hair in a ponytail—and her clothing when last seen—cut-off jeans, a pink Michael Jackson T-shirt, and pink sneakers with white soles. All I needed now were some words of wisdom from Brownie to put in the lead.

Al gave Don an especially sorrowful picture of a rosebush covered with red blossoms as big as a grapefruit dangling from the jaw of the Bobcat's bucket to accompany my story about Marilee's mysterious demise. We'd have every apprehensive parent and anthomanic gardener in the city sobbing in the morning.

I was just about to leave when my desk phone rang. "This is Donna Waldner," said the caller. "You wanted me to call you if my husband Fred knew what Jack Anderson did before he retired."

"Oh, yes," I said. "Thanks for the call."

"Will this get me another fifty bucks?"

"I'll see what I can do," I said, knowing the answer would be no. "What kind of work did Jack do?"

"He was a butcher in one of the Mall of America restaurants," she said. "You know, cutting up the steaks and stuff like that with big sharp knives."

* * *

I HAD AN IMAGE of big sharp knives in mind when Detective Lieutenant Curtis Brown stepped out of his office to greet the assembled reporters and photographers at the St. Paul Police Department. I pictured them in the hands of Jack Anderson, whose twenty-five-years-ago photos I'd seen while rummaging through the old stories. He was a wiry, athletic-looking man when those pictures were taken.

Brownie skimmed through some of the background on Marilee Anderson's disappearance that I had put into my story, but I was pleased at his omission of the names of the potential suspects who'd been interviewed. Let the others—and every news outlet in the Twin Cities was represented at the briefing—conduct their own research.

"Even though the Marilee Anderson missing person case is twenty-five years old, we have never closed it," Brownie said.

"We've had many tips over the years but none of them has produced either a dead body or a live missing person. This week's activity is in response to a tip from someone claiming to know that something, not necessarily Marilee's body, was hidden in one of the gardens that the Andersons began creating in the months following her disappearance.

"All of the gardens some of you saw today have been dug and planted since Marilee vanished. There was nothing but grass and a couple of shrubs in the backyard at the time of her disappearance. We are also sifting through several cartons of material removed from the house. This intensive investigation will continue until everything has been examined carefully. Unless, of course, we get quick results. Now I'll take any questions you might have."

Trish Valentine was in the front row, as she always is, and Brownie looked at her first, as male officials always do.

"Where are the Andersons?" Trish asked.

"They'd rather not talk to the media until they get back home," Brownie said. "So I can't tell you where they are."

"When will they get home?" I asked.

"Not sure. Maybe Wednesday."

"Will you notify the press?" asked the guy from Minneapolis.

"No, you're on your own on that," Brownie said. "We're not going to set off a mad rush to the house by issuing an APB."

"Can we stake out the house?" Barry Ziebart asked.

"As long as you stay outside the tape and don't pester the troops. If you start sticking microphones into people's faces—either ours or the neighbors'—we'll most likely ask you to leave. And if you happen to be there when the Andersons are brought back, they will be escorted past you and into the house by armed police officers."

"Can you describe what Marilee Anderson looked like?" Trish asked.

"She was fifteen years old, and, according to the medical chart from her school physical examination, she was five-foot-two and weighed a hundred and eighteen pounds. Her hair was blonde, usually done up in a ponytail, and her eyes were blue, and she had a mild case of acne, according to her mother."

"Was she . . . uh . . . physically developed?" Barry Ziebart asked. This brought snickers from some of the men in the crowd.

"If you're talking about breast development, the answer is very little," Brownie said. "From the photos we were shown, she was still pretty much a child, body-wise."

"Do you have those photos?" somebody behind me asked.

"All photos have been returned to the family," Brownie said. "You'll have to ask the parents if you want to see or reproduce them."

"That's what we need, an original photo," Al said in my ear. "The ones printed in the old papers aren't worth a damn."

I nodded. "How are we going to get one?"

"You're the investigative reporter. You figure it out."

After a couple of more questions, the session was over. When we were outside, walking back toward the office, I said, "We need to find out where her parents are and ask them to get us a photo we can use."

"Good luck with that," Al said. "You got any idea what hill Jack and Jill might have gone up?"

"Maybe we can find the source of their water."

"I pail at the thought of it."

"Jack had a brother named Eddie living practically next door, remember? What if Eddie is still somewhere close by?"

"It's possible. So how do we find out?"

"The same way we find out everything in the twenty-first century," I said. "Google it."

Damned if a Google search didn't turn up three Edward Andersons living within the St. Paul city limits and six more within a twenty-five-mile radius.

"We have a surplus of riches," I said.

"Who wants Riches?" Al said. "Aren't we looking for Eddies?"

Two of the Edward Andersons were close to Jack Anderson in age; one was sixty-three and the other sixty-eight. The younger Edward lived in St. Paul; the older one resided in the adjacent northern suburb of Roseville.

I looked up the phone numbers and tried the St. Paul resident first. A woman answered and I asked if Jack Anderson was there. "You've got the wrong number," she said. "This is the Edward Anderson residence."

"Does he have a brother named Jack?"

"He's got a sister named Jackie. Is that who you're looking for?"

"No," I said. "You're right; I've got the wrong number."

Next I called the Roseville number and a man answered. Again I asked, "Is Jack Anderson there?"

There was a moment of silence. Then the man said, "He's . . . uh . . . no, he ain't here. I mean, he don't live here." The receiver went down hard in my ear.

I smiled at Al and said, "Bingo. We get a car and go to Roseville as soon as I finish writing my story."

# Chapter Four

## Up the Hill

APPROPRIATELY ENOUGH, we had to drive up a short, steep hill to reach the address we'd found for Jack and Jill's hideaway. It was on a tree-lined side street off a heavily-traveled Ramsey County road. The neighborhood was made up mostly of cookie-cutter homes built during the post-World War II housing development boom.

The address we sought was a white, one-story rambler with a large picture window displaying the obligatory table lamp, right out of the cookie cutter. Three steps led up to a small concrete deck that held a trash barrel, a recycling bin, a bamboo fishing pole, and a round plastic container that I assumed contained dog food. There was a narrow pathway in between these items to allow access to the front door.

We went up the steps, and I opened the screen door and rang the bell. A dog started barking inside and a man's voice yelled, "Shut up, Boris." Apparently Boris was the latest successor to Bruno, who would have been 175 dog years older by this time.

A minute after Boris shut up, the inner door opened a crack and a man with stringy white hair and a white beard at the end of his long, narrow face peered out. The angular nose bore the tiny red lines that appear when a person consumes too much alcohol over too long a period of time. "Yeah?" the man said.

Without moving my upper body, I slid my left toe into the opening and introduced myself and Al. "We'd like to speak to your brother and his wife for a moment," I said. "We promise not to stay long; we just have a quick request."

Glenn Ickler

"Who do you think I am?" the man asked.

"Jack Anderson's brother Eddie," I said.

"What if I told you I ain't no Jack Anderson's brother?"

"I'd still think you were."

"So you're callin' me a liar?"

"I'm calling you a good protective brother who's doing his family duty. But as I said, we just have one quick request that won't take more than a couple of minutes. Just ask Jack and Jill if they'll give us that much time."

"Tell me what your 'one quick request' is and I'll run it by them."

"Fair enough," I said. I told him about our desire for a photo of Marilee, then asked, "Can we wait inside?"

He thought about this quick request for a moment. "Oh, I suppose that won't hurt." He opened the door and we stepped into a small living room that was dominated by a huge flat screen television set. The rest of the furnishings—a sofa, two armchairs, and a coffee table buried in newspapers and dirty coffee cups—had an aura of gray about them. "Nondescript" would be a kind way to describe the entire collection.

A medium-size black poodle with some gray around his muzzle bounded toward me and put his front paws up on my knees. "Get down, Boris," Eddie said. Boris tried to climb higher, sniffing my clothing every place his nose could reach. "He won't hurt you. Might lick you to death."

"He's okay," I said. "He probably smells my cat."

"He likes cats. Plays with the one next door. Folks are out back on the deck. You wait right there."

We didn't have to wait long. A gray-haired woman so thin that my fingertips would have met if I'd put my hands around her waist hobbled in with the aid of a cane. "I'm Jill Anderson," she said in a monotone. "What is this quick request you want?"

23

"We're very sorry about your daughter," I said. "We'd like to borrow a picture of her to use in the paper, if you have one with you. We'll take very good care of it and bring it right back."

"Something taken as close to the time she disappeared as possible," Al said.

"All I got in my purse is her seventh-grade school picture," Jill said. "It's kind of beat up and it isn't very big."

"We can use that," Al said. "We can even make you a bigger and better copy."

She sighed. "That would be nice. My purse is in the bedroom. Be right back." She walked slowly down a hall to our right and returned bearing a wallet-sized photo with the ragged edges and faded colors that come from being carried in a woman's purse for twenty-five years.

The photo showed the unsmiling face of a young girl with Nordic features and intensely blue eyes. I got the feeling that those eyes would be the first thing one would notice upon meeting her, even if she were, as Bart Ziebart had so delicately put it, physically developed.

Al took the photo and held it carefully by the yellowed border. I thanked Jill and said we'd return it the next day. I added that we'd like to talk to both her and Jack about the police activity currently going on at their home as soon as possible.

"I'm glad the cops are doing something after all these years," she said. "I'll talk to you when you bring the picture back. I don't know about Jack."

"Will you still be staying here with Eddie tomorrow?"

"Looks like it. That bald detective with the big ears said he'd send a car for us when they were done going through the house."

"You mean Detective Brown?" Al asked with a grin.

"Yah, I guess he did say that his name was Brown. Anyhow, he seemed to be the big honcho."

"He's a very big honcho," I said. "And if anybody can find out what happened to your daughter, it's him."

24

"It's time it all came out," Jill said. She turned away and walked slowly back toward the deck.

"What do you suppose she meant by that?" Al said.

"I don't think she was talking about spilling a pail of water," I said.

Al went to work on the photo as soon as we got back to the *Daily Dispatch*. He photographed Marilee's picture with a close-up lens on his camera so that he had a digital image to work with. Some electronic touching-up and enlarging time later he had a clean, crisp image and made several eight-by-ten prints.

"Marilee's mama should like this," he said, holding up one of the eight-by-tens.

"Wow, those eyes just burn into you," I said as I looked at the print.

"Bore a hole right through you," Al said.

"I feel like I've seen those eyes, but I can't imagine where it would have been."

"I don't think you'd forget them."

"Yeah, probably my imagination. What's that little smudge on her right cheek?"

"It's a mole or a birthmark, I think. It doesn't show up that much on the little original."

"I wonder what she'd look like now if she was alive," I said.

"I'm going to find that out," Al said. "I know a guy in my photography club who's a whiz at aging people's images. He can take an image of a ten-year-old and show you how he'll look at fifty a couple different ways—fat or skinny. I'll send him a digital copy of Marilee and ask him to work on aging her face by twenty-five years."

"That's a great talent."

"It's a great *lucrative* talent. Cops, private detectives, and families looking for lost relatives are willing to pay for that talent. Our police department's missing persons division has used him several times."

"Maybe they will again, on this case."

"Maybe. But we'll be a few days ahead of them."

"Meanwhile, Don has the teenage image of Marilee to run with my story. That's something that Trish Valentine won't have to show her audience while she's standing out in the street reporting live."

"Right. Well, my day is over. See you later." Al gave a little wave and headed for the elevator.

My day was over, too. I straightened up enough of the jumble of newspapers, magazines, notes, and old candy bar wrappers on my desk to avoid an overnight avalanche, made a note of Eleanor Miller's house number on East Geranium Street, and called it a day. My plan was to swing past Ms. Miller's house before going home. However, by the time I flopped into my car I felt too tired to go out to the East Side before heading west to the Lexington Avenue apartment I shared with Martha Todd, the gorgeous brunette who had been my wife for all of seven weeks, and my neutered black-and-white tomcat, Sherlock Holmes.

All I wanted to do was walk in the door, grab a drink of ice water, and crash on the sofa. I'd probably be asleep when Martha Todd, who had kept her maiden name rather than becoming Martha Mitchell, got home.

When people were rude enough to ask why Martha hadn't changed her name, we replied that it was because she had established herself as Martha Todd at the St. Paul law firm where she worked. The real reason was that she had changed her name for her first husband, who rewarded her by beating her up and dragging her across the kitchen floor by her hair, had changed it back after her divorce, and didn't want to go through the name-changing process a third time. I also suspected that she had an unspoken fear that another change might bring bad luck to our union.

Martha is the light of my life, both physically and emotionally. Physically, she is part Cape Verdean, with a knock 'em dead dazzling white smile, a silken complexion the color of coffee with a heavy dose of cream, and the most perfectly sculpted ass of any woman I have ever seen. Emotionally, we love each other with a passion that goes beyond anything I'd ever imagined.

Our apartment is the on left side of a two-story brick duplex. The right side is occupied by our landlord, a Liberian immigrant named Zhoumaya Jones. Zhoumaya's husband was killed and she was paralyzed from the waist down in a bizarre motorcycle accident about five years ago. They were buzzing along at sixty miles per hour when a tree fell across the road only a few feet in front of them. Now Zhoumaya gets around briskly in a motorized wheelchair. She works in an office in City Hall and has anonymously steered me to some meaty stories involving our city government.

The house looked blessedly quiet as I walked up the front steps. I put the key in the lock, yawned before turning it, and opened the door.

I was greeted with a blast of voices shouting, "Surprise!" I found myself facing at least a dozen grinning people, including Martha; Al and his wife, Carol; my mother; my grandmother; Zhoumaya; and several fellow ink-stained wretches from the *Daily Dispatch*. I took a step backwards and almost lost my balance.

"What the hell?" I asked.

"It's your birthday, dummy," said Al.

"Oh, God, that's right. It's the thirteenth of July."

"Party time," said Martha. She threw herself against me, wrapped me in her arms, and kissed my lips for a long time. "And there'll be a special party time later when everybody goes home," she whispered into my ear.

"Why the big party crowd?" I said. "It's not a special year, like forty or forty-five or, God help me when I get there, fifty."

"It is a special year, silly. It's your first birthday as my lawfully wedded husband."

# Chapter five

## Party Time

S OMEHOW MY ADRENAL glands produced enough of the ener-
gizing chemical to revive me and carry me through the fes-
tivities, which included grilling hamburgers in the
backyard and consuming an assortment of beverages. There was
wine and beer for those who could handle it and lemonade for
Mitch, the recovering alcoholic.

In order to avoid creating a fire hazard, Martha had decorated my birthday cake with only two candles. They were shaped
like the numbers four and two and stood about two inches high.
I drew a round of cheers by blowing them out with one puff after
formulating my secret wish. The cake itself was perfect: chocolate, with chocolate frosting. Martha responded with laughter
when I asked if she had made it from scratch.

After the cake was demolished, my eighty-eight-year-old
Grandmother Goodrich, who I call Grandma Goodie, took me by
the elbow, walked me away from the crowd, and expressed her
usual concern for the status of my soul. "You're a year older and
a year closer to the afterworld," she said. "Warnie Baby, you need
to pick a church and start going every Sunday to prepare your
soul for the day of reckoning." I have been Warnie Baby to her
since the day I was baptized Warren James Mitchell.

"You're just full of good birthday party cheer, aren't you?"
I said.

"I'm only thinking of your future, Warnie Baby. You need
to get yourself right with God before the Day of Judgment arrives." The only Sunday church service Grandma Goodie has

missed within my memory was when she was hospitalized with a gall bladder attack, and then the minister of the Methodist church and five members of the choir conducted a service, complete with hymns, prayers, and a sermon, in her room.

"I appreciate that, but churches and I don't get along very well." As a member of Alcoholics Anonymous, I had submitted myself to the care of a higher power, but I wasn't prepared to worship that higher power in a weekly Sunday morning service.

"Every week you let go by is another week your soul is at risk," she said.

"Maybe I should join the church Martha and I were married in," I said. A Unitarian-Universalist minister had been kind enough to conduct a wedding service for us two non-church-going backsliders.

"I don't know," Grandma Goodie said. "Some of those Unitarians think they're not Christian."

"Some of those Unitarians *aren't* Christian. That's their whole point: everyone is welcome no matter what they believe."

"I'm not sure that kind of thinking will get you into heaven, but I suppose it could be a start," she said. "At least it's a church."

Luckily for me, we were interrupted at that moment by someone who knows everything about churches—Franklin P. Butterfield III, who covers all newsworthy events pertaining to religion for the *Daily Dispatch*. Franklin is openly and gloriously gay, and is known affectionately at the office as Churchy LaFemme (with apologies, of course, to the late Walt Kelley, creator of the *Pogo* comic strip, which included a character of that name).

"Ready to start a mid-life crisis?" Churchy asked. "You've reached the magic age and you're halfway over the hill." His flowing dark hair was woven into a pair of pigtails and tied up with bows of yellow ribbon. His pierced ears displayed dangling earrings with an easily decipherable phallic design.

"I had my mid-life crisis standing at the altar on my wedding day," I said. "From here on in I plan to age gracefully and go gentle into that good night."

"Good plan," Churchy said.

"Good night," said Grandma Goodie, who had been studying Churchy's hair and earrings with a facial expression usually produced by sucking on a raw lemon. "If you'll excuse me, I'm going to round up your mother and head off to bed." She and Mom were staying in Zhoumaya Jones's guest room overnight because our second bedroom had been converted into a shared office for Martha and me.

"Night, night," I said. "And thanks for your words of wisdom."

"Don't be a smart aleck," she said. I really hadn't meant to be; not this time any way.

"Good night, dear lady," said Churchy, giving her an effeminate finger wave of farewell.

Grandma Goodie wrinkled her nose. "Night," she said, and off she went.

After the crowd departed, Martha and I adjourned to the bedroom, where she hosted the special party she had promised. An hour later, as we lay side by side in quiet reverie, I said, "You know something?"

"What?" she whispered.

"I know what day your birthday is but I don't know what year you were born."

"Sounds good to me." Seconds later she was asleep.

\* \* \*

AFTER A BREAKFAST TOPPED with the last two pieces of chocolate cake with chocolate frosting, I got into my Honda Civic and drove toward downtown. It was a cloudless, sunny day that promised to get hot and humid later, about the time I planned to check out the address of Eleanor Miller.

Maybe I could avoid the afternoon heat. I called Don O'Rourke and asked if my presence was required in the office at eight o'clock.

"Did you oversleep again?" Don asked. "Married life is wearing you out."

"It's not like that; I'm bright-eyed and bushy-tailed and eager to excel," I said. I explained that I wanted to take a run past East Geranium Street on the way to work and Don gave me the go-ahead. He said he remembered Eleanor Miller and that she would be a good person to interview if she was "still cogent."

The police roadblock was still up, so I parked in front of it and walked to Eleanor's house. As I passed the yellow tape ringing the Anderson residence, I waved at the well-fed cop who was again standing guard with his back against the tree. He nodded but did not wave back. He was holding a plastic coffee cup in one hand and two-thirds of a doughnut in the other. A suspicion confirmed.

I turned and went up the steps to the next house, rang the bell, and waited. I was about to ring the bell again when the inner door opened and a girl of about twelve stood facing me through the screen door. She was wrapped in a white terrycloth robe, which she held closed with both hands, and her long brown hair hung straight to her shoulders. Obviously I'd gotten her out of bed.

"Yes?" she said.

I held up my *Daily Dispatch* identification card and introduced myself. "I'm looking for Eleanor Miller."

This produced a puzzled look on the young face inside the screen. "Who?"

"Eleanor Miller. She lived here twenty-five years ago."

"Oh, that must be Great-Grammy. We moved in here when they put her in a home."

"What kind of home? A nursing home?"

"I guess," the girl said. "They feed her and help her get dressed and push her around in a wheelchair and all that kind of stuff."

"What's the name of the home?" I asked.

"Oh, jeez, I don't really know. It's out of town somewhere."

"Do you know where?"

"Not really. I go out there with my mom and dad sometimes but I don't look where we're going."

"Are either of your parents home?"

"Both working," she said. "My little brother is home but I'm pretty sure he don't know any more than I do."

"Maybe he does," I said. "Sometimes boys pay attention to where a car is going."

"You want me to wake him up?"

"If you would."

"Jeez! Okay, I'll see if I can rock him." She turned and went away. I tested the screen door with a gentle pull. It was locked.

I was about to ring the bell again when a boy wearing only a red shorty pajama bottom emblazoned with baseballs appeared. He was about eight or nine and looked as sleepy as the girl.

"Meghan says you want to know where Great-Grammy is," he said.

"That's right," I said. "Do you know?"

"I don't know if it's okay to tell you."

"Why wouldn't it be okay?"

"Daddy might not like it. He says he doesn't want people to bother her."

"Is it possible to call your father at work?"

"He sometimes gets mad when I do that."

"Tell you what," I said. "Why don't you give me his phone number and I'll call him. That way he'll get mad at me and not you."

"He might get mad that I gave you the number," the boy said.

"I won't tell him where I got it."

The boy thought a minute. "We-e-ell, okay. It's . . ."

"Just a second," I said. I pulled out my notebook and ball-point and the kid rattled off a number so fast I had to ask for a repeat. When I was sure I had it right I said, "Thanks."

"No problem," he said. Aargh! Whatever happened to "you're welcome" with this generation?

# Chapter Six

## Eleanor Remembers

WHEN I PUNCHED in the number the boy had given me, a recorded voice answered, "Thank you for calling Jefferson Realty." I had forgotten to get the father's name, so when I finally finished pressing a series of ones and twos and reached a female human I asked for Mr. Miller, hoping that he was the son of a son and not of a daughter.

I got lucky. "May I tell him who's calling?" she asked. I gave her my name and she put me on hold. A moment later a male voice said, "Andrew Miller. How can I help you?"

I explained who I was and how he could help me. His response was not encouraging. "I don't think it's a good idea, Mr. Mitchell. Grandma is not very strong and her memory is not very good."

"Sometimes people with memory problems can do quite well with older memories," I said. "What I want to talk to her about happened twenty-five years ago."

"I know, I know. She used to talk about the fuss over the missing girl a lot. Basically she felt it was, as they say, good riddance, but she felt sorry for the parents."

"If I can see your grandmother, I promise to be very gentle and to leave immediately if she seems to be getting tired or confused. I have a grandmother, too." I thought it best not to mention that mine was a hard-charging religious zealot who still walked without assistance.

Andrew Miller took a long time to answer. "If I don't tell you where she is, I suppose you'll find her any way," he said.

"I'll certainly try."

"Let me call the home and see how she's doing today. Some days are better than others. Give me your number and I'll call you back."

Eight minutes later, I was on my way to a nursing home in the northern suburb of Shoreview. According to Andrew, his grandmother was in good spirits and would love to have a visitor to brighten her day. I thanked him and he said, "No problem." So that's where the kid learned that response. It was a parental malfunction.

I called Don, told him where I was going, and said I hoped to have a story about Eleanor's recollections of the disappearance of Marilee Anderson.

"I'll send your twin out to take her picture," Don said. "Wait for him before you go in." Because Al and I so often work and laugh together, Don calls us the Siamese twins. He says we are joined at the funny bone, which in our case is the skull. I've told him several times that the term "Siamese twins" is politically incorrect in the twenty-first century, but he says he was born in the twentieth century and "politically correct" is not in his edition of Webster's dictionary.

Connected or not, Al and I don't even look alike. I'm six-foot-two and weigh 180 pounds (when I'm faithful to my exercise regimen), with a light brown moustache and light brown hair. Al is five-ten and 175 pounds (mostly muscle), with a moustache and beard that match his dark brown hair.

The nursing home was a long, L-shaped, one-story frame building. The clapboards were painted a light yellow and the trim was a complementary shade of blue. The grass was clipped, the shrubbery was trimmed, and the blacktop parking lot was smooth and free of potholes. I was impressed with the fresh—and expensive—look of everything and hoped Andrew Miller was selling enough real estate to pay for grandma's room and board.

When Al appeared with his camera bag, we went in the front door, picked up a phone beside the inner doors and told a disembodied voice who we were. The inner door buzzed, and we traipsed into the lobby. We were greeted at the reception desk by a middle-aged woman with a warm smile and hair so richly red it had to have been an overzealous dye job. She said Mrs. Miller was waiting for us in one of the parlors and flagged down a passing attendant to show us the way.

"I like the smell of this place," I said to Al as we followed our leader.

Al took two sniffs. "I don't smell anything," he said.

"That's what I like about it."

"Oh, yeah; my grandfather's nursing home always smelled like stale piss."

"A lot of them do."

"Here she is," said our guide. She led us to a tiny white-haired woman sitting in a wheelchair at a low table with a hand of Solitaire spread before her. She was wearing a mostly pink flower-print blouse and from the waist down was wrapped in a pale pink blanket. "Here's your visitors, Eleanor," the attendant said loudly and slowly. "Have a nice visit."

I thanked her and she said, "No problem." Some of my good feelings about the place went away.

We pulled chairs up to the other side of the table and, picking up on the attendant's cue, loudly and slowly introduced ourselves. I started to explain our mission and Eleanor interrupted with, "Yes, yes, I know. Andrew called me a few minutes ago and said you was coming." She peeled the six of hearts off the deck of cards in her left hand and played it on the seven of spades.

"Do you mind if I take your picture while we talk?" Al asked.

"Oh, gosh, I don't know," Eleanor said. "My hair's a mess and I don't have any earrings on." She played the nine of clubs on the ten of hearts.

"Maybe we can find somebody to help you comb your hair and bring you some earrings," I said.

"I'd have gone to my room and got gussied up when Andrew called if he'd said you was going to take my picture. I thought we was just going to talk."

"It's not Andrew's fault," I said. "I thought we was . . . were just going to talk, too. I didn't know the editor was going to send a photographer."

Eleanor played the eight of diamonds on the nine of clubs, turned up the ace of hearts from the deck and laid it in the proper place. "Andrew said something about they's tearing up the Andersons' house again. Is that right?"

"They've never closed the investigation of Marilee's disappearance," I said. "And after twenty-five years, they learned something new that has them lugging stuff out of the house and digging up the flowerbeds."

"I always wondered about them flowerbeds," Eleanor said. "They didn't have no flowerbeds until after Marilee went away. Next thing you know, old Jack is out there digging and Jill is planting rose bushes. Like I said, it made me wonder." She flipped through the rest of the cards, looking at every third one. Finding no winners, she reshuffled the deck.

"You wondered if Marilee was buried there?" I asked.

"Stranger things have happened," she said. "Ah!" She turned up the two of hearts and laid it on the ace.

"You're doing well," Al said, nodding toward the cards. "I'll go find someone to help you gussy up while Mitch talks to you."

"How well did you know the Andersons?" I asked.

"Not all that well. They was okay neighbors. Didn't bother anybody, except they yelled at each other a lot. All three of 'em." The eight of diamonds went onto the nine of clubs.

"What did they yell about?"

"Mostly about what that bratty little girl wanted to do or had already done. She was a handful, I tell you. I didn't miss her none when she was gone, but I felt sorry for Jill. She pretty much went into a shell. Quit her job and never did anything outside the house except take care of those gardens. Seemed like she made 'em bigger every year." The three of hearts appeared. "Oh, that's more like it." She put the three on the two and moved the four off one string and laid it on the three. "This hand's been pretty much crap up to now."

"Solitaire can be a very frustrating game," I said.

"You got that right. But there ain't much else to do here unless you want to watch TV all day. My eyes don't last long when I try to read, and I sure can't go for a walk." She pointed at the blanket-wrapped lower portion of her body. "Diabetes. First they cut off my toes, and then my feet, and then the bottom half of my legs, just below the knees. Next thing you know, they'll start chopping on this end." She tapped herself on top of her head. "Anyways, I can't get out on my own, I don't get much company and most of the folks living here ain't very talkative." She waved in the direction of three other women who were snoozing in wheelchairs around the room.

"Andrew and his family don't visit very often?"

"Andrew works crazy hours selling houses and his wife puts in a lot of hours on her feet at Target. And of course the kids ain't old enough to drive and they wouldn't come here to see an old lady who can't always remember their names if they was." She shuffled the remaining cards again.

"So what did you think of the Andersons?" I asked, trying to get back on track. "Did you think they might have been capable of killing their daughter?"

"The way they yelled at each other and called each other names sometimes, it did seem possible. But I guess the cops never found nothing that would pin it on them."

"Apparently not. Do you have any idea what might have happened to Marilee if she wasn't killed by her parents?"

"She might have just run off. She was always saying she was going to leave. She'd tell them that she knew they weren't her real parents, and that she was going to find her real family so she'd have somebody that loved her."

"Was there any truth in that?"

"I don't think so. Jack and Jill told her she was talking crazy, and I remember Jill looking pregnant with a big belly." She slammed the remaining cards down on the table. "This hand's nothing but a bunch of crap."

"Maybe the next one will be a winner."

"You never know. Anyway, I'm about ready for a nap. Been nice talking to you, Mr. . . . uh . . ."

"Mitchell. You can call me Mitch."

I looked around for Al and was glad to see him approaching with a young woman beside him. "Here's Al to take your picture," I said.

"You're going to take my picture?" It was almost a scream.

"Yes, remember? Al went to get someone to comb your hair and put on your earrings."

"Who's Al?"

I pointed. "This is Al."

"I don't know him," Eleanor said.

"He's my buddy," I said. "He's very nice and he's a very good photographer."

The woman, who said her name was Sara, took charge, soothing Eleanor while combing her hair and attaching a pair of clip-on gold earrings with stones that looked like diamonds.

"I'm not dressed for taking pictures," Eleanor said. Much of the color had been laundered out of the pink-and-blue flower print blouse, and the blanket was covering whatever she wore on the lower half of her body.

"I'll just take a picture of your face," Al said. "Your clothing won't show."

"Give Al a big smile," Sara said.

Eleanor shook her head, sat up as stiff as a table leg and stared soberly at the camera. Al took a couple of quick shots and said he was finished. Eleanor relaxed and smiled in relief, and Al got the image he wanted.

I took Eleanor's right hand between my palms and said, "We'll be going now."

"Come see me again," she said.

"I might just do that. Thank you for talking to us, Eleanor."

"You're welcome," she said. Thank heaven for the older generation.

"So what did Eleanor say while I was away?" Al asked on the way to the car.

"She suspected that Marilee's parents killed her and buried her in one of those gardens the police are digging up."

"So far everything's coming up roses for the cops."

"But the last rose of summer might hold a surprise."

\* \* \*

AFTER FINISHING MY STORY, rewriting a press release that Don dropped on my desk and downing a bite of lunch, I set about finding another East Geranium Street neighbor I really wanted to interview. Since Patrick O'Brian's last known residence was the federal prison in Sandstone, where he'd been sent after being convicted of rape and murder, the Sandstone facility seemed like a good place to start my search.

I found the prison's administrative number and punched it into my phone. Three prompts and two live human voices later, I found myself talking to an assistant warden who said his name was "Donald Shibelski." I asked for a spelling of his last name and he said, "P-r-z-y-b-l-s-k-i." Glad I'd asked.

I explained my cold-case mission and asked if Patrick O'Brian was still in custody, and if not, when he was released.

"When did you say he came in here?" Donald asked.

I gave him the date from the clipping and he said, "That's twenty-two years ago."

"You've got the math right," I said. "Now if you can find the history, I'll give you an 'A' for today's class."

"That's way before my time here and I don't remember anybody by that name being here when I started. I'll have to go through the records and get back to you."

I gave him my office, cell, and home phone numbers and said, "Call me anytime."

As I put down the phone a shadow came over my desk. Twisting and looking behind me, I saw the shadow was cast by Don O'Rourke.

"Grab your twin and get over to East Geranium," Don said. "The cops have found human remains."

"A body?" I said.

"Whatever's left of a body after twenty-five years."

"My guess is that it would be nothing but bones."

"So stop guessing and get your ass out there."

# Chapter Seven

## Blockade II

TWO YELLOW SAWHORSES supporting a weathered wooden sign that said ROAD CLOSED – POLICE in black stenciled letters stood across the middle of the street, stopping us two blocks from our destination. Looking down the block beyond the barrier, we could see so many flashing blue and red lights that it looked like Christmas in July.

Our Ford Focus joined three TV mobile units and half a dozen cars with press stickers. Inside the blockade we found an assortment of marked and unmarked police vehicles with lights flashing, an ambulance also with lights flashing, and a black hearse with its warning lights pulsing.

"Why would they call an ambulance if they found a skeleton?" Al asked.

"I don't know," I said. "Maybe we should bone up on police body recovery procedures."

"There might be skullduggery afoot," he said.

We joined a crowd of men and women bearing cameras, notebooks, cell phones, and microphones milling about in front of the line of yellow tape. The perimeter of the off-limits area had been expanded, so that now the Miller and Waldner homes flanking the Anderson property were included within the forbidden circle. This prevented any of us snoopy media types from seeing what was happening in the Andersons' backyard.

Al and I reached the tape just as Trish Valentine was signing off with her customary, "Trish Valentine reporting live."

"What did you report, oh lively one?" I asked.

"Not a hell of a lot," Trish said. "All we've been told is that the diggers found some human skeletal remains."

"If the remains are skeletal, why the ambulance?"

"Who knows? Maybe they're afraid somebody will pass out looking at the bones."

"Do they think it's Marilee Anderson's bones?"

"They won't say what they think, and they won't let us peek at what they're doing. We're sending a helicopter to fly over and get a look at the backyard."

"What we need is a drone," Al said. "I could mount a camera on it and fly it right over where they're working."

We didn't have to wait long for the sound of approaching rotors. This was quickly followed by the whooshing of another set of rotors. A minute later these two were joined by the racket from a third set of rotors. All three major Twin Cities TV stations had launched their eyes in the skies.

"My God, they'll have a mid-air collision," I said.

"I hope not," Al said. "Remember what we learned about mid-air collisions in Navy flight school?"

"Yes. A mid-air collision can ruin your whole day." This axiom, recited to us by a tongue-in-cheek Navy instructor, had actually been the answer to a question on a test.

Soon we had to shout in order to be heard above the clatter of the three choppers as they formed a tight nose-to-tail ring and took turns passing directly over the house. We were all covering our ears and looking up, and even the police officers who'd been watching us from inside the tape turned their attention to the skies.

Our focus returned to the ground when a scarlet-faced Detective Lieutenant Curtis Brown came trotting around the house and storming toward us. Waving his right arm in a circle and pointing at each TV reporter in turn, he yelled, "Tell your people to get those goddamn choppers out of here or I'll give an order to shoot them down."

Brownie stood watching until he was certain that Trish Valentine, Barry Ziebart of Channel Five, and Chris Collins of Channel Eleven were all on their cell phones. By the time Brownie was again out of sight behind the house, all three elements of the airborne armada were gaining altitude and veering away from the Anderson abode.

Trish broke the blessed silence that followed their departure. "Do you think he'd have really shot them down?"

"No, but he could have had them fined for flight violations," Barry said. "They were way too low and way too close together."

"And he could have made your job reporting on this story a hell of a lot harder," I said. "If Brownie's pissed at you, Brownie doesn't talk to you."

"That's discrimination," she said. "He should treat everyone equally."

"He would," I said. "He'd shut all three of you off with equal silence."

"The William Tell Overture" sounded in my pocket. Again it was Don. "What have you got?" he asked.

"Skeletal human remains and a roped-off crime scene a block wide," I said. "They've got us pushed back so far we can't see the whites of their eyes and they haven't told us anything beyond the bare bones."

"Very funny. I'll switch you to Corinne Ramey and you can entertain her with your puns and what little bit of information you have. Describe the scene and give it a little background. Have Al send some pix of the scene."

"Don wants some pix of the scene," I said while I waited for Corinne to pick up her phone.

"Already on the way," he said. "Got a good one of the three choppers practically hooked together, almost scraping the roof of the house. The folks at the FAA might enjoy that one."

For the second day in a row I dictated a short story about the Anderson case to Corinne Ramey. When she finished taking my story, I did not thank her. I knew it was no problem.

We went back to standing and waiting for some word from Brownie. The TV reporters took turns standing in front the cameras with their backs to the house, reporting breaking news "live from East Geranium Street in St. Paul."

At 2:55 p.m., Don called again. "I'm done for the day. Call Fred when you've got something." Fred is Fred Donlin, the night city editor, who comes on at 3:00 p.m.

"Have a nice night," I said.

"I'll be watching Trish Valentine reporting live," he said. "She'd better not be reporting anything that you don't."

"So how long do Al and I stay here?"

"As long as it takes. Or until Fred sends somebody out to relieve you."

"Thanks a bunch."

"Welcome. See you bright and early." I don't know how I'd have responded if he'd said, "No problem."

It was almost four o'clock when Brownie came around the corner again. Behind him were two men carrying a stretcher bearing a black body bag. All eyes and cameras turned toward the stretcher and followed it as it was laid on a gurney and rolled through the back doors of the hearse. As soon as the doors swung shut, people around me started yelling questions.

Brownie held up his hands for silence as he approached the tape, dragging his feet at a slow, weary pace. His face was wet with sweat, his shirt collar was unbuttoned, the knot on his tie was halfway down to his belt, and his shoulders were sagging.

When the clamor finally ceased, he spoke. "Here's what I can tell you: At approximately twelve fifteen this afternoon, one of the two men working with shovels contacted bones in a portion of the garden scraped to a depth of about four feet by the backhoe.

These bones were exposed further by careful hand removal of the soil around them. Eventually a complete set of skeletal remains was revealed. A medical examiner and a forensic specialist then examined the bones and confirmed that they were in fact human remains. These remains have been carefully placed in a body bag and taken to the laboratory for further examination."

He stopped talking and folded his arms. Trish broke the brief silence. "Is it Marilee Anderson's body?"

"I really can't say," Brownie said. "That will have to be determined by the forensic people."

"Do they look like the bones of a young girl?" Barry Ziebart asked.

"Never having seen the bones of a young girl, I cannot say," Brownie said. This drew a groan from the crowd.

"Are they the size of a young girl's bones?" I asked.

"Again, I couldn't say. The bones will have to be reassembled in the lab before the size of the remains can be measured."

"Are they female bones?" a woman behind me asked.

"That will also have to be determined in the lab. I can say that the remains have deteriorated substantially during the time they were buried."

"When will you have the lab results?" another reporter asked.

"I can't say for sure," Brownie said. "We could have a preliminary report in a couple of days or it could be longer. You'll be notified as soon as I have anything from the lab. Now if you'll excuse me, it's been a very long, hot, and unpleasant day and I'm heading for a long shower and a very cold martini. Maybe two very cold martinis." He turned and walked away, ignoring a hailstorm of questions and comments from the gallery.

I phoned Fred Donlin and said we were coming in with a story and pix. All three TV crews were lined up and reporting live as Al and I started toward our car.

"Did you get the feeling from Brownie's answers that the skeleton might not be Marilee's?" Al asked.

"Make no bones about it; I got the distinct impression that Brownie knows more than he was telling us."

"So it would be a grave mistake to tell our readers that Marilee has been found."

"I can't imagine who else would be buried in the Andersons' backyard, but I won't tell the readers that it's Marilee until I'm dead certain that it is."

\* \* \*

ON MY DESK WEDNESDAY morning was a message slip noting that I'd had a call from "Mr. Shibelski" about an hour after I'd left the office Tuesday. I punched in the number and was amazed to get a direct connection to the man with the Polish name.

"Our secretary mangled your name as badly as I would have," I said. "I take it you didn't spell it for her."

"She didn't ask," he said. "And I never volunteer it."

"What are you volunteering in the way of information this morning? Is there a chance I'll be able to interview Patrick O'Brian?"

"Afraid not, Mr. Mitchell. It seems your Mr. O'Brian was stabbed to death in his cell by a person or persons unknown about thirty days after his arrival here in the warm, welcoming arms of our residential institution. Apparently child rapists weren't popular with the other residents at that time."

"Damn. He was my very best suspect, although her parents are now in the spotlight."

"Yes. I heard on the TV news this morning that they found the girl's skeleton in their backyard."

"The police aren't verifying that it's Marilee until they get the lab tests, but I don't know who else they'd find back there."

"Cops like to err on the side of caution," Przyblski said. "But you're right—folks don't just go around getting buried in strangers' backyards."

Or do they?

# Chapter Eight

## Seeking Jack and Jill

M Y HOPE WAS TO talk to one or both of the Andersons before any other reporter got to them. Where would I find them? Were they still in seclusion with good old Uncle Eddie? Were they home on East Geranium? Or were they in police custody in downtown St. Paul?

I tried the home phone first. I got their voicemail and tried to leave a message. A cool feminine recorded voice said the message box was full. Why was I not surprised?

Next I called Uncle Eddie. Same result—no pickup and a full voicemail message box. Popular folks, the Anderson family.

That left only one possibility: the police. I punched in the number of Detective Lieutenant Curtis Brown's private line. There I finally got a message: Brownie's voice saying he wasn't at his desk right now, please leave a message. Interrogating the Andersons, no doubt. I left a message and looked at my other options for a story.

The convenience store clerk topped the list. But James Bjornquist had been only nineteen years old, and a nineteen-year-old man could have gone anywhere in the ensuing quarter century. He sure as hell wouldn't be working at the store anymore.

On the other hand, somebody at the store might know where he'd gone from there. The odds were against me, but I looked up the number and called it. The phone was answered by a man named Cole, who sounded like he was nineteen. I asked if he knew anything about a former employee named James Bjornquist.

"Jeez, Mr. Mitchell, I never even heard of the guy 'til yesterday," the young man said. "The thing with the missing girl happened before I was born. I suppose you could talk to the owner. He might know something."

"Is the owner there?"

"No, sir, he's not. He generally comes by about noon to pick up the morning's receipts."

"Do you have his home number?"

"Yes, but he said he'd fire my . . . my butt . . . if I ever gave it to anybody. It's strictly for emergencies, like me getting robbed or shot or something."

"I'll give you my number," I said. "Please ask him to call me."

"Okay."

He copied the number and I said, "Thanks."

"No problem." Aargh! I put down the phone and uttered a curse word out loud.

Corinne Ramey looked up from the next desk. "Problem?" she asked.

"Oh, no," I said. "There's never no problem."

"That's a double negative, Mitch."

"No shit?" I said.

"That's better," she said, and went back to writing her story.

A half hour later, Brownie returned my call and asked what I wanted. "Just wondering if the Andersons are in your interrogation room," I said.

"No, they are not," he said.

"So where are they?"

"You tell me."

"You mean you don't know?"

"Excellent deduction," Brownie said. "Jack and Jill seem to have gone up some hill that we don't know about."

"What about good old brother Eddie? Can't he tell you?"

"Good old brother Eddie seems to be among the missing, also."

"So now you have three missing adults in addition to one missing teenage girl and one unidentified set of bones?"

"That about sums it up. We've got people talking to the Andersons' neighbors again to see if they have any idea where Jack and Jill might have gone tumbling off to."

"When you find them, will you break Jack's crown?"

"You know we don't indulge in physical abuse in this department."

"I'm only kidding, but I have heard rumors about uncooperative people who've had accidental falls on the stairs of the city jail."

"Accidents sometimes happen to people who are drunk enough or stupid enough to attack an officer. I can't imagine either Jack or Jill Anderson being either that drunk or that stupid."

"I can't, either. Anyhow, please let me know when and where you find them."

"You and everyone else. Have a good day, Mitch."

I went to the city desk and told Don O'Rourke about the latest development in the Anderson cold case. "My God, who else can go missing?" he said.

Who, indeed? I had no answer at that moment.

I wrote a quick update for the online edition and was about to head for the cafeteria when my phone rang. "This is Mike Casey," said the caller.

"What can I do for you, Mr. Casey?" I asked.

"There's nothing you can do for me. You wanted me to call you."

"I'm sorry, but your name doesn't ring a bell."

"I own the convenience store on Arcade Street, near the corner of East Geranium."

The light in my brain went on. "Oh, of course," I said. "I'm sorry. Your clerk didn't tell me your name—just referred to you as the owner."

"That dummy can't remember his own name, much less mine. What was it you wanted me for?"

I told him I was trying to track down a former employee named James Bjornquist and asked if he'd ever known the young man.

"Before my time," Casey said. "I bought the store eight years ago from Adelbert Love, who had it for a long time before me. Bjornquist would have worked for Del."

"Any idea where I can find Adelbert Love?"

"Last I heard from one of the regular customers was that Del was in a nursing home. He'd be up in his middle nineties, if he's still alive."

"Do you know which nursing home?"

"Customer didn't say. Not sure he knew."

"Okay, I guess I'll have to check around. Thank you for your help, Mr. Casey."

"No problem." I clamped my teeth tightly together and put down the phone.

On a whim, I called the nursing home in Shoreview where I'd interviewed Eleanor Miller and asked the woman who answered if they had a patient named Adelbert Love.

"Oh, do we ever," she said. "Del is one of our favorites. He's a real hot ticket."

"Do you think he'd talk to a stranger?" I asked.

"Del would talk to a wooden fencepost if it didn't walk away," she said. "Come on out and visit with him." At last, a break.

"I'm on my way." I added, "Thanks for your help," and held my breath.

"You're very welcome," she said. I could have kissed her right through the telephone line.

# A Cold Case of Killing

I rose from my desk, intending to buy a sandwich to take out from the cafeteria and find out if Al was free to accompany me and hustle out to the nursing home. I had taken one step away from my chair when the phone rang. I picked up the receiver expecting to hear Brownie's voice telling me that Jack and Jill had come tumbling down home.

# Chapter Nine

## California Bound

I T'S MORRIE," SAID a dreary male voice. I almost screamed. Morrie is another person who belongs in a home—in his case it would be a residence with padded walls. Morrie is little white-haired man who walks the downtown streets with a little white shaggy-haired dog and imagines that—depending on the day—either a Russian radar operator or an American postal employee named Robinson is out to do him harm.

Somehow Morrie learned my name—I certainly didn't give it to him—and he usually asks for me when he makes one of his all-too-frequent calls to the *Daily Dispatch* customer service number.

"What's happening?" I asked, trying to calm myself.

"It's the Russians," he said. "They're beaming their radar at me again. I can feel the rays coming through the ceiling."

"Didn't I tell you to hide in the bathtub with the shower curtain pulled shut when that happens?"

"I did that, but I can still feel the rays. You've got to write an article about it so the Russians will stop."

"Tell you what," I said. "Put your little dog on a leash and take a walk around a few blocks, kind of zigzagging back and forth. The Russians will lose track of you and turn off the radar."

"You think that'll work?"

"I'd bet my last million-dollar paycheck on it."

"Okay, I'll try that. Thanks, Mr. Mitchell."

"No problem," I said. After all, he was not welcome.

Fifteen minutes later Al and I, with sandwiches in hand, were in a *Daily Dispatch* Ford Focus headed north. "How could you be so lucky as to find the guy in the same nursing home as Mrs. Miller?" Al said.

"Clean living and a humble heart," I said.

"If you're saying that with a straight face, maybe you belong in the same padded room as your pal Morrie."

"Please, anything but that."

"You could always tell him you're a Russian radar operator."

"Or Robinson."

"Who the hell is Robinson, anyway?"

"Who the hell knows except Morrie?"

At the nursing home, we went through the same rigmarole as our previous visit. We were led to a different, but similarly decorated, sitting room and introduced to a man with no hair on his head and a bushy white moustache on his upper lip. He was seated on a folding chair in front of a card table with a Solitaire hand spread before him. A metal walker with wheels on the two front legs stood beside his chair.

Adelbert Love stuck out his right hand and gave our hands a vigorous shake. "I'd get up, but you boys would have to help me get down again," he said. "Damn knees don't work so good anymore." He was short, with a potbelly and broad shoulders, and looked much younger than his middle nineties. He was wearing a gaudily patterned short-sleeved shirt, faded blue jeans, and orange canvas tennis shoes.

There were three additional folding chairs beside the table and Al and I each plopped into one. "Sorry to interrupt your game, but we're looking for somebody you used to know," I said.

"Oh, never mind the game," Love said. "I'm sick of Solitaire anyway. Who is it you're looking for?" He swept the cards together, stacked them, and set them aside.

"A young man who worked in your store on Arcade Street twenty-five years ago. James Bjornquist."

"Jimmy Bjornquist? How's come you're looking for him?"

I filled Love in on the warming of the cold case on East Geranium Street and he sat in silence for a moment.

"That seems like an awful long time ago," he said. "As I remember it, the cops came and questioned Jimmy the afternoon the girl was reported missing. He told them she hadn't been in the store. He seemed to be pretty upset about it, more than you'd expect. Made me wonder if he had something going with that little teeny-bopper. She came into the store pretty regular, so they might have got to know each other. Anyhow, when the cops were gone Jimmy asked if he could take the rest of the day off and seeing how shook up he was I said go ahead, and he went on home—he was living with his grandparents. Next day his grandmother calls and says Jimmy ain't coming to work no more, that he'd packed up his clothes the night before and said he was going to California. I never heard from him again. He didn't even come in for his last paycheck. I mailed the check to his grandmother and that was the end of it."

"So, as far as you know, Jimmy went to California?" I said.

"I guess."

"Might he have had Marilee Anderson hidden somewhere and taken her to California with him?"

"Oh, you know, I never thought of that," Love said. "I was afraid he'd done something bad to her and was running away from the cops."

"That's one of the possibilities that the police suspected at the time, according to the reports I've read."

"Either way, I never heard from Jimmy or his grandparents again."

"Do you know if his grandparents are still in St. Paul?"

"I think their address was in White Bear. I know Jimmy had to drive a ways down Highway 61 to get to work. Anyhow, if they're still around they must be at least as old as I am, which is going on ninety-six."

"What about Jimmy's parents? Where were they?"

"They were killed in a terrible car crash when he was ten years old. That's why he was living with his grandparents."

"Would the grandparents' name be Bjornquist, or were they his mother's parents?"

"Now that you ask about it, I don't think it was Bjornquist. I mailed the check to them, but I'm not absolutely sure about the name anymore. Like I said, it seems like a long time ago."

"Did Jimmy have any brothers or sisters?" I asked.

"Never mentioned any."

"Well, we should let you get back to your card game. Do you mind if Al takes your picture?"

"If he wants to risk breaking his camera, it's okay with me," Love said. He sat up straight and gave Al a big smile, and Al snapped the shutter a couple of times.

As I rose to leave, I said, "If you're really tired of Solitaire, I know of another Solitaire player who might be willing to switch to Cribbage."

"Oh, that would be great. Where is he?"

"She is right in this building. Her name is Eleanor Miller. I'll bet one of the nice ladies here would help you find her."

"And you say she plays cards?"

"She was playing last time I saw her."

"Was she playing with a full deck?"

"Literally and figuratively," I said. "Thanks for your time and your help."

"You're more than welcome," said Adelbert Love. As previously stated, I love the older generation.

"So Jimmy Bjornquist could be in California," Al said on the way out.

"And so could Marilee Anderson," I said.

"In that case, whose bones were in the Andersons' backyard?"

56

"That, my dear Watson, is a bona fide mystery."

As we crossed the lobby, Al spotted a familiar figure parked in a wheelchair facing the front window. "Isn't that Eleanor Miller?" he asked. She was sitting up as straight as she could manage, staring out the window as though waiting for someone. She was wearing a different flowered blouse but her surgery-shortened legs were encased in the same wrap as the previous day.

"Let's go over and say hello," I said. We walked to her side and, in unison, said, "Hi, Eleanor."

She looked up at us and studied our faces for an embarrassingly long time before she spoke. "Hello. How did you know my name?"

"We met you yesterday," I said. "Mitch and Al from the paper?"

"Yesterday?" she said.

"Yes," Al said. "You were playing Solitaire. I took your picture."

"You took my picture?"

I recalled what her grandson had said about Eleanor's fading short-term memory. "We're from the newspaper. We talked to you about your neighbors, Jack and Jill Anderson."

Her expression turned from puzzled to pleased. "Oh, yes, I know Jack and Jill," Eleanor said. "How are they?" Ah, the long-term memory was doing better than the short-term.

"They're, uh, they are having some problems, but they're okay," I said.

"Their daughter has disappeared, you know. Run away or kidnapped, or maybe her father strangled her for all I know, she was such a sassy little thing. I don't miss the girl—she did a lot of yelling and screaming—but I feel sorry for Jill. For her sake, I hope they find the girl okay."

"Right now we're hoping to find Jack and Jill," Al said. "They don't seem to be home today."

"Oh, they're probably up to the lake," Eleanor said.

That got my attention. "Do they have a cabin at a lake somewhere?"

"Oh, gosh yes, they go up every summer on Jack's vacation. They're big fishermen, both of them."

I decided to push my luck. "Do you know the name of the lake?"

"Oh, gosh, I've heard them talk about it but it don't come to me just now," Eleanor said. "It's up north." Up north in Minnesota covers several hundred thousand square miles of territory and a majority of the state's acclaimed 10,000 lakes.

"Do you remember the name of any town they might have mentioned?" Al asked.

"Oh, gosh, I should, but I'm afraid I don't."

"Might you remember if you thought about it for a while?" I asked.

"Oh, gosh, I might. I remember it had kind of a funny name." This would cover scores of Minnesota cities, ranging from Argyle to Zumbrota. It brought to mind a classic headline that once ran in our paper over a story about a woman from one northern Minnesota city being killed in an auto accident in a neighboring northern Minnesota city: "Fertile woman dies in Climax."

I wanted to give Eleanor my card and ask her to call me if the name of either the lake or the city popped into her head, but I wasn't sure that she would remember why she had the card. At least she had given us something to get started on. Another of the Andersons' neighbors might come up with the name.

We had said our goodbyes and were almost at the door when we heard Eleanor's voice. She couldn't muster a shout but it was loud enough to stop us and send us back.

"Did you think of something?" I asked.

"Is there a town up north called Bemidji?" Eleanor said.

# Chapter Ten

## Up at the Lake

HOMICIDEBROWN," said Brownie all in one word, as he always does when he answers his direct line.

"*Dailydispatch*mitchell," I said, as I always do when he greets me that way. "Just wondering if you've found the wayward Jack and Jill?"

"I should be so lucky," Brownie said. "Neighbors didn't have a clue where they might be hanging out."

"Did you talk to the Millers?"

"People across the street? Affirmative. Andrew Miller couldn't help us."

"How about his grandmother, Eleanor Miller?"

"No use. She's in a nursing home with Alzheimer's."

"Read your medical dictionary. Alzheimer's patients often have surprisingly good long-term memories."

"So you think we should talk to her?"

"Not necessary. Al and I already have."

"And you found out something?"

"She says the Andersons have a cottage up at the lake. She can't recall the name of the lake, but the name she does remember is Bemidji. You know, the place that bills itself as 'The first city on the Mississippi River.'" The mighty river trickles out of a lake southwest of Bemidji and flows north and east in a curving pattern, mostly through wilderness, before turning south and reaching that city.

"There's a whole shitload of lakes around Bemidji," Brownie said.

"Somewhere in all the stuff you hauled out of the Andersons' house might be documents pertaining to lakeshore property in the Bemidji area," I said. "Maybe even in their computer."

"Son of a bitch, you're right. I'll see what we can find."

"When you come up with something, remember you heard the word 'Bemidji' from this phone number first."

"You'll get the first call," Brownie said. "I'll even put you ahead of the Channel Four boob show. Have a good day, Mitch."

I have a tendency to doodle while I'm on the phone, and I had drawn two stick figures with fishing poles in a small boat. I was putting on the finishing touches when Al arrived at my desk.

"Nice artwork," he said. He was carrying my afternoon pick-me-up, a cup of hot black coffee, which he set down beside the drawing. "Was that Brownie on the phone?"

"Thanks for your critical assessment of my artistic endeavor," I said. "It was Brownie, and he was all ears when I told him about Bemidji."

"He's all ears all the time," Al said. Al's major problem in photographing the chief of homicide was Brownie's ears, because of the way they protrude at ninety degrees from his bald head. Al was always looking for an angle shot that lessened the impact of the ears.

"This is true. What I meant was that I got his attention. And the beneficial side effect is that if his troops can find something that locates the cabin in the stuff they took out of the house, he'll owe me one."

"Having the homicide chief owing you a favor is always a killer."

"Now our problem is what to do about James, a.k.a. Jimmy Bjornquist. Did he really go to California? Did he take Marilee Anderson with him? Or did he kill Marilee Anderson? And if he killed her, and the bones in Jack and Jill's backyard belong to Marilee, why in hell would Jimmy bury her in her parents' yard?"

"He couldn't have done that. The garden digging wasn't started until after Marilee disappeared, remember?"

"You're right. I'm thinking the only people who could have buried Marilee in that garden are Jack and Jill Anderson."

"Their crowning achievement."

"Right. It's no wonder they've decided to fall out of sight."

I thought about all the missing people in this cold case while I sipped my coffee. When my cup was empty, I dragged out the city directory and thumbed through the "B's" until I reached "Bjornquist." There were seven listed in St. Paul. I started calling them, hoping that one might be a relative of the missing Jimmy.

"Please leave a message after the tone," said the first name on the list.

"Never heard of a Jimmy in our family," said the second.

After two more voicemails, I got another "never heard of him" response.

Next came another voicemail, followed by a third "never heard of him."

I left messages on all four voicemails saying who I was and why I was calling. I had no expectation of getting a return from any of them. Thus I was surprised when my phone rang as I was clearing the trash off my desk prior to departure at 5:00 p.m.

But the caller wasn't a Bjornquist. It was Brownie. "Got a Minnesota map handy?" he asked.

"Hang on a sec," I said. I dug into the bottom drawer of my desk and came up with a ten-year-old Minnesota road map. "I have a map and it's open," I said.

"Find Lake Bemidji; it's big enough you should see it easy."

I did, and said, "I've got it."

"You can see that the city is on the south end of Lake Bemidji," he said. "A few miles off the northeast corner of Lake Bemidji is a much smaller lake called Big Bass Lake. On the northeast corner of Big Bass Lake is a half-acre piece of land deeded to John G. and Jill L. Anderson. Several vehicles bearing officers from the Minnesota State Patrol are moving toward that parcel even as we speak."

"Got it," I said, circling the little odd-shaped blue blob on the map with a red ballpoint. "How'd you find it?"

"Monday morning we took one of those portable safes—you know, the ones that people put their valuables in because they're told that thieves can't get them open—out of the Andersons' closet. Today we opened the safe and found the deed to a parcel of land in Beltrami County, which happens to be the county in which Bemidji is located. I called the county clerk and she looked up the parcel on the county map and bingo, we had a winner."

"And the troops are on the way to arrest the Andersons?"

"The troops are on the way to persuade the Andersons to accompany them back to St. Paul to chat with me. I hope an arrest isn't necessary, because we really don't have anything to charge them with."

"How about leaving the scene?"

"What scene? Having a body found in your garden isn't a crime unless there's evidence that you put it there. We don't have any such evidence as yet, which is the main reason we want to talk to John G. and Jill L. Anderson."

"So the body in the ground isn't grounds for arrest?"

"Cute. You can put that in your headline," Brownie said. "We'll be notifying the media when the Andersons have been returned to St. Paul. Meanwhile, you're the only one who knows where they are and what's about to happen. Have a good day, Mitch."

I looked at the map. According to a little graph at the top, Bemidji is 239 miles from St. Paul. Big Bass Lake appeared to be another fifteen miles beyond the city. The state cops wouldn't be there for a few minutes yet. It would take the cops at least fifteen minutes to get the Andersons into a vehicle and a little over four hours to return to St. Paul unless they drove at high speed with lights and sirens, which didn't seem necessary. That meant *Daily Dispatch* readers would be seeing my online-edition story about finding the Andersons four and a half hours before Brownie's office intended to notify the rest of the media. And it was already too late to make the early evening TV news. Indeed, I was having a good day.

I had doodled the face of a clock with the hands showing 9:00 p.m. I told Fred Donlin, the night city editor, what I had and wrote the story. Some lucky night-side reporter would get to pick up the action when the St. Paul police announced the Andersons' return.

"You're late," Martha Todd said when I finally got home. "I was beginning to wonder if you were joining the missing persons list."

"No such luck," I said. "You're stuck with me for at least one more night."

"Then we'd better stick very close together tonight," she said. And we did.

# Chapter Eleven

## Dodging Publicity

WHILE EATING BREAKFAST Thursday morning, I turned on the TV and learned that all three Andersons had returned to St. Paul willingly, driving their own SUV with a three-car Minnesota State Highway Patrol escort. Their reason for going up to the lake? To avoid publicity.

How did this work out for them? The front page of every newspaper in Minnesota was carrying the story of the police finding them, and every TV and radio newscast was leading with their so-called "apprehension," accompanied by tape of the caravan arriving at police headquarters. Bemidji's TV station had a helicopter flying above the cabin on Big Bass Lake, taking aerial shots that were going viral on the Internet. Jack and Jill and Uncle Eddie were becoming household names all across the country. Their attempt to dodge the media had turned this into the hottest cold case in twenty years.

Of course, Don O'Rourke was looking for a fresh story when I arrived in the newsroom at eight o'clock. "See if you can get an interview with any of those three Anderson nutjobs," were his instructions. "Take your twin along to get some fresh pix."

I started searching for the Andersons' current whereabouts with a call to Detective Lieutenant Curtis Brown's direct line. I was shunted to his voicemail. Apparently he wasn't talking to anybody at the moment. I left a message, hoping he'd still remember who steered him toward Bemidji.

Next I called the number of the house on East Geranium Street. No answer. Not even voicemail. Apparently they'd turned off the machine. Did that mean Jack and Jill were at home?

Eddie Anderson was next. Same thing: no answer and no voicemail. We needed to get in a car and make a personal visit.

Al and I arrived at East Geranium to find the street open but the Andersons' house and yard still ringed with yellow police tape. TV trucks from all three Twin Cities stations were parked in front of the house. Two women who looked like newspaper reporters and a couple of TV reporter/camera crews were standing near the tape. Three uniformed police officers were visible inside the tape. Two were flanking the front steps and one, my paunchy acquaintance from our first visit on Monday, was propped against his favorite tree.

We approached Trish Valentine, and I asked, "What's the story?"

"Jack and Jill are under police protection," she said.

"Protection from what? Us?"

"Exactly. They don't want to talk to us and the cops are keeping us from knocking on their door. They're violating our First Amendment rights."

"They can justify it with the Fourth Amendment," I said.

"What's that?"

"The Andersons' right to privacy."

"They should repeal that one."

"Maybe we should try Eddie Anderson's house," Al said.

"Won't do you any good," Trish said. "We had a crew there and the cops ran them off. I guess Eddie doesn't like talking to reporters, either."

"Either that or the cops don't want any of the threesome talking to us until after they've questioned them," I said.

I called Don O'Rourke on my cell phone and told him about the standoff. "No use wasting your time out there," he said. "Have Al get a shot of the cops guarding the door and then come back to the office and try to get through to Brown. Find out when the Andersons are being questioned if you can. We need some kind of a story."

We went back and I called Brownie's number again with the same result. It looked like all we'd have for a new lead on the cold case story was the police guard at the two Anderson residences. How exciting was that?

I'd almost given up hope of hearing from Brownie when the phone rang. It had to be him. I gave the caller a cheerful, "Good morning."

"It's Morrie," said the voice.

Somehow I resisted the urge to slam down the phone and controlled the volume of my reply, which was spoken through clenched teeth. "What's your problem this time?"

"It's Robinson," Morrie said. "You have to write about him harassing me so he'll have to stop."

"What's he doing?"

"He's broadcasting lies about me all over town. I can hear him."

"I'll write a story as soon as I hear what he's saying."

"Don't you hear him? It's all over town."

"I'm wearing a telephone headset so I can't hear anything but you," I said. "Hang up and I'll go outside and listen."

"You promise?" Morrie said.

"On a stack of AP stylebooks. Now please hang up."

I set the receiver down so hard that Corinne Ramey looked up from the next desk. "Crank call?" she asked.

"Morrie," I said.

"Oh, God. Which was it, radar or Robinson?"

"Robinson. Morrie says you can hear him all over town."

"Guess our building must be soundproof, huh?"

"Oh, good idea. I'll use that the next time the little creep calls."

"Be careful what you say or he'll come here to get away from the sound."

The potential horror of having Morrie cowering under my desk was going through my mind when the phone rang again. This absolutely had to be Brown.

"*Dailydispatch*mitchell," I said as fast as I could.

There was a brief silence, then a timid male voice said, "Is this Warren Mitchell?"

"It is," I said. "Can I help you?"

"I might be able to help you," he said. "Did you leave a message on my voicemail?"

"That depends on who you are."

"My name is Roger Bjornquist."

Oh, yes, I definitely had left a message on his voicemail.

# Chapter Twelve

## All About Jimmy

J IMMY BJORNQUIST IS my cousin," Roger Bjornquist said. "Or maybe I should say he *was* my cousin. I don't know if he's still alive."

"When was the last time you knew he was alive?" I asked, grabbing a notebook and a ballpoint.

"I saw him a couple of days before he supposedly took off for California."

"Supposedly? Do you think he didn't go to California?"

"I don't know what to think. He went somewhere, but California seems kind of far for a kid with no money. Wherever he went, nobody here ever heard from him again, as far as I know."

"Not even his grandparents?"

"If they did, they never said anything about it."

"Is it possible for me to ask them?"

"No. They're both gone. Grandma passed away just a month ago, in fact. She was a hundred years old."

"She did very well. So what can you tell me about Jimmy? Did you see him the day Marilee Anderson disappeared?"

"No. The last time was the day before she disappeared."

"Do you think Jimmy left because he did something bad to Marilee?"

"Just the opposite. I think he took her with him, wherever he went. He had something going with her, you know."

"I didn't know. She was only fifteen and he was nineteen. What did they have going?"

"I'm pretty sure he was screwing her," Roger said. "She hung around the store a lot while he was working and she was one wild little bitch."

"You knew her?"

"Oh, yah. I hung around the store some, too, when Jimmy was working."

"And you thought she would let Jimmy have sex with her?"

"Let him? Hell, she'd have been the one to start it. She grabbed him by the nuts . . . I mean the crotch . . . more than once when there was no customers in the store."

"What was she like otherwise?"

"What do you mean?"

"Was she smart? Dumb? Happy? Unhappy? How was her life?"

"She was no dummy. No Einstein, either, understand, but she was smart enough. She wasn't happy at home, that's for sure. And she was scared stiff of her father."

"Why was she scared of her father?"

"He had a hell of a temper. Beat the crap out of her more than once. She'd run next door to her Uncle Eddie after her dad whipped her, and Eddie would hug her and cuddle her and comfort her, you know."

"Did you ever think that Uncle Eddie might be doing more than hugging and cuddling?"

"Oh, jeez, no. I never thought about that. I was the same age she was, fifteen, you know. But now that you ask about it, Uncle Eddie was kind of, uh . . . I don't know . . . strange might be a good word."

Oh, great, a funny uncle. "What did he do that makes you think he was strange?"

"I guess the way he hugged Marilee. I only saw it happen once, but he pretty much ran his hands over everything."

"Everything including . . . ?"

"Oh, jeez, you know. Butt, breasts, belly, you name it."

"What do you think happened to Marilee when she disappeared?" I asked.

"I think she ran off with Jimmy," Roger said. "She wanted to get away from her family real bad and he wanted to get away from the damn boring life he was leading working in that stupid store."

"You don't think he would have hurt her in anger or anything?"

"No, never. Jimmy would never hurt anybody, especially not a girl."

"How about Uncle Eddie? Could he have done something to Marilee?"

"I guess that's possible. Like I said, he was strange."

"Any other thoughts about Jimmy or Marilee, Mr. Bjornquist?"

"No, not really. I just thought you might like to know that Marilee and Jimmy had a thing going."

"You were right about that."

"Are you gonna put this in the paper? What I said?"

"I'd like to use what you said about Jimmy," I said. "Your comments about Marilee I'll save as background."

"Oh, jeez, I don't want my name in the paper," Roger said.

"Suppose I refer to you as a family member who doesn't wish to be identified?"

He thought for a moment. "I guess that would be okay."

"Great. Thanks very much for calling."

"No problem." Aargh! A pox on the forty-year-old generation.

This conversation left me with at least five possible scenarios. I wrote a list: (1) Marilee ran off to parts unknown with Jimmy Bjornquist; (2) Jimmy and Marilee quarreled—maybe she was pregnant and he wanted her to get an abortion—and he killed her; (3) Marilee resisted Uncle Eddie's sexual advances and he killed her, either accidentally or intentionally; (4) Jack Anderson beat Marilee to death in a fit of rage; (5) Marilee took off by herself and never wanted to be found.

The bones in the backyard seemed to point the finger at number four, but the police had no evidence as yet. Still, one other question was haunting me as I began to write a story about my conversation with a James Bjornquist family member who didn't wish to be identified. What had Jill Anderson meant when she said, "It's time it all came out," as she handed me Marilee's picture Monday afternoon?

\*   \*   \*

MY CALL FROM BROWNIE finally came at 2:58 p.m. as I was shuffling through layers of old notes and newspapers on my desk for possible mass disposal. The police had smuggled Jack and Jill Anderson out their back door and into a squad car parked in the alley without being detected by the TV crews still parked in front of the house. The couple had been separated at police headquarters and they were being questioned individually about what they might know about the burial of the backyard skeleton.

"What did they say?" I asked.

"Wouldn't you like to know," Brownie said. "You'll find that out if we bring one or both of them into court."

"Any charges yet?"

"No. The interrogations are still going on. I just took a break to pee and return your call."

"I'm thrilled to hear that my call came in a close second to nature's."

"When you gotta go you gotta go. Have a good day, Mitch."

He ended the call before I could ask if and when they'd be questioning Uncle Eddie. I completed my half-finished doodle of a skull and crossbones and went back to shoveling off my desk. "It's time it all came out," kept running through my mind.

\*   \*   \*

FRIDAY WAS MY day off (our days off rotate so the newsroom is always equally staffed) and I waved goodbye to Martha from a prone position between the sheets as she left for work. I rose some time later and was consuming a bowl of Cheerios and blueberries when the phone rang. The caller ID said "city editor."

"Hi, Don, what's up?" I said.

"I hope you are," Don said.

"I am, but this is—"

"I know it's your day off, but you might want to change it. The coroner is going to give a report on the Anderson backyard bones at ten o'clock in the police station. If you cover it, I'll give you a whole day's comp time you can use whenever you want."

"I'll be there." I wasn't about to let some other reporter move in on my story. "What about Al? It's his day off, too."

"I'm calling him next. You can meet him there."

Knowing there would be a mob of reporters and photographers, I arrived early. So did everyone else. The briefing room was packed by 9:45 a.m. and the air conditioning system was overwhelmed. The atmosphere grew heavy as various brands of deodorant lost their grip on sweating bodies. I was in my usual spot behind Trish Valentine when Dr. Lyle Lundberg, the Ramsey County medical examiner, appeared before us. He was accompanied by Brownie and Police Chief Casey Riley. All three wrinkled their noses and they huddled together for a whispered conference. I'd have bet my paycheck they were discussing the locker-room smell in the air.

Brownie made some introductory remarks and turned the show over to Dr. Lundberg. His opening line produced a chorus of gasps and a synchronized row of dropped jaws.

"Ladies and gentlemen," Dr. Lundberg said. "I have examined the remains found buried in the backyard of the John H. Anderson residence and determined them to be those of an adult male."

# Chapter Thirteen

## Skeleton X

YOU COULD HAVE heard a pin—hell, a feather—drop after the gasps died. The M.E. was a showman; he played the silence to its maximum endurable length before continuing. "Our problem now is identifying the remains," he said. "We are checking dental records of missing adult males back to the time the makeshift grave was dug, but some of the teeth were out of their sockets and we're not sure we have them all. We are also going through police reports of missing adult males from that period. So far, we have had no success. We have taken a DNA sample from the remains and are searching for a match among known missing persons on whom we have data. We are asking you to broadcast our plea to families of missing adult males. We're asking them to come forward with information about their missing person—things like height, weight, et cetera—that could help us determine the identity of these remains."

He held up a card with an 800 phone number and said it was the number to call if you knew of a missing person who disappeared during the summer twenty-five years ago or soon thereafter.

"So how tall would this person have been?" Trish asked.

"We're estimating him at about six feet," Dr. Lundberg said. "Give or take an inch or two."

"If he was that tall, it seems like you could have told us earlier that the bones weren't Marilee Anderson," Barry Ziebart said.

"The remains were just a mass of scattered bones," the doctor said. "All the connecting tissue had long since decayed, plus the bones were disturbed by contact with the backhoe when we exhumed them. The skull was actually a couple of feet away from the neck. We really couldn't tell how tall the deceased had been at that point."

"Any estimate of the dead man's age?" someone asked.

"The bones have been softened and bleached a bit, but they appear to be those of a young person. We're estimating somewhere from late teens to early twenties."

"What was the cause of death?" I asked.

"We haven't determined that as yet," the doctor said. "There are no obvious indicators, like bullet holes in the skull for example."

Chief Riley stepped forward. "We really could use your help in this. The more you repeat our request, the greater the number of people who will hear it or read it. We're obviously searching all our missing persons files but not everyone who goes missing gets reported to the police. We're referring to the remains as Skeleton X, and people can use that identifying code when they call."

"Have you asked the Andersons about it?" I asked. What could be more basic?

"Neither of the Andersons professes to have any knowledge of the buried remains," the chief said.

"Do you believe them?" someone behind me asked.

"Yes and no," said Riley.

"Does that mean yes for one Anderson and no for the other?" I asked.

"I'll drop it at that," the chief said. "You may interpret it any way you wish."

Trish Valentine turned her head halfway toward me and said, "I'll bet he believes Jill and not Jack."

"That's my guess," I said. "Did you get that comment live?"

"Trish Valentine is always reporting live," she said. "See you when they dig up another body." She motioned to Tony, the man with the camera, and followed the trail of the dispersing crowd.

"You look like you're deep in thought," Al said when we were outside. "Your brain must be working; I can smell wood burning."

"I'm just wondering how tall Jimmy Bjornquist was," I said.

* * *

No one answered the phone at the Roger Bjornquist residence. I left another message, specifically asking about his cousin Jimmy's height, on the voicemail. I hung up thinking what a frustrating business reporting is—always waiting for someone to return a call. It becomes even more frustrating when you know that the person doesn't want to talk to you and hell will freeze over before he or she makes a return call.

My interview with Roger was in our online edition, which meant that other editors and news directors could read it and tell their reporters to find the unidentified Bjornquist family member and call him. Phones had to be ringing in every Bjornquist household in the Twin Cities metropolitan area. Maybe Roger had been flooded with calls and was no longer answering the phone. Whatever. There was nothing to do but wait and hope I'd be the first to learn if Skeleton X, which matched Jimmy Bjornquist's age, also matched his height.

I wrote my story and sent it to Don. He sent back an e-mail suggesting that I spend some time in our library looking for stories about missing adult males from twenty-five years ago. As I passed Don's desk on my way to the library, a light went on in my brain. Don might have interviewed Jimmy Bjornquist.

"No such luck," Don said. "The kid went home right after the cops questioned him, and his grandmother wouldn't let any reporters near him that day. And then of course he skipped the following day. I've always thought he killed Marilee and hid the body, but maybe she did go off to California with him if the cousin is right about them getting it on in the sack."

Another light went on. "I have one more possibility," I said. "His boss at the store: Adelbert Love."

I called the nursing home and asked to speak to Mr. Love. "I'll direct your call to Mr. Love's room," said the nice lady who had answered my call. The phone in the room rang ten times before I gave up. I called the nursing home again and told the nice lady that Mr. Love apparently was not in his room and that he didn't seem to have a means of leaving a message.

"Oh, he always turns off his voicemail when he leaves the room," she said. "Says he can't hear what the callers are saying, so why waste the electricity?"

"Does he turn it on when he's in the room?" I asked.

"Yes, he does. If he doesn't recognize the voice of the person leaving the message he doesn't pick up the phone."

"Is there any way to talk to him when he's not in the room?"

"I'll see if one of the attendants can find him and have him call you back."

I gave her my number and thought again about the frustrations of constantly waiting for return calls.

This one came more quickly than most. I was debating leaving my desk and going to search old missing men files in the library when my phone rang. I picked it up and gave my usual greeting.

"This is Bert Love," he said. "Who'd you say you were?"

I explained that I was the reporter who'd talked to him about the Marilee Anderson case on Wednesday.

"You the guy that told me about the old lady that plays Solitaire?"

What pot was calling the kettle old? "That's me. Did you find her?"

"I did. She's a shark at Cribbage. Beat me three out of five yesterday. Only problem is that when I went back today she didn't remember who I was. Then she beat me three out of five again."

"Well, I've got a question that will test your memory," I said. "Do you remember how tall Jimmy Bjornquist was?"

"Who?"

"Jimmy Bjornquist. The young man who was working for you in the store when Marilee Anderson disappeared."

"Oh, Jimmy. Yeah, he was about eighteen or nineteen I think."

"No, I'm not asking his age. Do you remember how tall he was?"

"I ain't hearing you so good. Did you say how tall?"

"Yes. How tall?"

"Well, I can't say exactly. He was taller than me."

"And how tall are you?"

"Now or back then?"

"Back then. How tall were you when you stood next to Jimmy?"

"Oh, I'd say he was a good four inches taller than me."

"And how tall were you?"

"I was that much shorter than Jimmy."

This was turning into "who's on first?" I clenched my teeth, turned my head away from the phone and emitted a sigh of frustration before saying, "Can you give me your height in feet and inches?"

"Back then?"

"Back then."

"Well, I'd guess I must have been about five-eight back then. Now I'm more like five-four, they tell me. Old farts like me keep shrinking, you know."

"I've heard that that happens," I said. "So you were five-eight and you say Jimmy was four inches taller?"

"About that," Love said. "Give or take an inch or so. Hard to remember exactly that far back."

"That's close enough. Thank you very much for your help, Mr. Love."

"You're very welcome," he said. Bless the nursing home age.

So Jimmy Bjornquist had been nineteen years old and stood six feet tall, give or take an inch or so. And Skeleton X had been in his late teens or early twenties and stood six feet tall, give or take an inch or two. I wondered if the cops were checking the Bjornquist DNA. I picked up the phone to call Brownie.

# Chapter Fourteen

## Looking for a Match

To MY AMAZEMENT, Brownie answered on the first ring. "Homicidebrown."

"*Dailydispatch*mitchell," I said. "Got a question for you."

"You're a reporter and you have a question? I'm shocked. Stunned, in fact."

"I knew it would amaze you. The chief said you're checking for DNA matches. I'm wondering if you're checking with the Bjornquist family."

"You're thinking Skeleton X might be the long-gone Jimmy?"

"Skeleton X comes very close to Jimmy's height and age."

"You been hacking into our records? How'd you know Jimmy's height?"

"A little birdie told me. No, I haven't been hacking. If I was a good enough hacker I'd never have to call you about anything."

"Well, Mitch, I can't comment on whose DNA we are testing. All I can say is that you are right about the similarity in Jimmy Bjornquist's and Skeleton X's statistics."

"So you haven't ruled out Jimmy Bjornquist as the potential victim found in the Andersons' backyard?"

"We haven't ruled out any adult male with those statistics."

"I wouldn't be wrong in speculating that Skeleton X might be Jimmy?"

"Speculate all you want. Have a good day, Mitch."

When I put down the phone I realized that Al was standing beside me with a coffee cup in each hand and a manila envelope clamped under his right elbow. "Was that Brownie?" he asked.

"It was," I said, taking the proffered cup of coffee.

"What did you find out from him?"

I took a sip of coffee. "He thinks Skeleton X might be Jimmy Bjornquist but he can't say so on the record."

"Why would Jimmy Bjornquist be buried in the Andersons' backyard?"

"One scenario I can think of is that Jimmy killed Marilee, and Jack Anderson found out and killed Jimmy and buried him in the backyard."

"So where's Marilee's body?"

"Only Jimmy Bjornquist could have told us that."

"Frustrating," Al said. He put his coffee down on a small square of open surface on my desk and pulled out the manila envelope. "Maybe Jimmy can't talk, but what I have here will tell us something."

He pulled an eight-by-ten sheet of paper out of the envelope and handed it to me. It was the photo of an attractive blonde woman with intense blue eyes. "Marilee Anderson at age forty?" I asked.

"Exactly. My camera club friend delivered this just a few minutes ago."

"Did you show it to Don?"

"I scanned a copy into the computer and sent it to him. He wants you to write a short piece to explain what it is and how we got it."

"Including 'courtesy of Jill Anderson,' I assume. Which reminds me, we've still got the original."

"That I don't know. You could ask Don."

"Those blue eyes still stand out, even in the twenty-five-year projection."

"The eyes have it. Like light bulbs on a Christmas tree."

"This is fabulous. We'll have our readers staring at every blue-eyed blonde between the ages of twenty and sixty in the Twin Cities."

"She cleans up pretty good as a forty-year-old."

"She does indeed. Better looking than I'd have guessed from the original."

"Maybe Jimmy Bjornquist could see into the future."

"I'm sure we'll start getting calls from people who are positive that they've seen her."

"I'll let you handle them. I'm heading out. See you later."

I wrote a brief story asking readers to phone the police if they'd seen this woman and noting that the original photo, which we'd be running alongside the new one, was courtesy of Jill Anderson, and sent it to Don. Minutes later, the before-and-after display was in the online edition. A few additional minutes later I was putting my computer to bed and preparing to go home when I received a call from a totally unexpected source.

# Chapter Fifteen

## Lauralee

THE VOICE WAS FEMALE but deep and husky, the kind of voice that would make any man eager to see the lips from which it came. I'm thinking Lauren Bacall in those old black-and-white movies with Humphrey Bogart.

"You're the one who's been writing about the Marilee Anderson cold case, right?" she said.

"Right. And you are?" I said.

"I'm Lauralee Baker."

I waited for further explanation. Receiving none after an embarrassing passage of time, I said, "May I ask why you're calling me?"

"I thought you'd like some inside information about Marilee."

"I'd love to get some inside information about Marilee. What do you know about her?"

"You don't know who I am, do you?"

"Other than your name, no. Should I know more?"

"If you'd done all your homework, you would. I'm Marilee's cousin. Her mother and my mother are sisters."

Ouch! I'd been chasing Marilee's relatives on the Anderson side but hadn't even thought about those on the mother's side. "You're right," I said. "I haven't done all my homework, and I'm embarrassed. Were you very close to Marilee?"

"We were buddies since we were babies," she said. "We were born only one day apart and our mothers gave both of us names ending in Lee, which was their maiden name. We were almost like twins when we were little girls. I've missed her every day for twenty-five years and now that the case is in the news again, I'd like to help find out what happened to her."

"Your help would be most welcome. Can I meet you somewhere?"

"I'm teaching summer school in Roseville and I live in an apartment near the high school," Lauralee said. "You could meet me there."

I'd have gone a lot farther than Roseville, which touches on St. Paul's northern border, to meet the owner of that voice. "Sounds good," I said. "When can we meet?"

"How about tomorrow right after school. Say about three o'clock."

"Give me directions and I'll be there."

\* \* \*

I'D BEEN RIGHT ABOUT phone calls. When I arrived in the newsroom Friday morning, Don handed me a list of thirty-six people who had left messages on our call-in line Thursday evening claiming to have seen Marilee Anderson. "It's your story—check them out," he said.

My e-mail contained a message from Brownie saying the police had been swamped with something like eighty-eight calls, and why the hell hadn't I warned him that the photo was running.

I replied that I had e-mailed him a copy of Marilee's image as a forty-year-old the previous afternoon at the same time we'd put it online, which was less than thirty minutes after it had been placed in my hands.

Either Marilee Anderson was covering a lot of ground or there were a lot of fortyish blondes with intense blue eyes running loose in the Twin Cities. I called the first number on the list of call-ins and got a woman's voicemail. I anticipated getting a lot of voicemails; it was, after all, a work day.

I worked my way down the list and talked to people of various ages and IQs who had seen the spitting image of Marilee in the supermarket, at a Twins game, at the airport, at the Como Park zoo, on a street corner, in the candy store, in a Lutheran church, in a Catholic church, on the beach at Lake Phalen, in a liquor store, at the beauty parlor, on the bus, standing at Seven Corners, at a high school concert, and at the movies. The times of the sightings ranged from "just a couple of days ago" to "sometime in June, must have been seven years ago." The descriptions of what the woman was wearing ranged from a yellow bikini swimsuit to a black dress that made her look kind of like a nun. I thanked them all for their help, and when I had accumulated eighteen comments I wrote a story about some of the possibilities, omitting the names of the callers.

"Really gets around, doesn't she?" Al said, looking over my shoulder at what I was writing.

"It's a wonder her parents or her cousin Lauralee didn't see her in one of those places," I said.

"Did any of them sound legitimate?"

"Most of them sounded loony. But there were a couple that might bear checking. I e-mailed their information to Brownie. It might make up for our not giving him a longer warning time before we ran it online."

"He's pissed about that?"

"Somewhat. They'd had eighty-eight phone calls by the time I got in this morning, and I got the impression that he hadn't opened the e-mail with the photo attached that I sent him yesterday afternoon."

"That'll teach him to look at his e-mail more often."

"Can't teach an old detective new tricks, but it taught me to call him when I'm sending something like that."

"They say you can learn something new every day. Right now I need to learn what time we're meeting cousin Lauralee."

"At three, near the high school," I said. When I'd told Don about this new development he'd assigned Al to accompany me. "We'll need to leave about two thirty."

*   *   *

AT 2:17 P.M. THAT DAY, the driver of a red convertible with Wisconsin plates cut off a semi-trailer on I-94 about two miles east of the St. Paul city limits. The truck driver's evasive maneuver caused the semi to jackknife and tip over, scattering a load of fresh ripe tomatoes from the broken trailer. Truck parts and squished tomatoes spread across the highway, blocking all three of the eastbound lanes. The driver of the red convertible with Wisconsin plates went merrily on his (or her) way to the Cheesehead State, while seven cars and two pickup trucks molded themselves into a pile of twisted metal behind the flattened semi and a sea of juicy red pulp. Behind this instant junkyard, scores of eastbound vehicles came to a screeching halt.

A photographer was needed and the only ones in the building were Alan Jeffrey and Daniel Hendrickson. Daniel Hendrickson is also known as Downtown Danny because he suffers from an emotional affliction that makes it impossible for him to leave the boundaries of St. Paul. The crash was in Lake Elmo, so obviously Don could not send Danny. Thus Al was ordered to the scene of the wreck.

My interview was in Roseville, also beyond the confines of St. Paul, so Don could not send Danny with me. Thus it was that I stood alone as I rang the bell at Lauralee Baker's apartment on the third floor of a building near Highway 36.

When the door opened, I was amazed at what I saw.

# Chapter Sixteen

## Summer Heat

KNOWING THAT LAURALEE Baker was Marilee Anderson's cousin, and having heard Lauralee describe herself and Marilee as virtually twins, I was expecting the door to be opened by a blue-eyed blonde of medium height.

What greeted me instead was a jade-green-eyed brunette who stood nearly six feet tall. Her dark, nearly black hair was pulled back in a waist-length ponytail and large gold circles dangled from her ears. She was wearing a shiny red, yellow, and orange robe that was held together by a matching belt knotted around her stomach. The robe was short on both ends, revealing a generous portion of two sensational breasts at the top and stopping six inches above her knees at the bottom. Below the hem were two extra-long legs shaped like those you see in TV commercials for short shorts and bikini swimsuits.

Apparently my face reflected my amazement because the spectacular woman in the doorway said, "Are you okay, Mr. Mitchell?" The low, silky voice was the one I'd heard on the phone.

I realized that my mouth was hanging open so I closed it. Finding it difficult to speak in this configuration, I opened it again, and words tumbled out. "I was expecting you to look more like your cousin."

"Blonde, you mean?" she said. "My mother is light, like her sister, but my father is dark like me. His genes seem to have won the battle." She stepped aside, gestured me in and waved me toward a deep brown leather chair. "Please sit down, Mr. Mitchell."

86

"Please call me Mitch," I said. I caught a whiff of a pleasantly spicy perfume or bath salt as I passed her on my way to sitting. Lauralee settled herself into a matching chair facing me and crossed her legs, showing enough thigh in the process to make me wonder if she was wearing anything under the red, yellow, and orange robe. Merely a reporter's curiosity, of course.

Other than the chairs we sat on, I can tell you nothing about the apartment. My focus was so locked on Lauralee and her abbreviated apparel that I wouldn't have noticed an elephant on the other end of the living room.

"Mitch, I hope you don't mind that I got into something comfortable," she said. "It's a hot day outside and I don't like to run the air conditioning at the freezing point."

"What you're wearing is just fine," I said. "I don't like too much air conditioning myself, either."

"I love bright colors, don't you?" She stretched out her arms, pulling the silky material taught against her breasts. I decided that she was not wearing anything under the robe on the upper part of her body.

"They look very nice on you. Goes really well with your dark hair." I felt like I was babbling foolishness.

"Can I get you a drink of something before we chat, Mitch? A beer or a gin and tonic or whatever?"

"No, I'm just fine, thanks. Better if I don't drink anything while I'm working." No point in discussing my membership in Alcoholics Anonymous.

"How about some water then, or some iced tea? You look a little warm."

She was right, I was a little warm. I loosened my tie and undid my collar button. "I'll be okay," I said.

She smiled and leaned back in the chair, causing the hem of the robe to slide upward another two inches. I felt my temperature rise another degree and decided to get down to business.

Opening my notebook with sweaty hands, I asked if she knew anything about Marilee's relationship with Jimmy Bjornquist.

"I know she was putting out for him," Lauralee said. "She told me all about how it was when she did it for the first time with him, because up to then we were both virgins."

"I know young guys brag about having sex with girls but I didn't know girls talked about it."

"Marilee and I talked about everything, right down to how it felt when he put it in the first time. It didn't sound that great to me, but I still tried it the first chance I had. That wasn't so great, either."

This was more information than I needed; certainly more information than I could put in print. As I was trying to think of my next question, Lauralee slowly uncrossed her legs and crossed them in the other direction. At this point, I was betting that there was nothing but Lauralee anywhere underneath the robe.

I wiped a trickle of sweat off my forehead with the back of my left hand. "Do you think they got serious about each other, or was it just hormones?" I asked.

"I don't know about Jimmy, but Marilee had feelings for the guy. I mean, she had no loving at home—her father beat her on her bare ass and her mother was such a wimp she let him do it. The only person she was ever close to was me until Jimmy started talking to her in the store. Eventually she started sneaking out at night to see him and they'd do it in the backseat of his car."

"So, do you think that she hid somewhere and went with him the next day when he took off for California or wherever?"

"I've always thought of a couple of possibilities. One is that they did what you just said. The other was that Jimmy blew up and killed her when she wouldn't have an abortion."

Two of the same scenarios that I had imagined. "She was pregnant?" I asked.

"She missed two periods, so she went and got one of those test kits at the drug store," Lauralee said. "The stick turned the right color—or maybe I should say the wrong color in her case. I was there when she did it."

"So she told Jimmy she was pregnant, and he wanted her to have an abortion?"

"He said he couldn't afford to have a kid. Didn't want a kid even if he could've afforded it. They argued about it. She never said that Jimmy got violent, but you never know. The timing is pretty suspicious."

"I guess I'm surprised that she refused the abortion."

"She wanted the baby. She wanted somebody that would love her. And she'd been brought up Catholic and believed that abortion was a sin."

"Makes sense when you put it that way. So which of those two scenarios do you think is the most likely?"

"I hate to say it, but I think the one where he kills her. Might have been by accident, you know, in a fit of rage. But I think if she was alive she would have contacted me somewhere along the line. Like I told you, we were like twins."

"If that's what happened, what do you think Jimmy did with the body?"

"I'm thinking he hid it in the trunk of his car and took it with him when he ran off the next day. He could have buried her anywhere between St. Paul and California."

"Have you ever told this to the police?" I asked.

"The police have never asked me anything," she said. "Like you, they went after Marilee's parents and her creepy uncle."

"What about the uncle? Why do you call him creepy?"

"Because he *was* creepy. Marilee said he was always feeling her up every chance he got and pressing his dick against her when he hugged her. He did practically everything but rape her; I think he was scared to go that far."

"She really had a wonderful family life. A father who beat her—did you say on her bare ass?—and an uncle who mauled her."

"Yes, I said bare ass. The bastard would pull her pants and panties down, lay her across his lap and smack her on the ass as hard as he could. I think he got off on it."

Again, more information than I could print. "You don't think Marilee's dad might have killed her?"

"I have thought of that. I really did think that when they dug up the bones in the backyard the other day, but now they say it was a man?"

"It was. Any idea who it might be?"

"Not a clue. That's really weird. All I can think of is maybe Jack killed somebody, but who? And why? It doesn't make any sense at all."

"Could it be Jimmy?" I asked. "Could Jack have found out that Jimmy had knocked up his daughter and killed him?"

"Oh, shit, I hadn't thought of that," Lauralee said. "But in that case, what happened to Marilee?"

"As I said to my photographer buddy yesterday, only Jimmy could tell us."

Lauralee sat in silence for a moment with her hands steepled in front of her face. "I haven't been much help to you, have I?" she said at last.

"Oh, no, you've been a lot of help," I said. "You've confirmed my suspicion that Marilee might have been pregnant and you've given me information about her father's spankings, her uncle's roaming hands, and her feelings about Jimmy."

"But that doesn't explain what happened to her. None of it does."

"It gives me pieces that might make sense if I find another piece or two."

Lauralee smiled, uncrossed her legs and slowly crossed them the other way, showing me further evidence that she might be naked beneath the robe. "Let's talk about you for a while," she said.

"Me? Why? I'm just a reporter doing his job."

"Are you a married reporter?"

"For almost two months. I tied the knot with my longtime lover just before Memorial Day."

"That's too bad."

"Why do you say that?" Being a sharp-eyed, ever-observant reporter, I had an idea why.

"You're a very attractive man. You're tall and strong and virile looking, and I haven't had a man in my bed for a long time." She stood up and the robe spread open far enough for me to get a flash of her bellybutton and everything below it before she pulled it shut. I'd been right; there was nothing inside that robe but Lauralee.

"I suppose you're the non-cheating type of newlywed," she said.

At that moment, I wasn't so sure, but I said, "You're right. I am." Another ribbon of sweat trickled down my forehead and I wiped it away with the back of my left hand. I could feel pools of water in my armpits.

Lauralee let the robe fall open all the way, revealing two suntanned breasts with dark burgundy nipples standing taught, and a flat tummy that tapered into a velvety-smooth, bikini-waxed V at the juncture with her equally well-tanned thighs. A gold stud winked at me from the top of the path to paradise. This was one smoking forty-year-old.

"Sure I can't tempt you, Mitch?"

My whole forehead was beaded with sweat and I was feeling action where I shouldn't have been feeling action. I rose from the chair and said, "You're gorgeous and I'd love to be tempted, but I just can't do it." I started backing toward the door.

She pulled the robe together and shook her head. "Just my luck to get a man with morals. If you ever change your mind or your wife decides to dump you, you have my number and my invitation."

"Thanks, I'll remember that," I said. I had reached the door and turned the knob, but the door wouldn't open.

"I took the liberty of locking the door behind us," Lauralee said. She walked past me, letting her robe flow freely in the breeze and giving me another whiff of her spicy fragrance as she went by. She unlocked the door, turned toward me, grabbed my face between her hands, pressed her lips against mine for about three seconds, and then released me and backed away. "Bye, bye, moral married man," she said and opened the door. I almost tripped over my own feet going out.

"Come again when you can stay and play," she said. The robe still hung open.

"Thanks for everything," I said.

"No problem," she said, lazily closing the door. Coming from her, I had no problem with that response.

\* \* \*

"So what did you do today, sweetie?" Martha Todd asked as we sat on our porch sipping our before-dinner ginger ale cocktails. Martha has no problem with booze and has been known to tip a glass of wine at dinner with friends or a party, but she rarely indulges in anything alcoholic when it's just the two of us.

"Talked to a bunch of people who think they've seen Marilee Anderson," I said. "I don't think any of them have."

"Weren't you going to interview Marilee's cousin today?"

"I was and I did."

"What was she like?"

"Very cooperative." I immediately wished I'd chosen a different adjective.

Martha's back stiffened. "Oh? Cooperative in what way?" she asked.

"In the way of answering questions. She told me a lot about Marilee and Jimmy the store clerk, and about Marilee's dad and her creepy uncle. The dad spanked her bare butt and the uncle groped it, along with everything else."

"Nice home life."

"That's what Lauralee said."

"What's Lauralee look like?"

"Oh, you know. Your average forty-year-old female."

"What do you call average?"

I saw I could be headed for trouble here. "Oh, you know. Average."

"Am I average?"

"God, no. You're a way-above-average, super-sexy, gorgeous female who doesn't look a day over twenty-nine."

"Did Al take pictures of Lauralee?" Martha asked.

"No, Al got sent out to the big crash on I-94. I had to go without a photographer."

"So I won't be able to see Lauralee's face in the paper?"

"Afraid not." *And you won't see her naked body in the paper, either,* I thought.

"So I have to take your word for it that she's average looking."

"Afraid so."

"Is she sexy?"

"Some men might think so."

"But not you?"

"Hey, I'm married to the sexiest woman between St. Paul and Cape Verde."

Martha got off her chair, leaned over me and kissed me on the lips. "Okay, you smooth-talking stud muffin, let's go have supper." I wiped the sweat off my forehead with my left hand

and followed her into the house. I was glad that I'd washed up and changed clothes when I got home so Martha detected no lingering essence of Lauralee.

*   *   *

"WHAT DID I MISS yesterday?" Al asked as he brought coffee to my desk Saturday morning.

I noticed Corinne Ramey look up at the next desk. "Let's take this coffee into the cafeteria and get some doughnuts to go with it, and I'll tell you all about it," I said. Corinne's eyes returned to the press release on her desk as we walked away.

"You missed the photo-op of the century," I said when we were seated at a table in a corner of the cafeteria.

"Oh, yeah? What did she do? Take off her clothes?"

"How did you guess?" I gave a minute-by-minute, inch-by-inch description of Lauralee's strip show while Al interjected monosyllabic profanities. When I was finished, Al said, "And while you were watching a private strip show, I was spending two goddamn hours shooting bloody faces and mangled metal and mushed tomatoes out in the sun on a boiling blacktop road. Life is not fair."

"I could set you up for a photo shoot with Lauralee. I've got her number."

"And we'd explain this to Carol how?"

"Tell her that duty calls."

"Seems more like booty calls."

"Carol doesn't have to know the naked truth."

# Chapter Seventeen

## A Day of Rest

O

N SUNDAY I ALWAYS—well, almost always—call my mother and Grandma Goodie. They are both widowed and live together on the family farm near Harmony, a small city in southeastern Minnesota. The milking stanchions in the old dairy barn stand empty, but the hay mow is still used for storage by a couple of neighboring farmers who rent the cropland and grow hay, corn, and oats.

I enjoy talking to my mother, who gives me a crop report—the corn was more than knee-high on the Fourth of July this year—and tells me what's wrong with the Minnesota Twins—the manager knows nothing about handling prima donna athletes.

Grandma Goodie is another story. As she did at my birthday party, she usually zeroes in on her favorite topic, which is my absence from anything resembling a church every Sunday. Her concern for my salvation is touching, but her harping on the subject is aggravating. It was her insistence on a church wedding that persuaded Martha, who is as averse to organized religion as I am, and me to find a minister who would conduct the ceremony in a church. The fact that the only minister liberal and compassionate enough was Unitarian-Universalist didn't sit very well with my more conventional grandmother, but she accepted it as being better than a justice of the peace in the Como Park Pavilion.

"Did you go to church this morning, Warnie Baby?" Grandma Goodie asked as soon as Mom passed her the phone.

"I think you know the answer," I said. "I didn't get there today."

"Warnie Baby, you need to think of your immortal soul. You need to be right with the Lord when the Day of Judgment arrives."

"You know I'm counting on your prayers to take care of me when that day arrives, Grandma."

"Well, Warnie Baby, I won't be around forever to ask the Lord for your salvation. I'll be eighty-nine in December, you know, and the doctor says my heart isn't the strongest he's ever seen on an eighty-eight-year-old lady."

"Yes, but your heart is in the right place."

"A lot of good that will do when it stops beating."

"I think you'll make at least a hundred," I said. "Maybe a hundred and five."

"Oh, Warnie Baby, what an awful thought. With my aches and pains and whatnot."

I quickly changed the subject to the Twins, who were also Grandma's favorite target for constructive criticism, and the conversation was more pleasant until the end, when she closed with, "I expect to hear that both you and Martha have been to church when you call here next Sunday."

I wanted to say, "Forgeddaboutit," but I simply said, "Bye, I love you," in my cheeriest tone of voice and hung up. I had in fact attended a Methodist service with Mom and Grandma about a year earlier and it wasn't the best of times. The minister chose that Sunday to blame the press for most of the problems of both the religious and the secular worlds, and my post-sermon conversation with him had been as strained as the coffee in our cups.

"Let me guess," Martha said. "Grandma Goodie wants you to go to church next Sunday."

"Lucky guess," I said. "But only half right. She wants you to go with me. She's worried about your soul, too, Marty Baby."

"She didn't call me that."

"No, but don't faint if she does. Lucky for you, she never saw you in diapers."

"Too bad for you that she saw you in your birthday suit."

"How would you like to see me in my birthday suit?"

"Now? It's the middle of Sunday afternoon."

"Got anything better to do?"

Martha thought it over for about three seconds before grabbing my hand and towing me toward the bedroom. I offered no resistance.

\* \* \*

MY FIRST CALL MONDAY morning was to Detective Lieutenant Curtis Brown. To my amazement, after the first ring I heard, "Homicidebrown."

"*Dailydispatch*mitchell," I said. "What's new on Skeleton X?"

"Stubborn bastard still hasn't told us his name," Brownie said. "Toughest interrogation I've ever had."

"Have you tried the extra bright lights and the rubber hose?"

"Lights don't even make him blink, and he just gives the hose a big toothy grin."

"With some of the teeth missing, according to the doctor of forensic dentistry."

"We've got two guys on their hands and knees in the rose garden running dirt through a sifter like the archeologists use to see if we missed any."

"Wow, that's a great lead for my story: 'Kneeling coppers seek skull's choppers.'"

"Probably won't get you a Pulitzer," Brownie said.

"That's why I'm putting the bite on you; I'm trying to extract something with more teeth," I said.

"I can't give you anything much to chew on, Mitch. Still haven't determined a cause of death, either."

"Are you getting any help from Skeleton X's' above-ground hosts?"

"You mean the Andersons? We'll be talking to them today."

"As suspects?"

"Negative. Not even as persons of interest. As of this moment we have nothing that would tie either of them to Skeleton X except the proximity of his gravesite. No prosecutor would hang a charge on that."

"Are you working on the Bjornquist DNA?"

"I can't comment on that at this time. All I can say is that basically we are now working on two cold cases, one of which was never hot in the first place. Have a good day, Mitch."

I interpreted Brownie's closing comment to mean that investigators had found no other missing person from that timeframe who matched Skeleton X's size and age. That meant that all things were pointing to Jimmy Bjornquist as the late possessor of Skeleton X, subject to DNA confirmation. This could be done with his cousin's cooperation. But it wouldn't tell us who planted Jimmy in the rose garden. Was it Jack Anderson or still another missing person?

This question brought another bizarre scenario flashing like lightning through my clouded brain. What if, instead of Jimmy killing Marilee, Marilee had killed Jimmy and run away, leaving her parents to cover up for her by burying Jimmy's body?

This was too much to deal with. I decided to leave the puzzle of Skeleton X to Brownie for the rest of the day and turned my attention to the list of people who'd thought they'd seen Marilee Anderson sometime in the last twenty-five years. Seven more names had been added overnight, but I wanted to follow up on one of the previous thirty-six. The woman who'd said she'd seen Marilee in a Catholic church wearing dark clothing had sounded sober and non-delusional when she left the message. Maybe she could provide me with some details.

Helen Hammersley lived in Newport, a suburb just south of the city. She answered on the third ring.

I told her that I'd like to hear more details about when she had seen the woman she thought was Marilee. She thought for a moment, and said, "It must have been in April, because I was taking care of my sister in her house in north Minneapolis. She'd had surgery and I was staying over to do the cooking and the housework for a few days. We're both in our seventies, you know, and she lost her husband about two years ago so she's all alone in that big old house. My husband wasn't too happy with me being gone for almost a week but I told him family is family and what else can I do, you know?"

I now knew more than I wanted to know about Mrs. Hammersley's family life, but I plunged ahead. "You went to church near your sister's house in April?"

"Yes, I went to the second Mass there on Saturday night and met this woman on her way out from the early Mass. I noticed her especially, first because she was dressed in black, almost like a nun, you know, and second because of her blue eyes. The dark clothes—she had on a hoodie, you know—really set off her eyes."

"You're saying she was dressed so that she looked like a nun but that she really wasn't a nun?" I asked.

"That's right. She had on a black hoodie over a black skirt, you know. But when I saw the picture of that missing girl in your paper, the blue eyes made me think of the woman I saw coming out of the church that night. I tried to imagine the face in the picture with a black hood around it, you know, and I said to my husband, I'd better call the paper like it says."

"What about her hair? Was she a blonde?"

"Oh, now I can't really say. The hood covered up her hair, you know, so I couldn't tell you if she was light or dark. I'm sorry about that."

"That's okay, Mrs. Hammersley. No need to apologize. You say you saw her just this past April? This year?"

"Oh, yes. That's when I was staying with my sister in north Minneapolis because she had had surgery and needed help."

"What was the name of the church?"

"It was, um, oh, gosh, now you're asking hard questions of an old lady," Mrs. Hammersley said. "It was, uh, Saint somebody, but then most of them are, you know. It was close to my sister's house on Fifteenth Avenue North if that helps you any."

"It does. I can look up which Saint somebody church is in that area."

"Wouldn't that be something if it really was the missing girl? I mean, after all those years to find her right there in Minneapolis."

"Yes, that would be something. I'll certainly follow up on this."

"Is there any kind of a reward for helping to find her?" Ah, there was mercenary thinking behind the moral compunction to do what's right.

"No, I'm afraid not, Mrs. Hammersley. The only reward would be knowing that you've done something nice for someone."

"Well, I suppose that's worth something, isn't it? Anyhow, I'll be watching the paper to see if that girl turns up in north Minneapolis."

"You do that—keep reading our paper. And thank you very much for your help."

"You bet," she said. I gritted my teeth, but at least "you bet" sounded more Minnesotan than "no problem."

I put down the phone and it rang immediately. Maybe it was Brownie, waiting on the line to tell me Jack Anderson had confessed to killing Jimmy Bjornquist.

"It's Morrie," said the voice. "I been waiting on hold to tell you that I just saw your missing girl."

This would be the last person from whom I would expect lucid assistance. But I asked the question anyway: "Where?"

"In the skyway," Morrie said. "She was walking her dog in the skyway."

"I didn't think that was allowed."

"Oh, she had a dog on a leash all right. Blonde woman with something like a little Shih Tzu on a leash. She was smiling. The woman, that is."

Something about this picture rang a bell but I wasn't sure what. "Where in the skyway was this?"

"Over your way. Just after you cross Cedar Street when you're coming from my apartment."

The bell was ringing more clearly. "It wouldn't have been in front of that store that sells pet food and supplies, would it?" I asked.

"Yeah, now that you mention it, it was right in front of there," he said.

"Did you speak to the woman?"

"Oh, no, I would never speak to a strange woman in the skyway."

Just what I suspected. "I hate to tell you this, Morrie, but that woman is a mannequin and the dog is a stuffed imitation. It's the store's advertising gimmick."

Morrie was silent for a moment. "Oh," he said at last. "Yeah, now that you mention it, I've seen her and her dog there before."

"I'll bet she was smiling then, too."

"Yeah, she was. I just thought of that picture in the paper when I saw her today."

"Tell you what, Morrie. You go back and talk to that woman, and if she answers you, give me a call because that will be a real news story." I put the phone down harder than necessary and drew a quizzical look from Corinne Ramey.

"Morrie," I said.

"I thought it might be," Corinne said. "You always get red in the face when you're talking to him. You should have your blood pressure checked."

The little bell on my computer that alerts me to incoming e-mail dinged. I punched in my password and clicked the mailbox open. The e-mail had been forwarded to me by City Editor Don O'Rourke. The original sender was Ramsey County medical examiner, and the subject was Skeleton X.

# Chapter Eighteen

## A Nick on the Neck

"ATTENTION ALL MEDIA," the message began. "Further close examination of Skeleton X reveals an indentation on the inside of a vertebra which could have been caused by a sharp object striking the bone. This vertebra was high up in the neck, just below the base of the skull, and would have been located behind the victim's throat. An extremely sharp and heavy blade might have penetrated to that depth if the victim's throat had been cut by a strong person using a powerful stroke. Therefore I am making a tentative determination that the cause of death for Skeleton X was a severing of the throat with a sharp object. Our office will continue to examine the remains in an effort to either confirm or discredit this supposition."

The notice was signed by Dr. Lyle Lundberg, Ramsey County medical examiner.

I picked up my phone and punched in Brownie's number on speed dial. I got his voicemail and left a message. He was probably still talking to Jack Anderson, who had been employed as a butcher when his daughter and her young lover had disappeared. How had Donna Waldner put it? Oh, yes, something about his job entailing cutting up steaks and things with big sharp knives.

Brownie did not return my call until an hour after lunch. "If you're calling about the cause of death I can't tell you anything beyond the ME's statement," he said.

"How are you coming with questioning Jack Anderson?" I asked.

"He insists he knows nothing about Skeleton X. He finally got tired of answering questions and lawyered up."

"Is he in custody?"

"Negative. We have nothing to hold him on."

"Any heavy, sharp knives in the stuff you took out of his house?"

"You think he'd keep the murder weapon laying around the house for twenty-some years if he cut a man's throat?"

"Might have been a knife he used every day on his job," I said. "He was a butcher, remember?"

"I do remember, but you should remember that I can't comment on what we took out of his house," Brownie said.

"Just a passing thought."

"Well, you'd better pass that thought into the wastebasket. You'd be sticking your neck out for cutting if you printed what you're thinking."

"Okay. So tell me, who'd Anderson hire as a lawyer?"

"Nobody from your wife's firm." That was always a possibility because the firm was headed by Linda L. Lansing, St. Paul's number one defense attorney. "His name is Harold Smalley. Has an office on the East Side, over near where the Andersons live."

"Thanks. I'll give him a call."

"I predict he'll say 'no comment.'"

"So do I, but I have to make the call."

"Anything beyond 'no comment' would be more than I got. Have a good day, Mitch."

I looked up Harold Smalley's office number and made the call. The guardian of his gate, a woman with a silky smooth voice, said he was consulting with a client and would I like to leave a message. I left a message, and I was still waiting for Smalley's return call when I shut down my computer, rose from my chair, and got on the elevator. I hoped the client with whom

he was consulting had sufficient funds to pay for all those bill-
able hours.

* * *

MY MONDAY NIGHT ritual consists of eating an early supper, attending a meeting of my Alcoholics Anonymous group in a
church basement on Grand Avenue, and having a ginger ale
after the meeting with fellow alcoholic Jayne Halvorson in a
place called Herbie's Bar. Jayne is five or six years older than I
am and is the divorced mother of two teenage girls. Together we
find something invigorating about slurping ginger ale in an es-
tablishment where everyone else is drinking what to us is forbidden fruit.

Jayne has been a positive force in my life. Not only has she
reinforced my abstinence at times of temptation, but she has also
often shown me a way to solve a problem that seemed unsolv-
able. The best thing she's ever done was to drag my quivering
ass into the jewelry store where I bought an engagement ring
for Martha Todd.

"Showing an age-advanced picture of the missing girl was
a great idea," Jayne said after her first sip. "Did it produce any
results?"

"It was Al's idea. He knows the guy who did the aging," I
said. "And did it ever produce results." I told Jayne the number
of calls that the paper and the police had received and she expressed amazement.

"Did any of them sound real?" she asked.

"Most were off the wall, but one woman's sighting really
intrigued me. She saw a woman of about forty with features like
Marilee's, including the bright blue eyes, coming out of a
Catholic church. Marilee was Catholic, so it could be possible.
The only question is her hair color. She was wearing a black

hoodie, so the woman couldn't see if she was a blonde. Anyhow, I need to talk to the priest at that church to see if the person the woman saw is a member of that congregation."

"What about Skeleton X?" she asked. "Do you have any idea who he might be?"

"I do, and I think the cops do, but as yet they don't have the DNA match they need to confirm it. I'm ninety-nine percent sure it's the young man who worked in the convenience store where Marilee was going for bread the morning she disappeared."

I told Jayne about Marilee's pregnancy and Lauralee's and my suspicions. "I'd just really like to talk to Marilee's mother alone," I said. "She said something about it being time for things to come out, which makes me sure she knows what happened. I just can't figure out a way to get in to see her. There's a cop at the Andersons' front door keeping reporters away."

"Could you get in if Mrs. Anderson gave her permission?"

"I don't know. And I don't know any way to get her permission."

"Didn't you and Al borrow a picture of Marilee from her to use for the age enhancement?"

"We did."

"Have you returned it?"

The light came on in my brain. "We have not. What a great idea. Why the hell didn't I think of that?"

"You're too close to the events. Sometimes an outside mind can think of things that an insider doesn't see."

"Once again, you've lit up a dark alley for me. I'll be on East Geranium on the morrow with Marilee's picture in hand thanks to you."

Little did I know how early I'd be on East Geranium on the morrow.

# Chapter Nineteen

## Blockade III

THE PHONE BESIDE our bed rang before our alarm clock Tuesday morning.

The glowing numbers on the clock said 5:49 a.m.

I said, "What the hell?"

Martha said, "Moomph!"

The phone rang again. I rolled over, picked up the receiver, and mumbled hello.

"I need you to get over to East Geranium right now," said Don O'Rourke. "I'm calling your twin to meet you there. The police radio says there was a shooting at the Andersons' number a few minutes ago." He hung up while I was saying, "okay."

I dragged my body out of bed and made the required trip to the bathroom. Still half asleep, I pulled on some underwear, a short-sleeved shirt, and the first pair of pants I encountered in the closet; stepped into a pair of loafers without putting on socks; kissed Martha, who had never opened her eyes, and dashed to my car. At the red light on Arcade and East Geranium, I cruised to a stop behind a familiar-looking gray Subaru. The Subaru turned right onto East Geranium and I followed it. When it stopped beside the curb, I stopped behind it. Al was standing beside the Subaru waiting for me when I jumped out of my Honda.

Two yellow sawhorses supporting a weathered wooden sign that said ROAD CLOSED – POLICE in black stenciled letters stood across the middle of the street, stopping us half a block from our destination. Looking down the block beyond the barrier, we could see so many flashing blue and red lights that it looked like Christmas in July.

"I wonder who shot who," Al said as we skirted the saw-horses and hustled toward the flashing light show.

"Whom," I said.

"What?"

"The correct usage is 'who shot whom.'"

"Thanks for the grammar lesson, but I'll let you shoot the pronouns while I stick to shooting the pictures of whoever or whomever I want to."

I saw no need to comment on the fact that he'd ended his sentence with a preposition. Al was right, his camera would not be recording his grammar.

The Andersons' property again was circled by yellow plastic police tape. The street again was crammed with emergency vehicles: five squad cars, an ambulance, and a hearse, the latter being the only one not displaying flashing lights. Uniformed police officers were going in and out the side door of a one-car garage at the end of a short driveway beside the Andersons' house. The overhead door of the garage was down, blocking our view of what was happening inside.

I approached a young uniformed officer who stood just behind the tape watching for intruders. "What happened in the garage?" I asked.

"Guy apparently put a handgun in his mouth and pulled the trigger," the officer said. "It ain't a pretty sight."

"Was it Jack Anderson?"

"Don't know. And I ain't authorized to tell you if I did."

"Who is authorized?" I asked.

"Nobody yet," he said. "Word is that an investigator is awake and on the way."

A car horn sounded behind me and I turned to see headlights at the barricade. "That must be him," the cop said. "I have to open the barricade. You'll stay on your side of the tape, right?"

"Right," I said. "Go do your job."

The cop left and Al asked if I wanted to crash the tape.

"No reason to piss off the cops," I said. "Plus, I have no desire to conduct a personal inspection of the mess in the garage, do you?"

"I can live without it. Blood and brains before breakfast isn't my cup of tea."

"Not part of my diet, either. I'll settle for a second-hand report from the investigator."

Said investigator parked his black, unmarked Crown Vic and came hustling past us, followed by the cop who had moved the barricade. We both said "hi" as the man, dressed in a light green shirt and khaki pants, was ducking under the yellow tape and he waved his right hand in response. We watched him trot up the driveway and go into the garage.

"What's happening?" said a familiar female voice behind us. I spun around to face Trish Valentine and her trusty cameraman.

"A man shot himself in the head inside the garage," I said. "We're told it's not a pretty sight."

"Nice of him to do it in the garage and not mess up the house," Trish said. "Is it Jack Anderson?"

"Don't know for sure. We have to wait for the investigator to give us the official word, but I can't imagine who else it would be."

"You're sure it's not whom else?" Al said.

"What do you mean by that?" Trish said.

"It's an inside joke," I said. "You had to be there to hear it."

"I can never follow what you two are saying," she said. "Your boss should split you up."

"He's threatened to do that with a big sharp axe," Al said.

"That's what I mean," Trish said. "You're always talking nonsense."

"We're not reporting live," I said. "We have time to clean up our work before the public sees it."

"Good thing," Trish said. "I'd hate to see your act on live TV."

This reminded me that I needed to call Don O'Rourke and let him know what was happening. While we talked, more members of the media, both print and electronic, straggled in. Soon we had a substantial group of sleepy-looking, sloppily dressed people standing around the yellow tape waiting for the investigator to emerge from the garage. Even Trish, whose hair and make-up were always the picture of perfection, looked pale and droopy in the early morning light. I heard her complain to another TV reporter about the dead man choosing such an ungodly early hour to blow himself away.

While we waited, another investigator who'd taken the time to put on a dark pinstripe suit with a striped necktie pushed his way through the crowd. He ignored our greetings and our questions and proceeded silently to the garage.

"Who's that jerk?" Trish asked.

"That's Mike Reilly from homicide," I said. "Don't know why he's here at a suicide. But you're right about him being a jerk." Al and I had a history of run-ins with Reilly, who bore a deep dislike of all reporters and photographers.

Some forty minutes later, Reilly and the original investigator came out of the garage and walked toward us. Reilly ducked under the tape and walked away without a word while the other man stopped inside the tape and held up his hands to silence the barrage of questions fired at him.

"My name is Tony Albright and I am investigating this shooting incident," he said when he could be heard. "All I can tell you right now is that we have the body of a man who apparently took his own life by placing the barrel of a handgun in his mouth and pulling the trigger."

"Who is he?" at least a dozen voices yelled in unison.

"We won't be releasing the victim's name until his family has been properly notified," Albright said.

"Isn't it Jack Anderson?" Trish Valentine said.

"I'm sorry but I can't release his name until the family members are notified."

"But Jack's closest family member is right there inside the house," I said.

"I'm sorry, but rules are rules," Albright said. "Any other questions?"

"What kind of gun did he use?" a man behind me asked.

"A .38-caliber Colt revolver. It was found near the victim's right hand with one bullet fired."

"What time did it happen?" asked another reporter.

"St. Paul police were called at 5:36 a.m. today by a neighbor who heard a gunshot."

"Which neighbor?" Trish asked.

"We've been asked not to identify her . . . I mean the neighbor," Albright said. Well, guess which neighbor that was. We would all be storming Donna Waldner's front door the minute the question-and-answer session broke up. Realizing his gaffe, Albright's face turned red.

"Why was a homicide detective here?" I asked. "Aren't you sure it's a suicide?"

"Detective Reilly was asked to look at the scene for confirmation," Albright said. "We have no doubt that it's a suicide."

"Any note by the body?" Barry Ziebart of Channel Five asked.

"No note has been found at this time," Albright said. "We will continue searching for a note within the victim's residence."

"After you've officially notified Mrs. Anderson?" I asked.

"After we've officially notified the victim's family," Albright said. Damn! I'd hoped to catch him in another slip.

I turned to Al. "Got enough pictures?"

"I've got shots of the garage and the helpful Mr. Albright," he said.

"Then let's get out of the crowd. I want to talk to Donna Waldner before the TV mob swarms around her door."

We retreated from the noisy scene and I took out my cell phone. I had added Donna's number to my contacts, as I always do with people I interview. I store the numbers until I'm sure I won't need them anymore and then I delete them.

Donna Waldner answered on the second ring. I identified myself and asked if she was watching out her window. "I am," she said. "Is it Jack?"

"Cops won't say, but I can't imagine who else would shoot himself in Jack's garage," I said. "The investigator said a neighbor heard the shot. Am I right in assuming that neighbor was you?"

"I don't want my name in the paper," Donna said.

"I'll say that you didn't wish to be identified."

"Then yah, it was me. I was up because Butchy needed to go out."

"Is Butchy your dog?"

"Yah. She sometimes needs to take an early pee."

"What kind of dog is she?"

"Shih Tzu," she said. "And don't make no funny remarks about that word. I've heard 'em all."

"I'm sure you have, Mrs. Waldner," I said. "Tell me what you heard this morning."

"I heard a sort of poppin' sort of a bang comin' from next door. It wasn't all that loud, but it was loud enough to make me think maybe it was a shot, so I called 911."

"Did you go over to Andersons' to check on the noise?"

"Oh, no, I didn't want to go over there and find somebody who'd been shot, or maybe even run into some crazy loon with a gun in his hand. I stayed right here in the house 'til the cops came, just like the operator said for me to do."

"Have the police talked to you?" I asked.

"Some," she said. "They asked some questions and then told me there was a dead man in the garage who'd shot himself. They wouldn't say who it was but I figured it must be Jack."

"Can you think of any reason Jack would shoot himself?"

"Not off the top of my head. I don't know what kind of problems he's been havin', but with all that's been goin' on the last few days, with the buried body and all, maybe he just went off his nut."

"Well, if you think of any other possibility, please give me a call. Do you still have my card?"

"Oh, yah, it's still around somewhere."

"Good. Now I see a couple of TV crews heading toward your front steps, so I'll say goodbye."

"Oh, shit," she said. "I mean . . . oh, darn. I'm gonna go hide upstairs until they go away. And you remember now, I don't want my name in the paper."

"I'll remember. And thanks for your help."

"No problem," she said. I gritted my teeth and ended the call.

"Anything good?" Al asked.

"She has a Shih Tzu named Butchy who had to take an early pee and she heard a popping sort of a bang. Also, she thinks Jack might have just gone off his nut."

"That's a cracking good quote," Al said.

"Sums it up in a nutshell," I said.

\* \* \*

"HEY, YOU GUYS ARE really dressed up today," said Virginia Donaldson, the *Daily Dispatch* receptionist, when Al and I walked past her desk on our way to the newsroom. "Something special going on?"

I'd forgotten about my sloppy attire, and Al had dressed as quickly and casually as I had when the early morning call came in.

"Very special," I said. "We always try to look our sartorial best when we're called before sunrise to go out and cover a shooting."

"Oh, wow! Who got shot?" Virginia asked.

"Guy out on East Geranium," Al said. "At the place where they dug up the bones a few days ago."

"Oh, gosh. Another big mess out there? I've got a friend that lives in the next block and she says the neighbors are sick and tired of looking at cops and tape and flashing lights all the time."

"Well, they got another dose of it this morning," I said. "The guy shot himself at about five thirty and the cops, tape, and flashing lights were all there a few minutes later. Where does your friend live?"

"Like I said, in the next block. She knows the place because of the big gardens out in back. She and the woman belong to the same garden club."

That got my attention. "Your friend knows Jill Anderson?"

"Sort of," Virginia said. "I don't think they're what you'd call friends or anything like that."

"But she does know Jill."

"Yes, she does."

"What's your friend's name and phone number?"

"Oh, God, are you going to call her?"

"I'm calling everybody I can find who can tell me anything about that family."

"Molly won't want her name in the paper."

"I won't put her name in the paper. I'm looking for background, not quotes."

"Okay, her name is Molly Stewart. I'll have to look up her number and send it to you with an e-mail."

Five minutes later I was punching Molly Stewart's number into the phone on my desk.

# Chapter Twenty

## A Quiet Woman

MOLLY STEWART WAS NOT pleased to receive my call. "I'll bet Virginia Donaldson gave you my name, didn't she? Wait'll I see her. I told her I didn't ever want to get a call from any reporters where she works."

"I'll neither confirm nor deny your suspicion," I said. "Anyway, I'm not looking for quotes. I'm just trying to learn more about the Andersons—what kind of people they . . . are." I'd almost said "were."

"I can't help you much with that," Molly said. "The only contact I had with Jill was at garden club meetings and I never once met her husband."

"What was your impression of Jill at the meetings?"

"I don't think I ever had an impression. She was super quiet, never said 'boo' about anything. Never hosted a meeting at her house or ever invited us to come look at her gardens, either. We all thought that was kind of strange, especially since she had all those big beautiful roses to show off. Now, if you'll excuse me . . ."

"She had those gorgeous gardens and she never invited club members to see them up close?"

"Not once. If she knew there was a body buried there, I guess I can understand why she didn't want visitors. Does that answer all your questions?"

I wasn't going to let her go that quickly. "So do you think Jill knew about the body?" I asked.

"I haven't a clue what she knew about anything. All I know is that she came to meetings, listened to the speakers, got ideas from us, and never shared one damn thing with the group. She'd say 'hi' and 'goodbye' and almost nothing in between. We all thought it was because she was depressed about losing her daughter, but maybe it was more than that. Always kind of hung her head like she was afraid to say anything to people. What were the cops doing there this morning, by the way?"

"A man shot himself in the garage early this morning," I said.

"Oh, no! Was it Jill's husband?" Molly asked.

"Cops haven't confirmed it yet, but everybody is ninety-nine and nine-tenths percent sure that it was."

"Jesus, that poor woman. She'll really be hanging her head now. He's dead, I suppose?"

"He is. And you say that you've never had a conversation with Jill, or been in her garden or her house?"

"That's right. And now, if you'll excuse me, I have to get out of here and get to work. Please don't put my name in your paper, Mr. . . .uh?"

"Mitch," I said. "Mitch Mitchell. Thanks for your time."

"No problem," Molly said as she hung up. Really? It seemed to me that there was a problem all the time we were talking, but who am I to judge her?

The "You've Got Mail" light on my computer was flashing. The email was addressed to a long list of media and came from the St. Paul Police Department, and read: "John L. (Jack) Anderson, age sixty-five, was found dead, apparently from a self-inflicted gunshot wound, in his garage at approximately 5:45 this morning. A .38-caliber Colt revolver was found beside the remains. The official cause of death will be announced upon completion of an autopsy by the Ramsey County medical examiner. Mr. Anderson is survived by his wife, Jill Anderson, and a brother, Edward Anderson."

"And maybe a daughter, Marilee Anderson," I said to myself as I copied the e-mail into the story I'd begun writing.

As I wrote the story of Jack Anderson's suicide, I recalled Jill Anderson saying that it was time that it all came out. Had Jack shot himself because it all was coming out? If so, what was the "all" that was coming out? Was it related to the skeleton found in the rose garden?

Another thing I wondered about was the presence of homicide detective Mike Reilly at the suicide scene. Was there something about Jack's death that the investigator hadn't told us about? I called Detective Lieutenant Curtis Brown's private number.

"Homicidebrown," Brownie answered in his usual one-word response. "Can you hold for a minute?"

"*Dailydispatch*mitchell," I said. "I can hold."

I held for a minute that lasted for approximately 360 seconds. When Brownie finally came back, I asked about Reilly's role at the suicide scene. "Did something look like it might not have been suicide?"

"The investigator, what's his name? . . . Albright . . . had a question about the position of the gun in relation to the victim's hand," Brownie said. "Detective Reilly checked it out and was satisfied that the weapon could have fallen where it did."

"So Albright was wondering if somebody else might have placed the gun near Jack Anderson's hand?"

"I assume that was his concern. Detective Reilly found nothing to indicate that anyone else had handled the weapon. It's clearly a suicide, Mitch. Don't try to blow it up into anything else."

"You know me, Detective. I'm always asking all the questions."

"And you're always looking for the biggest, most sensational story. Sorry to disappoint you on this one."

"I'm always looking for the true story, sensational or not," I said. "I've got one more question: Is anyone at the St. Paul PD planning to ask Jill Anderson about why Jack shot himself?"

"You'd have to ask Albright about that," Brownie said. "I assume they'll be talking to her, but I imagine they'll handle her gently. Apparently the deceased didn't leave a note, so she might not know why he did it."

I briefly considered telling Brownie about Jill's bothersome comment, but decided to keep it to myself for the moment. "You've been questioning Jack about Skeleton X. Could his suicide have something to do with that?" I asked.

"I'm not about to speculate on Mr. Anderson's motive."

"Okay. But speaking of Skeleton X, any luck with identification?"

"Nothing yet. We'll let the media know when we find out who he was. Now I've got another call to take. Have a good day, Mitch."

I had one more call to make. I punched in the number for the house on East Geranium Street. A man answered.

I identified myself and asked the man for his name. "This is Edward Anderson," he said. "And we've got no comments for the press."

"'We' being you and your sister-in-law?" I said, assuming that Uncle Eddie wouldn't be using the royal "we."

"Exactly," he said. "We've just lost a dear family member and we've got nothin' to give to the press."

I decided to try the route suggested by Jayne Halvorson. "Actually, I have something to give to Mrs. Anderson," I said. "I'd like to return the picture of Marilee that I borrowed a few days ago, and also give her the enhanced enlargement that my photographer friend made from it."

"Not the one that shows what Marilee supposedly looks like now?" Edward said.

"No, no. It's a copy of the school picture that we borrowed."

"Jill cried for hours after she saw the one that showed what Marilee would look like if she was still alive. That was a terrible thing to run in the paper. Made Jill bawl her eyes out and gave me the creeps."

"We were hoping that Marilee is still alive and that someone might have seen her recently."

"Well, we're pretty damn sure she's not alive and it was awful for Jill to see that picture of her little girl looking like she was forty years old."

"I'm very sorry about that," I said. "But as I was saying, I'd like to return the picture we borrowed. Would it be possible for me to come to the house?"

He thought for a moment. "If it was up to me, I'd tell you to go to hell. But let me ask Jill. It's her picture. Hang on a minute."

I hung on. It was another long minute—296 seconds by the sweep hand on my watch—before Edward said, "You still there?'

"I am," I said.

"She says it's okay for you to bring the picture here this afternoon. But no cameras and no notebooks to write down anything she says."

"Fair enough. What's a good time?"

"Better make it late, like three o'clock or so."

"Three o'clock it is. Thank you for your help, Mr. Anderson."

"You're welcome," Edward said. Now there was a well-mannered man, even if it didn't sound like he really meant it.

*   *   *

At exactly 3:01 p.m., I rang the Andersons' doorbell. The barricade was gone, allowing me to park right in front of the house, and the yellow tape had been removed, permitting me to walk up the steps to the front door. No TV crews or police officers were in sight.

In my left hand, I carried a manila envelope containing the original photo of Marilee and the eight-by-ten copy that Al had made. In my shirt pocket, I carried my tiny tape recorder loaded with a fresh tape.

Uncle Eddie opened the door and I introduced myself. "Oh, yah, I remember you," he said, stepping aside. "Come on in. Jill is in the livin' room." His tone was as welcoming as it would be for a visit from Satan.

He turned his back to lead the way and I switched on my pocket tape recorder as I followed him through an oak-paneled archway into the living room. The beige-carpeted room was surprisingly bright, thanks to the wide floor-to-ceiling bay window that faced the street and two tall windows that looked toward the garage.

Jill Anderson was seated on a faded floral print sofa facing the bay window. Her eyes were red from crying and her shoulders and upper body were slumped in exhaustion. In front of the sofa was a dark wooden coffee table covered with a scattering of magazines. Most had flowers on their covers.

I offered my condolences on her husband's death and held the envelope toward her. She reached out and took it, laid it on the coffee table without opening it, and waved toward an armchair set at a ninety-degree angle to the sofa, upholstered in the same pattern. "Please sit down, Mr. Mitchell," she said. "Thank you for returning the picture of my dear daughter."

"You're welcome," I said. "I'm just sorry about what's happened here."

She emitted a long sigh and let her head droop until her chin touched her chest. "Yes, it's all coming out, just like I said it would," she said.

I decided to risk asking the obvious question. "What's coming out?"

Another sigh. "The body in the garden. What Jack did. What Jack and I did together. Everything . . ."

Edward, who'd taken a standing position at the end of the sofa, jumped in. "Jill, hold it right there. Don't say no more."

Jill raised her head and looked at Edward. "It's okay, Eddie. I've been doing some thinking, and I've decided that I want to tell this gentleman what really happened twenty-five years ago. Nothing I say can hurt Jack now. And what have I got to lose? My daughter is still missing, my husband is dead, and my beautiful garden is gone. What else can happen to me?"

"This man's a reporter," Edward said. "Don't you understand? He'll put the whole damn mess in the paper."

"Maybe that's the best place for it," she said. I wanted to voice my enthusiastic agreement but I clamped my jaws shut.

"You're makin' a big goddamn mistake talkin' to him," Edward said. "If you blab about everything that happened back then, it'll ruin you for the rest of your life."

"What life do I have left?" Jill asked. She turned toward me. "You don't have anything to take notes on, do you?"

"I have a great memory," I said. *Not to mention an hour's worth of tape in my shirt pocket,* I thought.

"Eddie, please get this man a notepad and a pen from my desk."

"Jill, I think it's stupid and crazy for you to do this," Edward said.

"I need to do this," Jill said. She sat up straight and her voice grew stronger. "I've been holding all this shit inside me for twenty-five years and I'm tired of it. I'm sorry, Eddie, but I just can't hold it in anymore. Jack is gone where he's safe now and I don't give a damn what anybody does with me."

I could feel my excitement rising as she talked. My armpits were getting wet with sweat and my forehead was hot and damp. I had all I could do to keep from telling Eddie to do what he'd been told.

Eddie stood looking down at Jill for a long moment. Her eyes met his and held steady. At last Eddie blinked. He turned to me and said, "Be right back." He walked stiff-backed out of the room and returned a minute later with a legal pad and a ballpoint pen. He held them out to me while looking past me toward the bay window. I took them and thanked him and he just grunted in response. Good manners disappear when a man is really pissed.

"Are you ready to listen, Mr. Mitchell?" Jill asked.

"Any time you're ready to speak," I said. Edward had walked to the bay window and was staring out with his arms folded and his back to us.

Jill sighed yet again and looked down at her lap, where her hands were folded. "It all started thirty years ago when Jack took his first trip to Canterbury."

She paused and I said, "The horse race track?"

"The horse race track. That visit started all the troubles that ruined our lives."

# Chapter Twenty-One

## It's All Coming Out

"JACK WENT TO CANTERBURY for the first time with a friend who went there all the time," Jill said without looking up. "The friend talked him into betting on every race, which he hadn't figured on doing, and he won enough times that he came home with a couple of hundred dollars more than he'd left with. Now you'd think that would be a good thing, wouldn't you?"

She looked up at me and I nodded. "Sounds good to me."

She looked down again at her folded hands. "It sounded good to Jack, too. Sounded like easy money. So good and easy that he started going back two or three times a month. Then it got to be every weekend, both Saturday and Sunday, and then he started taking sick days off from work so he could go to the track. He even used up all his vacation days out there betting on those damn old horses. Sometimes he won more money than he lost, but most days he lost everything he had. Then he'd go to the ATM to get some more, which he would also lose.

"He cleaned out our savings account—every last dime—and then took out cash loans on both of our credit cards. I tried to talk sense into him. I even went to Eddie and had Eddie talk to him. But it wasn't any use. There was just no stopping him.

"It was like Jack was sick with a terrible disease that he couldn't cure and didn't really want to cure. I tried to block the door one day when he was starting to leave for the track and he threatened to knock my head off if I didn't get out of his way. The man never once hit me in all our married years, but I think he would have done it that day if I hadn't given up and stood to one side. That's how sick he was."

She paused and looked up at me, turning her head from side to side. "That happens to a lot of people," I said. "A gambling addiction can be as bad as alcoholism or being hooked on dope."

Jill nodded and looked past me to Edward, who still had his back toward us. "That's the way it was," she said. "An addiction. There was no stopping it. No cure for it. When he'd maxed out the credit cards, he started skipping payments on bills. Pretty soon we had calls about the electric and the water and even the mortgage. I was about out of my mind, but Jack was still going to that damn track every chance he had and telling me he was going to win it all back and get us out of debt.

"I didn't know it, but he also borrowed money from some people he met at the track. People who charged a big rate of interest and who made sure they always got paid back. I found out about that when one of those people came around one Thursday night just before supper time and had a session in the garage with Jack. After the man left, I wouldn't give Jack a second's peace until he told me what was going on.

"Marilee heard us going at it and she got into it, too. She and Jack were always fighting, so naturally she jumped in on my side. That made Jack even madder—so mad that he finally told us that he owed the guy twenty thousand dollars and that the guy was coming to collect on Saturday.

"Of course we didn't have twenty thousand dollars. Hell, I doubt if we had twenty dollars in cash by that time. But Jack said not to worry, that he'd made a deal with the guy that didn't need cash. We both asked him over and over again what the deal was but Jack wouldn't tell us. He finally told us both to go to hell, walked out of the house and drove away, probably to the goddamn track."

Jill paused and looked up, and I saw tears beginning to flow from both eyes. I wanted to say something but couldn't find any words that seemed appropriate. She pulled a white hanky with blue flowers around the edges from her jeans pocket and wiped away the tears.

"Jack didn't come home until after I was asleep that night, and he was late coming home from work on Friday. I did not speak to him at all that night and neither did Marilee. We had eaten supper before he got home and I didn't offer him anything. I went up to bed early and was sound asleep when Jack finally came up.

"I didn't know what to expect Saturday morning. Marilee and I were in the kitchen when Jack came in and began to apologize for the way he'd been acting. He like to broke down crying he was so sorry about the whole thing. We finally all settled down and Jack gave Marilee some money and asked her to go to the store to pick up some things. She went out the door and . . . she never came back."

The tears were running like twin rivers down Jill's cheeks now, and she tried to dam the flow with the flower-rimmed hanky. I could feel my eyes growing moist in the corners but I refused to acknowledge this by drying them. I just told myself that reporters do not cry.

Edward broke the silence. "I suppose you're gonna bring out all the rest of the shit now." He had turned around and was glaring at us, his wrinkled face screwed into a scowl.

"I am," Jill said. "Like I said, it can't hurt Jack and I don't give a good goddamn about myself anymore."

"What about me?" Edward asked. "What can happen to me?"

"You're not involved," Jill said. "You didn't find out what Jack had done until days afterward, and you don't even know the worst of it."

"What do you mean the worst of it?" he asked.

"Why don't you just shut your mouth and listen," Jill said. "You've got a big, nasty surprise coming."

Edward shrugged and sat down in a chair beside the bay window. "Okay, spill your stupid guts. We're both listenin'." He stretched out his legs and folded his arms.

Jill looked at me again. "You know a lot about what happened in the next few days. You've written about it in the paper. How Jack went looking for Marilee and how we both were crazy with worry all day and how the cops ignored us for a while because Marilee had taken off without telling us a couple of times before. But what you don't know, and Eddie here doesn't know, either, is what happened that Saturday night."

"So what happened?" Edward said.

"I'm about to tell you," Jill said. "Jack and I were in the kitchen. I was making a couple of grilled cheese sandwiches for our supper and Jack was honing one of the big butcher knives he used at work, when the door opened and the man who wanted the twenty thousand dollars came charging in. He was raving mad, hollering that 'the bitch' had gotten away and was hiding somewhere and he couldn't find her. He kept yelling about 'the bitch' being gone and that if she was hiding here in this house he wanted her back right now.

"Jack told him that 'she' wasn't here and that he had no idea where 'she' was. The man said if that was true, he wanted his twenty grand, and walked up to Jack with his hand out. Jack had that big sharp butcher knife in his hand and he swung it right across the man's neck. Like to almost cut his head off . . ."

Edward was out of his chair, yelling, "Jesus Christ, you mean Jack killed that man?"

"Faster than you can say the words," Jill said. "Just like that the man drops to the floor and blood goes flying everywhere, all over the floor and the cabinets and the stove. I was so shocked I actually peed in my pants."

"And you guys never told me about that?" Edward said.

"What would you have done if we had?" Jill said. "Would you have called the cops on us?"

"God, no," he said. "I'd have kept your secret."

"Maybe," she said. "And maybe it would have got to be too much for you, like it has for me right now. Jack said right away we shouldn't say anything to anyone, especially to his brother, because his brother could never keep his mouth shut."

Edward slumped back into the chair. "I can't believe it. Jack killed a man. Right here in this house. Cut his throat right here in this house."

"What happened next?" I asked. I was beginning to see where this was going and I needed to get Jill back on track.

"We stood there looking at the mess on the floor for a while, Jack with the knife in his hand and me with piss dripping down my legs," Jill said. "When I finally could talk, I asked Jack what the crazy fool was talking about. Who was 'the bitch' that he was looking for? Jack told me to sit down. I asked him why and he said to just sit down and he'd tell me.

"When I sat, Jack put the knife in the sink and started the water running to wash away the blood that was on the blade. Then he turned and looked at me and said that the bitch was Marilee. He had given our daughter Marilee to that awful man to cover his twenty-thousand-dollar debt." She stopped talking and dropped her chin back down onto her breast.

"My God, what did you do?" I said.

"At first I didn't know what to do. Then I exploded. I went up to Jack and I started hitting him with my fists and screaming at him and calling him terrible names. He just stood there and took the beating until my arms got so tired I couldn't hit him anymore. Then he put his arms around me and held me while I cried, and he said everything would be okay because Marilee had gotten away, and she'd be coming home after hiding out from this guy for a while. Then he said what we had to do real quick was hide this creep's body and clean up the kitchen so's there wouldn't be any blood when Marilee got home.

"When I couldn't cry no more I realized that he was right, that we had to do something with the body and then clean up the mess. I asked Jack, 'what if someone comes looking for this guy,' and Jack said, 'we'll say we don't know where he could be.' The guy was just a sleazy crook who'd come to Minnesota from out east somewhere and no family was going to be missing him, Jack said.

"Anyhow, Jack had a big blue sheet of plastic in the basement that he'd used for a drop cloth when we painted the house, so he brought that up and we rolled the guy up in it and lugged it out to the garage and stuffed him into the trunk of Jack's Buick. I was glad he was a skinny guy because he was still awful heavy. Then we stayed up all night scrubbing up every speck of blood we could find in the kitchen. We thought we covered every square inch, but even so I'd find a spot somewhere for the next couple of weeks. If the cops had ever searched the house, I'm sure they'd have found enough blood spots to put us in jail for life."

"Maybe not, if they didn't know a man was missing and didn't find a body," I said. "How and when did the body get from the car trunk to the backyard?"

"We didn't know what to do with it. We knew we couldn't keep it in the car very long because it would start to stink pretty quick in the hot weather. Jack said we had to bury it somewhere but we couldn't think of a safe place where nobody would see us or find the grave.

"I actually came up with the idea of digging up a garden plot and burying the body there. I'd always wanted a rose garden and the idea just kind of popped into my head. So on Monday, between talking about Marilee to the cops and the reporters and the neighbors, we dug up part of that big plot in the back where they found the skeleton last week. I suppose we raised some eyebrows starting a rose garden in July, but people looked at us as kind of strange anyways because we weren't all that sociable. By Tuesday night we had dug up a spot big enough to bury the body without it looking funny, so we lugged him out there at two o'clock in the morning and put him in and covered him up. Not deep enough, I guess."

"And then you planted roses on top of him?" I asked.

"Yup," Jill said. "We'd bought a whole bunch of plants and we put them in real close together all over that piece of ground. You can't say we didn't decorate that bastard's grave." She actually chuckled at that.

"Oh, my God, Jill, that's sick," Edward said. "I can't believe you guys did such a gross thing. My own brother . . ."

"What else could we do?" Jill said. "Can you imagine telling the cops we'd killed a guy that Jack had sold our daughter to?"

"Self-defense," Edward said. "You could have pled self-defense. Didn't you say the guy came at Jack?"

"We weren't about to risk that," Jill said. "We just wanted to get everything cleaned up and out of the way for when Marilee came back home."

"But she never came," Edward said.

"That's the only thing I feel bad about," Jill said. "Looking back at it now, I'm not a bit sorry that Jack killed that son of a bitch."

"You've really never heard anything at all from Marilee?" I said.

"Never," she said. "Not one word. Either something bad happened to her or she was so mad at us she didn't want to come home. I hope it was that, but I've always been afraid that some other pervert found her and did something awful to her. It's hard to believe that she would stay away from her family this long if she was alive."

I had been scribbling notes like crazy in case the tape ran out. I finally put the notebook down by my side and clicked shut the ballpoint pen. I couldn't think of another question to ask Jill.

Edward rose and walked up to me. "So, what are you going to do now, Mr. Newspaperman?"

"I'm going to write a story about what I've just heard, and I'm afraid I'm going to have to run the facts past the chief of homicide as a courtesy before the story goes into print," I said. I could imagine Brownie's reaction if this bombshell appeared in the paper without his prior knowledge. I'd have to go back to covering art fairs and writing obituaries because I'd never get another word out of him or anyone else in the St. Paul PD.

"That means they'll be comin' after Jill," Edward said.

"They're planning to talk to her anyway about Jack's suicide," I said. "This will just give them a little broader subject matter." *Yes*, I thought, *the conversation will broaden to such topics as accessory to murder, unlawful disposal of a body, and conspiracy to conceal a criminal act.* She would need a very good lawyer and I had one in mind. I pulled my billfold out of my rear pocket and withdrew a business card.

"I'd recommend calling this law firm before you talk to the police," I said, laying the card on top of the manila envelope on the coffee table. "Ask for Linda L. Lansing. She's the best there is at helping people who need a strong defense. Tell them I told you to call."

"I don't really care if I go to jail," Jill said.

"I think you've already been punished enough," I said. "You shouldn't have to go to jail, but you probably will if you don't have the proper defense. I'll tell Linda you'll be needing her services. And thank you so much for trusting me with your story."

Jill rose from the sofa and reached out for my hand. I dropped the ballpoint onto the coffee table and took her hand in mine. Her grip was much stronger than I expected.

"You're so very welcome," she said. Ah, there was a woman with proper manners, even under duress.

*  *  *

I WAS FLYING HIGHER than a space probe when I got back to the *Daily Dispatch* newsroom. I told Don O'Rourke what I had and he almost jumped out of his chair and kissed me. "Get it done now," he said. "This is amazing after all these years."

"I'll have to run it past Brownie," I said. "He'll kill me if we drop it on him without any warning."

"Tell him you're making no changes," Don said.

"Of course. It's just a courtesy call."

"Has your twin got any shots of Jill Anderson?"

"He got some the day we borrowed Marilee's picture."

"I'll go see him," Don said. "You get writing."

I wrote the story almost word for word as Jill had told it, practically floating on air above my chair as I pecked away at the keyboard. When I finished, I sent a copy to Don and picked up the phone.

"Homicidebrown," said Brownie.

"*Dailydispatch*mitchell," I said. "I am about to e-mail you a story we'll be running on page one. I'd suggest you sit down while you read it. If you have any comment to go with it, give me a call. I'll be here the rest of the day."

"What the hell is it?" Brownie said.

"I had a chat with Jill Anderson this morning. You'll be very interested in what she said."

"She actually talked to you?"

"She did. For quite a long time, as you'll see."

"Okay. Send it along. Have a good day." I wanted to say that I was having a wonderful day, but he'd already put down the phone.

My phone rang ten minutes after I'd sent the e-mail to Brownie. Looking forward to his reaction, I picked up the receiver and said, "So, how'd you like it?"

"It's Morrie," said the dreary voice. "I don't like it."

I wanted to scream, but I kept my voice down to about ninety decibels. "Goddamn it, Morrie, I don't have time to talk right now."

"But the Russians are beaming their radar at me. You need to write about it."

I had to get rid of him quickly. "Listen, Morrie, go into the kitchen and eat a sandwich," I said.

"Why a sandwich?"

"It will confuse the Russians. They'll think it's lunch time and turn off the radar and go eat some borscht."

"That's a great idea. I'll make a ham sandwich right away."

"Put Russian dressing on it if you've got some. Bye, now." I slammed down the phone.

Corinne Ramey was staring at me from the next desk. "Who's going to eat borscht?" she asked.

"The Russians who are beaming their radar at Morrie," I said. "It's a diversionary tactic."

"Sometimes I think you're as nutty as he is."

"Oh, really? Next time I'll transfer the call to you."

"Never mind. You're the man, Mitch, you're the man."

My phone rang again. This time it was Brownie.

"How the hell did you ever get that woman to spill her guts like that?" he asked.

"Her guts just couldn't hold the crap inside anymore and I was the lucky person on hand to collect the contents," I said. "Do you have any printable comments to go along with it?"

"Not really. You can put in a sentence that says that I said we'll be talking to her if you want to. Other than that, the less I say about it right now, the better."

"I'll add that tidbit. Anything else?"

"No. Oh, wait! Did she happen to give you the dead guy's name?"

"No, she didn't. I doubt if she knows it, but you can ask her."

"Believe me, I will. We thought old Jack knew a lot more about Skeleton X than he was telling us but we couldn't get him to crack. I am amazed that the woman let it all come rolling out. Anyway, thanks for the head's up and have a good day." He hung up while I was saying, "You're welcome."

*  *  *

WHEN I GOT HOME at a few minutes after five, I practically ran into the apartment to tell Martha about my amazing day. I bounced into the living room ready to shout out my story, but throttled down my excitement level when I found our next-door neighbor Zhoumaya Jones sitting in her wheelchair in our living room. Even though her expression hinted that this was not a pleasure-filled occasion, I remembered my manners enough to greet her and say, "To what do we owe the pleasure of your visit?"

"Your wife is holding my hand, Mitch," Zhoumaya said. "I've had a serious death threat today."

# Chapter Twenty-Two

## The Who and the Why

IT'S AMAZING HOW quickly the winds of happiness can drop out of a person's sails when a friend says she's threatened to be obliterated by a hurricane. My tale of journalistic triumph was put on hold while we talked about the threat to Zhoumaya's life.

The death threat had been delivered via e-mail from a computer in a public library in Chicago. It had been sent the previous evening and she'd found it this morning when she booted up her office computer. The message told Zhoumaya that the sender planned to put her on a slow, painful road to hell, where she could be reunited with her husband. This was followed by personal references that convinced Zhoumaya that the writer knew her and was serious about sending her to join her late husband, Doliakeh Jones. She said that the e-mail had not been signed, but had ended with: "you know who and why."

"And do you know who and why?" I asked.

"I can only think of one person who might hate me that much, but he's in prison in Liberia," she said.

"Are you sure he's in prison?"

"He was when Doliakeh and I left Liberia."

"That was several years ago. He might be out by now."

"The man was sentenced to twenty years. He shouldn't be eligible for parole this soon."

"Okay," I said. "Why would this man want to kill you?"

"Because I sent him to prison," Zhoumaya said.

"How'd you do that?"

Before Zhoumaya could answer, Martha rose from the sofa and said she would bring us all some iced tea so we could get comfortable and talk about Zhoumaya's problem. Left alone with Zhoumaya, I found it extremely difficult to make small talk.

Obviously Zhoumaya did, too, but after a couple of awkward minutes she tried. "So, how was your day?"

"It started awfully early but it turned out very good," I said. "Until I heard about your trouble, that is."

"Sorry to be the day spoiler," she said, making me wish I hadn't added the "until" part of the description.

"Nothing to be sorry about," I said. "I'm glad you came over to tell us about it. I assume that you've called the police?"

"I have. I gave them the man's name and they said they would check into his present whereabouts. I can't imagine that he would be free, but I didn't know where else to start."

"Any chance he might have broken out?"

"In Monrovia? Not likely. The security there is . . . well, let's say it's efficient."

Martha appeared bearing a tray loaded with three tall glasses of iced tea and a plate of chocolate chip cookies. "You'll spoil my dinner," I said as I grabbed a cookie.

"I'm sure you'll find room," Martha said. She patted my stomach, calling my attention to an expansion that had been taking place in that area. I needed to get back to a regular schedule of jogging.

Zhoumaya smiled and accepted a glass of tea and a cookie. She took a sip from the glass and waited for Martha and me to seat ourselves on the sofa. When we were settled and looking at her in anticipation, she took another sip and began.

"As you know, I worked for the city government in Monrovia for several years before Doliakeh and I left Liberia and came to the United States," she said. "About two years before we left, I discovered some inconsistencies in one of the city's money accounts. I went to my supervisor with my discovery and together we carried out a quiet investigation. What we found was that this man, Robert Obachuma, had set up a separate personal bank account under a fictitious name and was funneling a small portion of his department's receipts into it each month. It was a very sophisticated arrangement; he was a very well-educated, clever man. The total amount stolen was nearly half a million dollars when we went to the police and had him arrested." She paused to sample the chocolate chip cookie.

"So he was charged with embezzlement?" Martha asked.

"He was charged and convicted, mainly on my testimony," Zhoumaya said. "The day he was sentenced to twenty years in prison he swore he would get even with both me and my supervisor. By normal parole standards, he wouldn't be eligible for several years yet, so I can't imagine how he could be free."

"But the e-mail message fits his threat," I said.

"That's why I went to the police. If he did get out some way and is e-mailing from Chicago, he could be on the way here to make good on his promise."

"So maybe you should disappear somewhere for a while," Martha said.

"I'm planning to do that," Zhoumaya said. "But I came over to tell you about it and to tell you what Robert looks like in case he shows up here." She took a big bite of her cookie.

"Okay, what does he look like?" I asked.

"Mmm," she said, and swallowed her cookie. "He's tall, probably about your height, and very strong-looking. At least, he looked very strong the last time I saw him in the courtroom. He's middle-aged, I'd say he'd be a little over fifty years old by now. And he's full-blooded Liberian, which means he's as black as I am."

"Well, if he shows up on the porch I won't invite him in for iced tea and cookies," I said. "When are you planning to bail out of here?"

"Probably some time tomorrow. I'm going to visit a friend—I won't tell you where—but I'm hoping to get some kind of report from the St. Paul police before I go. If they find out that Robert is still in jail I've got a whole different person to worry about—one that I've got no clue about who he or she could possibly be."

"Why don't you stay here with us overnight?" Martha said. "This is a fold-out sofa bed that we're sitting on."

"Oh, I couldn't put you to that much trouble," Zhoumaya said. "I'll lock up tight in my place and keep my gun handy next to the bed."

"You've got a gun?" I said.

"Yes, I have. A lovely little snub-nosed revolver that can fit into my handbag. And I have a permit to carry it."

"You never cease to amaze me."

"A girl never knows when she might need a gun. Especially when the girl has dark skin and is stuck in a wheelchair."

"At least you could stay for dinner," Martha said. "It's pasta with a tomato and veggie sauce and there's enough for six people, much less three."

"That I will accept," Zhoumaya said. "I'm so shaky right now I can't imagine trying to cook anything." I saw her hand tremble as she raised the last bite of cookie to her lips.

*　*　*

ZHOUMAYA RELAXED A bit after dinner, and even joined Martha for an after-dinner glass of wine. I drank sparkling cider while they sipped their merlot and the conversation finally turned to my triumph of the day. I had just about reached the part where Jack Anderson slashed the bad guy's throat when our doorbell rang. "I'll get it," I said.

# A Cold Case of Killing

When I'd arrived home, I'd left the inside door open so the evening air could come in through the screen door. Now on the other side of the screen I saw a tall man of about my height who wore a light blue shirt, black pants, and an open navy blue blazer. He looked as strong as a Vikings linebacker and had a Twins baseball cap on his head. He appeared to be middle-aged—maybe a little over fifty. His skin was deep black.

"I'm looking for Mrs. Jones," he said in a rumbling bass voice. "Do I have the right number?"

# Chapter Twenty-Three

## Wanted Man

LL THAT WAS between us was an unlocked screen door. I thought about backing up quickly, grabbing the inside wooden door, slamming it shut and locking it. Instead, I said, "May I ask who you are?"

"Sure," the big man said. "And I'll tell you." He put his right hand into the inside pocket of the open blazer and I took a step back and started to reach for the wooden door. But before I could grab the door, his hand came out bearing a leather wallet with a shiny metal shield. He held the shield against the screen and I read "FBI" on the top line in large letters. Below "FBI" it said "Clarence Jordan," and below that, "Special Agent."

"The St. Paul police asked for our help with a problem involving Mrs. Jones," he said. "Do I have the right number?" He was smiling ever so slightly, as if my reaction to his hand movement had amused him.

I realized that I'd been holding my breath ever since the moment I first saw Clarence Jordan standing at my door. I let the old air out, sucked in a gulp of new air and said, "Right number, wrong door. But you're lucky; she's visiting us this evening. Come on in." I was smiling ever so slightly in embarrassment.

I pushed gently on the screen door and Jordan grasped the knob and pulled it open. He was still carrying his ID in his right hand when we reached the living room, and he held the shield up while he introduced himself to the women. Zhoumaya, who had stiffened at first sight of him, relaxed when she saw the shield. "The St. Paul police asked us to step in because of the international nature of this case, Mrs. Jones," he said.

"You mean because I asked them to check on a man in Liberia?" Zhoumaya said.

"Exactly," Jordan said. "It seems that the man in question, Mr. Robert Obachuma, was granted an early parole because of his exemplary behavior in prison. It seems that they needed more space for incoming inmates and so they released some of the residents who were judged to be less dangerous to society. Apparently their judgment wasn't a hundred percent correct."

"So you think that's who sent the death threat?" Zhoumaya said. "You think he's in this country?"

"We don't know where he is, Mrs. Jones, but it certainly is possible. Tell me, did you know a woman named Ellen Sankawulo in Monrovia?"

"Why, yes, she was my supervisor. We investigated the embezzlement together. We still exchange Christmas letters every year."

"It's my sad duty to tell you that you won't be doing that anymore," Jordan said. "Ms. Sankawulo was found dead in her home two days after Mr. Obachuma was released from prison. Monrovia police have a warrant out for his arrest on suspicion of murder."

"Oh, my God," said Zhoumaya and Martha in unison.

"How was she killed?" I asked, ever the crime reporter.

"Not very pleasantly," Jordan said. "Monrovia police indicated that she was tortured in some manner before the final blow was struck."

"Maybe we shouldn't talk about that," Martha said. Zhoumaya had bowed her head and was covering her face with her hands.

"You're right," Jordan said. "What we need to talk about is keeping Mrs. Jones safe and apprehending Mr. Obachuma if he comes to St. Paul." He put a hand on Zhoumaya's shoulder and she uncovered her face and straightened up.

"I assume you would recognize this man if he appeared," Jordan said.

"I certainly would," she said. "I hate to say it, but I think he looks a lot like you. About the same height and build and age. His skin's a little darker than yours and he used to shave his head."

"Well, the look-alike ends at the hairline," Jordan said. He removed the Twins cap to reveal a full head of close-cropped black hair. "But I have to agree with you otherwise. Monrovia police e-mailed a photo and I was amazed at how much he looks like what I see in the mirror. The photo was taken upon his release and the biggest difference between us was that he still shaves his head."

"Zhoumaya had told us what he looked like and I damn near wet my pants when I saw you at the door," I said.

"You did look a little shaken," Jordan said. "But I get that a lot from white people, so I thought . . ."

"I'm not one of those white folks who are scared of black men and think they all look the same," I said. "It was a reaction to Zhoumaya's description of Obachuma. She had just finished telling us what he looks like, and there you were."

"Whatever it was, don't worry about it. The important thing is that we've put a twenty-four-hour police watch on this building," Jordan said. "We can either give you a police escort everywhere you go, Mrs. Jones, or you might want to consider vacating the premises until the situation is resolved."

"I've already made arrangements to stay with a friend up north for a few days," Zhoumaya said. "I'm not telling anybody where it is."

"I'd suggest you tell me," Jordan said. "And I also suggest that Ms. Todd and Mr. Mitchell move out temporarily, if possible. We don't know how far this man will go with innocent bystanders and you don't want to wind up as collateral damage."

Martha blushed and looked at her feet. "I was saving this news for later, when Mitch and I were alone, but I'll be leaving for Moorhead tomorrow morning to try a case for my law firm. The trial is sure to run over into next week. I was planning to come home over the weekend but I could stay in Moorhead if the man hasn't been caught by Saturday."

This hit me like a punch in the gut. "Whoa! When did that come up?"

"Just this morning. One of the two attorneys on the case was banged up in a car crash last night and Linda asked me to take over because I'd been helping them with the preliminary work. Like I said, I was going to tell you about it when we were alone and could, uh, discuss being apart for several days."

I assumed the planned discussion would climax with an appropriate goodbye, but I simply shrugged and said that the timing for her leaving couldn't be better.

Jordan turned to me. "What about you?" he asked.

"I'll keep the door closed and my eyes open," I said. "No more screen door chats until this guy is behind bars again."

"Couldn't you go stay with Al or somebody?" Martha said.

"I'll be okay. Sherlock Holmes and I will hold down the fort."

Jordan's expression turned quizzical and I explained that Sherlock was my faithful feline companion who had shared more than one adventure with me in the past. "Sherlock has disappeared a couple of times and been kidnapped twice but he has at least five lives left," I said.

"That's four more than you have," Martha said. "I really wish you'd move out until that man is caught."

Clarence Jordan chatted with Zhoumaya a few minutes longer before escorting her to the other side of the duplex. Before departing, he told us that the gray Chevy parked half a block away contained a pair of St. Paul police officers charged with watching for Robert Obachuma. "I had to badge them before I walked up and rang your doorbell or they'd have had me in cuffs for sure," he said.

Alone at last, Martha and I discussed her impending departure while she packed a suitcase. As I'd expected, the discussion climaxed at about eleven o'clock with a very appropriate goodbye. Two very appropriate goodbyes, in fact.

# Chapter Twenty-Four

## Saved by the Bell?

EDNESDAY WAS MY day off. After kissing Martha goodbye seven times, one for each day of probable absence, I spent the hours behind locked doors with Sherlock, peeking out the front windows every so often to check on the pedestrian traffic.

The only pedestrian who turned in and climbed the porch stairs was a middle-aged black woman who went to Zhoumaya's door. Five minutes later, Zhoumaya emerged in her wheelchair with the woman behind her towing a suitcase big enough to carry Zhoumaya's wardrobe plus the kitchen sink. They went down the ramp and the woman helped Zhoumaya get into a black Lincoln SUV. She stowed the wheelchair in the back and they drove away, leaving Sherlock and me alone in the building.

Twice during the day I ventured onto the porch to assure myself that the police watchdogs were still on the job. The gray Chevy was replaced by a darker gray Ford in mid-afternoon as the shifts changed. Otherwise traffic on Lexington Avenue was normal.

Every two hours I received a phone call from Martha. Her purported purpose was to tell me where she was along the 240-mile road to Moorhead and assure me that she was safe and well. I suspected that her real purpose was to assure herself that I was still safe and well enough to answer the phone.

Late in the afternoon I called Al, who also wasn't working, and told him about Zhoumaya's danger. He offered me a spot on the sofa in their rec room but I declined. I was a big boy who could take care of himself. Besides, I had a cat to feed.

\*   \*   \*

THURSDAY MORNING, I STEPPED out and looked in all directions before locking the door and checking it twice. My head continued to oscillate in 180-degree sweeps as I walked down the porch steps and slid into my Honda Civic, which was parked at the curb in front of the duplex. The gray Chevy was back in the surveillance spot, and I waved at its occupants as I drove past. My hope was that we'd hear about the capture of Robert Obachuma on the *Daily Dispatch* police radio sometime during the day.

Al and I arrived at the *Daily Dispatch* front door at the same time, and on the elevator going to the fourth floor we talked about Zhoumaya's death threat, the visit from the FBI, and the possibility of a suspected killer coming to my door. Again Al offered overnight shelter, and even included dinner. The dinner invitation made it a difficult decision, but again I graciously declined.

We took a detour through the cafeteria to acquire some coffee and continue the discussion. Al agreed that the timing of Martha's trip to Moorhead was good, and we went our separate ways, me to my desk and he to get an assignment from the photo boss.

My first phone call of the morning went to Brownie, who put me on hold for a minute that lasted 180 seconds. This was shorter than many of Brownie's minutes, and when he came back to me I asked if he had talked to Jill Anderson. He answered in the affirmative.

"Did she tell you anything that wasn't in my story?" I asked.

"She brought along your lawyer buddy, Linda L. Lansing, and didn't even tell us as much as was in your story," Brownie said. "Guess Mrs. Anderson didn't think her husband's lawyer was good enough to handle her defense."

"I confess to referring her to Triple-L," I said. "I didn't think her husband's lawyer was good enough." I'd watched Linda in action while covering several trials, and we'd been friends for years before she took Martha Todd into the firm.

"Many thanks for making our job tougher."

"I just feel sorry for Jill in this mess. Are you charging her with anything?"

"That will be up to the D.A. So far most of what we've got to go on is from your story in the paper. You can count on being a star witness if she is charged with anything and it goes to trial."

"Just what I need—fifteen minutes of stardom."

"You'll be on the stand a lot longer than that. Teach you to stick your neck out so far for a story. Damn good one, by the way."

Wow, a compliment from the head of homicide. "Thanks. Anything new on Skeleton X's identity? I assume Jill didn't give you his name."

"She said she has no idea who he was and I believe her. I doubt that even her husband, who made the rotten deal, knew the guy's real name. Unless somebody comes forward saying they had a pimping relative who disappeared twenty-five years ago in July, he's going to remain Skeleton X in our records."

"Skeleton X doesn't strike me as the kind of guy that any-body would miss."

"You got that right. Have a good day, Mitch."

\* \* \*

I HAD GIVEN UP on having a good day when Al appeared at my desk a little after 3:30 p.m. Not a word had been heard about the capture of Robert Obachuma, and nothing new had developed in the Marilee Anderson cold case investigation.

"I just had the strangest phone call ever," Al said. "I still can't believe it."

"Somebody likes one of your pix?" I said.

"Even stranger. Somebody claims to have recognized the person shown in one of my pix."

"You mean you had one in focus for a change?"

"I bet you'll stop making negative comments when I tell you who was in the picture that he recognized."

"Only if it's Marilee Anderson," I said.

"Bingo! How'd you guess?" Al said.

I did stop making negative comments. In fact, I stopped making any kind of comments. I just stared at Al.

"It was a man with a voice that sounded like he was a hundred years old," Al said. "Wouldn't give me his name, said to just call him John Doe. He told me that he had seen the picture we ran showing what that missing girl would look like now. He said he has seen that face and can tell us where to find the woman." Al paused for dramatic effect and I rediscovered my missing voice.

"Where did he tell you she is?"

"He didn't. He wants to meet with you and me in person. And he wants money for his information."

"That's a nasty complication. Did you offer him the fifty bucks we give people who call in tips that turn into stories?"

"I did, and he said fifty bucks wasn't even in the ballpark for an important story like this. He wants to negotiate what he calls 'a suitable fee' in a face-to-face meeting, and then he will tell us where to look."

"How about a fist-to-face meeting," I said. "We could go beat it out of him."

"I'm hoping Don will have a less brutal solution," Al said. "Anyway, he said he leaves for work at eight, so I set up a meeting for seven thirty tomorrow morning at his apartment in Falcon Heights. Now we need to talk to Don to see how much we can offer him, if anything."

Don O'Rourke was not much help when we asked about money. "You know we don't go out buying news stories from the public," he said. "Offer him a double tip fee—a hundred dollars—and tell him that's tops for a tip that I'm ninety-nine percent sure will turn out to be nothing we can use in the paper."

I still had mock mayhem in mind. "Would it be okay if we beat it out of him?" I asked.

"You're not a beat reporter," Don said. While Al and I rolled our eyes at the pun, Don added, "Just use your professional powers of persuasion. Play on his sympathy—just think how happy Marilee's mommy would be if we found Marilee alive and well and living in St. Paul."

Thus Al and I agreed to use guile rather than gelt to extract the information from the mysterious Mr. Doe. We both left the office hoping that Don would be proven ninety-nine percent wrong the next morning.

*   *   *

THE FORD HAD replaced the Chevy in the police watch site when I arrived home. I was glad to see they were still on the job, and was hoping they wouldn't have anything to do during the night. My thought was that the next day—after I'd safely made my early morning exit from our apartment to meet with John Doe— would be a great time for them to apprehend Robert Obachuma.

I was bending down petting Sherlock Holmes when the doorbell rang. I straightened up so suddenly that Sherlock crouched and laid back his ears. I went to the front door, approaching from the side so I couldn't be seen peeking out the window at the top of the door.

I could see the top of a woman's head down to her eyebrows. The eyebrows were dark brown, as was the hair above the forehead. I could not place either the eyebrows or the hair on any woman I knew.

What the hell, it wasn't Robert Obachuma ringing the bell. I opened the inner door and looked out through the screen door. There stood Marilee Anderson's cousin, Lauralee Baker. I stared at her in silent amazement.

"Hi, Mitch," she said in that dusky voice. "Aren't you going to invite me in?"

"Uh, yeah, sure," I said. "Come on in." She sauntered in and I closed and locked the inner door behind her. Ever the gracious host, I said, "How the hell did you find out where I live?"

"I have my ways," she said. "Google is a wonderful thing."

"You found my address on Google?"

"Eventually. You know you have a ton of bylines on Google."

I did know that, but I didn't think my home address was in any of them. I decided not to pursue the how and get to the why. "What brings you here?" I said.

"I need to talk to you. Is your wife home?"

"No, she's away for a week, trying a case in Moorhead." Her reaction told me that I should have stopped with a simple no, omitting the distance and duration of Martha's absence.

Smiling a smile as broad as the grin on *Alice in Wonderland*'s Cheshire cat, Lauralee said, "Well, what a shame. Could we go sit somewhere?"

I pointed her toward the sofa and sat myself down in a chair facing her. She was wearing a filmy white blouse that was open well into her succulent cleavage and a pair of jeans that must have been applied with a paint brush. I wanted to ask how anybody could squeeze into such tight jeans but I was afraid she might peel them off and demonstrate.

"What do you need to talk to me about?" I asked after finishing my visual inventory of her below-the-neck assets and shifting my gaze upward to her face. I realized that I should have recognized her long, luxurious dark hair from our previous meeting. Apparently that day I'd been concentrating so intently on anatomical revelations at a lower level that her hair had not registered in my memory.

Lauralee crossed her jeans-encased legs, right over left, flashing a pair of bright red shoes with spike heels as she moved.

"Originally I came to tell you that I've had a death threat," she said, leaning forward to open the window for a more expansive view of her breasts. "But since you're here all alone for a whole week, I might talk about something more pleasant."

I latched onto the original intent and ignored the possible pleasantry. "You've had a death threat?" I said in too loud a voice.

She sat back in surprise at the strength of my response. "Yes, I have."

"Excuse my reaction, but death threats seem to be going around. Any more and we'll have an epidemic."

"Who else has had death threats?"

"My next-door neighbor had one yesterday. Hers came all the way from Chicago. Where did yours come from?"

Lauralee uncrossed her legs and the red shoes flashed again as she crossed them again, this time left over right. "I don't know," she said. "It was left on my voicemail while I was at work. It was a high raspy voice—I think it was female—and it said she knew from what she'd read in the *Daily Dispatch* that I'd been talking to the press about Marilee Anderson, and that if I did it again it would be the last talking I ever did."

"How would anyone know that you'd talked to me?" I said. "I've never used your name or referred to you as an anonymous relative in a story."

"I don't know. You must have put in something that only I could have told you, but who would know that? Anyway, I thought you should know about it."

"I'll have to go back and look at my stories. But as you said, who would know?"

"All I know is that I'm scared. What if that creep reads another one of your stories and decides to come after me even if I don't tell you any more about Marilee?"

"Have you reported the threat to the police?"

"No. Do you think I should?"

"Absolutely. They might put a watch on your apartment, like the St. Paul police have done for my neighbor next door. She's moved out while the cops are watching for the guy who made the threat."

Lauralee tilted her head and smiled. "Maybe I should move," she said. "Maybe I could sleep here for a few nights. Keep me safe and keep you company while the little wifey is away."

"Like hell you'd be safe. The little wifey would break every bone in your body if she came home and found you in our bed. Better that you go home to your mama or some close friend."

She leaned forward again. "I've seen you staring at my boobs. Don't tell me you wouldn't like to wrap those big strong hands around them."

My sweat glands were beginning to function along my hairline and in my armpits again. "I won't deny that it's tempting, but it's not going to happen. I think you should toddle along and find a nice unmarried man to spend a few nights with."

"I wish I knew one as hunky as you. How about just one night here? Your wife would never have to know."

"I'd know," I said. "It took us a long time to learn to trust each other—several years in fact—and I'm not about to do anything that would leave me feeling guilty."

I stood up and held out both hands to assist her off the sofa. Instead she grabbed them and yanked me forward so that I landed on top of her as she fell backward on the cushions. Her breasts were pressed against my chest, her lips were jammed against mine, and her legs were wrapped around me. I could feel something come to life where our lower bodies met and I was sure she could feel it through the skin-tight jeans.

One of Lauralee's hands was clamped around the back of my neck and the other was inside my pants gripping my ass. I realized that I should have been struggling to break free, but I wasn't. I told myself I had to get loose, and I was trying to peel her fingers off my neck when the doorbell rang. Saved!

Lauralee released my neck and jerked her lips away from mine. "Who's that? Is it your wife?"

"Could be," I said, knowing damn well that Martha would have unlocked the door and walked in without ringing the bell.

Lauralee unwound her legs from around my waist and withdrew her hand from my pants, allowing me to roll off her body and onto the floor. "I better hide," she said. "Where can I go?"

"Out the back door," I said, pointing the way. "There's a little deck back there. If you hug the wall, nobody will see you."

We scrambled up and went our separate ways—she out the back door and me to the front door. I looked through the window and in the fading twilight I saw the familiar figure of a tall black man wearing a navy blue blazer and a dark baseball cap. I opened the door and through the screen I said, "Hi, Clarence. Come on in."

He pulled open the screen door and walked in. He stopped in front of me, studied my face for a moment, and said, "Who the hell is Clarence?"

# Chapter Twenty-Five

## Not So Safe

O BVIOUSLY I HAD made an egregious tactical error. In my fervor to free myself from Lauralee, I had tossed caution into the jetstream and opened the front door without due diligence. I was now standing in the entryway face-to-face with a man who was, as they say, the spittin' image of Special Agent Clarence Jordan, but whose baseball cap bore the logo of the Chicago White Sox, not the Minnesota Twins.

"Clarence is a friend who looks a lot like you," I said. "Who are you?" I tried to make it sound like I really didn't know.

"Does it matter to you who I am? Don't all black people look the same to you white folks?" he said. I heard a slight British accent in his speech.

"Not to me. Clarence really does look a lot like you, Mr. . . . ?"

"Just call me John."

I resisted the urge to say, "Another John Doe?" Instead I asked him what brought him to my door.

"I'm looking for someone," John said. "Someone who lives at this number."

I decided to play as dumb as possible, which was appropriate since I'd been dumb enough to let this man in. "Does this someone have a name?"

"Jones. Mrs. Jones. Is she here?"

"No, she's not. This is a duplex. Her door is the one on the other end of the porch. You could go over there and try ringing her bell." If I could just get him out of my apartment I could lock the door and call 911. Which reminded me, where the hell were the cops in the Ford? Had John done something to them?

"Who else is in this apartment?" John said.

"Just me," I said. "I'm here all alone."

"You wear those?" He pointed past me toward the living room. I turned and saw a red spike-heeled shoe on the sofa and another on the floor.

"Oh, those are my wife's. She's out of town for a few days. Didn't pick up after herself before she left." I tried to give him a disarming smile but it came off so weak it wouldn't have disarmed a chipmunk carrying a peanut.

"You sure nobody else is here?" he said.

"Absolutely. Wife is away and I don't have kids."

"And Mrs. Jones?"

"Like I said, she lives next door. Why don't you go ring her bell?"

"I think I'll do that. Why don't you come along with me?"

"Why would I do that? I've got nothing to talk to Ms. Jones about."

"I'll show you why you'll do that." His right hand slid into his coat pocket and slid out holding a switchblade knife. He clicked the button with his thumb and a silver blade long enough to go halfway through my gut flicked out. The tip of the blade was pointing toward that very gut.

"No need for that kind of persuasion," I said. "I'll be most happy to go with you." Where were those goddamn cops?

John jerked his head toward the door. "Let's go. Before the cops watching for me get back."

"Cops?" I tried to sound completely ignorant of their presence.

"Quit acting like a dummy. You know damn well they've been sitting out there watching the house. But right this minute, they're tending to a little fire show I lit off just for their benefit down the block a ways."

Instantly my pulse shot up to over a hundred beats per minute. The help I'd been counting on wouldn't be coming. I felt my face grow hot and my armpits become wet. All I could do was cooperate and hope John would decide to leave when we found Zhoumaya's apartment empty.

I had taken a step toward the door when the cell phone in my pants pocket rang. I turned toward John, shrugged, and pulled the phone out of my pocket. The caller ID said it was Alan Jeffrey calling.

To John I said, "It's my wife in Moor . . . uh, in Duluth." Hoping he hadn't noticed the mid-word geographical switch, I said, "I'd better answer it or she'll be worried about me."

"Let her worry," John said.

"She'll call a friend to come over here and check on me."

"Oh, shit, answer it," he grumbled. "But make it quick. And be very careful what you say." He emphasized "careful" by twisting the knife blade in a semi-circle an inch from my belly.

I backed off a couple of steps, turned my back to John and spoke into the phone. "Hi, sweetheart," I said. "Are you all settled down safely in Duluth?"

"This ain't your sweetheart," Al said. "It's just me checking on our meeting time in the morning."

"What? You say you have a problem?" I said. "What's the trouble?"

"What the hell are you babbling about?" Al said.

"Somebody broke into your car? You'd better call 911."

"What's going on with you?" He took a quick breath. "Oh, God, do you have a visitor? The guy you were talking about?"

"Exactly. That's the first thing to do."

"You want me to call 911?"

"That's what I'm telling you. It's the only way to deal with that kind of thing."

"Gotcha. Hang in there." The phone went dead.

"Bye, sweetie," I said. "Let me know how it comes out. Love you."

I made kissy sounds, closed the phone, put it back in my pocket, and turned to face John. "Somebody broke into her car in the motel parking lot and stole her GPS. Nice welcome to Duluth."

"Seems like there's crime everywhere you go," John said. "Ain't that a shame? Now let's us go call on Mrs. Jones."

"Okay," I said. "Mind if I get a drink of water first?"

"Yes, I mind. If you think you're going to throw water in my face and grab the knife you're even dumber than you've been acting."

I had no such thoughts; I was merely stalling for time. I shrugged again, opened the door, and went out onto the porch. Off in the distance to my right I could see the flicker of flames in the street. That had to be the diversionary fire that had lured away my uniformed watchdogs.

"Move your ass," said John.

I moved it across the porch toward Zhoumaya's side of the duplex. John was two steps behind me with the knife pointing at my spine. As I reached the porch steps and Zhoumaya's wheelchair ramp, I calculated my chances of turning, running, and going into the street. I didn't like the odds—one lunge with that knife could cost me a kidney or a spinal cord. I kept walking straight and stopped in front of Zhoumaya's door.

"Ring the bell," John said. He was close behind me, but not so close that I could have spun and deflected the knife if I'd been capable of such a move, which I was not. I rang the bell.

We waited. After a suitable interval I rang it again. "Maybe the bell doesn't work," I said after another wait.

"Try knocking."

I knocked. No answer. What a surprise. "Maybe she's asleep."

"Maybe she's not home," John said. "Maybe she's gone where she thinks it's safe. Maybe you can tell me where that is."

"Maybe I can't. In fact, definitely I can't. I have no idea where she is."

"Let's go back to your place and talk about it."

"Nothing to talk about. I honest to God don't know where the woman is."

"Move it. Back to your place. Now." I felt the tip of the knife prick my back, directly behind my left kidney. I moved.

"Let's go sit in the living room," John said as I opened my front door. I kept walking through the archway into the living room. It had grown dark while we were standing outside Zhoumaya's door, so I switched on the light and got still another surprise. Lauralee Baker was sitting on the sofa, putting on the red spike heels.

"Oh, shit, I thought you were gone," Lauralee said.

"I thought you said your wife was away," John said.

"This isn't my wife," I said.

"How cozy," said John. "Now we can all have a nice little chat about where I might find Mrs. Jones."

"Who the hell is Mrs. Jones?" asked Lauralee.

# Chapter Twenty-Six

## On the Cutting Edge

HAD A QUESTION also. Mine was, "Where the hell are the cops who should be responding to Al's call?"

I didn't ask it out loud. Instead, I explained to Lauralee that Mrs. Jones was my next-door neighbor and that this man, who said his name was John, was hoping to talk to her. Seeing the fright already present in Lauralee's eyes, I thought it prudent not to mention that John was the author of Zhoumaya's death threat.

"So why is John holding a knife?" Lauralee said.

I turned to John. "Yes, why are you holding that knife? I've already told you that I have absolutely no idea where Ms. Jones is."

"Maybe she gave you a hint where she was going," John said.

"Definitely she did not," I said.

"Maybe if I ask again, something will come to you," he said. He gestured toward Lauralee with the tip of the blade. "Stand up and come over here, cutie pie."

The color drained from Lauralee's face as she rose and walked toward him. When she got within arm's reach, John grabbed her with his left hand, spun her around, and pulled her against his body. She screamed. He said, "Shut up," and clamped his left hand over her mouth.

Placing the knife blade across Lauralee's throat, John turned to me. "Now, Mr. I Don't Know Anything, let me ask you again: where is Mrs. Jones?"

"Let me tell you again that I do not know where she is," I said. "Now please take that knife off of Lauralee's throat."

158

"Lauralee, huh? Nice name. Pretty girl. Be a shame if her throat got a big wide cut in it." He pressed the knife tighter against Lauralee's throat and her eyes bugged out so far I thought they'd go beyond the tip of her nose.

I decided it was time to tell a lie. Where had I said Martha was? Oh, yeah, Duluth. "Okay, okay," I said. "Ms. Jones went with my wife to Duluth. Now please let go of Lauralee."

"Duluth, huh?" John said. The knife stayed at Lauralee's throat. "Where's Duluth?"

"Up north. Almost 200 miles. Now please take away the knife."

"Damn it. I've got to get another car." He lowered the knife to his side, moved his left hand from Lauralee's mouth to her back and pushed her away from him so hard that she fell to her hands and knees.

I helped Lauralee to her feet and led her back to the sofa. She was shaking like an Eskimo sitting bare-ass on an ice floe.

"Why do you need another car?" I said to John.

"Because I burned up the one I got in Chicago," he said. "What do you think those cops are looking at out there, Mr. I Don't Know?"

"You torched your car to decoy the cops?"

"Yeah, that's what I did. You think Budget will be pissed off at me?"

"You probably won't get your insurance deposit back," I said.

"Very funny. Now, let's all go get into your car."

"My car? Okay, I'll give you the keys. You can take it." I reached into my pocket and pulled out the keys.

John shook his head. "I need a driver who knows the way to Duluth," he said. "A driver who knows where Mrs. Jones is staying in Duluth."

"She's not in the motel with my wife," I said.

"But your wife will know where she is. So let's go see your wife in Duluth, Mr. I Don't Know." He motioned toward the front door with his knife. As I took a step toward the door, wondering why in hell the cops weren't coming through it, John turned to Lauralee. "You, too, cutie pie."

I stopped. "Why her? She's not involved in this in any way. She was just visiting when you came in."

"Yeah, just visiting on the couch with her shoes thrown all over hell," John said. "I wish I'd seen what was going on when I rang the bell. She's coming with us because we're one big happy family off on a road trip to visit your wife and Mrs. Jones. Come on, cutie pie, get off your tight little ass and get moving. Right behind your don't-know-anything boyfriend."

Instead of moving, Lauralee bowed her head and started to cry. John grabbed her left arm, hauled her to a standing position, and flung her toward me. If I hadn't caught her by the shoulders she would have gone down on the floor again, maybe landing on her face this time.

"Move it, goddamn it!" John yelled.

With my right arm around Lauralee's shoulders, I started toward the front door. We were still a couple of steps away when we were halted by thunderous knock that shook the door and a voice shouting, "Police! Open this door." Then another loud knock rattled the door.

"Guess you're too late," I said to John.

"Son of a bitch," he said. With the speed of a striking rattlesnake he knocked Lauralee away from me, grabbed me from behind, and wrapped his left arm around my chest. The knife's blade slid against my throat. "Okay, Mr. Don't Know Anything, tell the bastards to come in."

"It's locked," I told him in a voice gone soprano.

"Then you open it." He pushed me forward so I could reach the knob. As I pulled the door open, John hauled me back a couple of steps. We were facing a porch full of policemen in full riot gear with weapons drawn. At least half a dozen assorted gun muzzles were pointing at me.

"Don't shoot," I said as loud as I could squeak in my state of terror. It probably sounded silly to the cops, but it was all I could think of at the moment.

All the guns stayed locked onto me as the officer closest to the door told John to drop the knife and step away from the man he was holding. John did neither.

"This gentleman and I are going for a ride in his car," John said. "We are going to walk past you and get into that car. If any of you makes a move to stop us this gentleman's throat will be sliced all the way to his neck bone." For emphasis, he pressed the razor-sharp blade tighter and I sensed that the skin had been penetrated.

"The second you do that, we'll blow you away," the lead officer said.

"I'm counting on you and your men to have the good sense not to force me to slice this gentleman's head off."

"You should have the good sense to give it up right now," the cop said. "You're not going to leave here, whether you hurt the hostage or not."

"Any attempt to stop me means this gentleman is dead," John said.

"Hey," I said to the officer. "This is my life we're talking about. Please just let us walk to the car with my throat in one piece."

"You think he won't kill you after we let him get away?" the officer said.

"I'll take my chances on that," I said. "Just let us go to the car."

"The man's talking sense," John said. "Better listen to him if you don't want his blood on your hands."

I could feel a thin, warm stream of that very blood trickling down my neck from where the blade had nicked me. "Please, Officer, he's right. You don't want my blood on your hands," I said.

"You aren't going anywhere," the officer said. "Drop the knife and release this man right now."

I felt John's muscles tighten and the blade press harder. I was about to scream at the damn fool policeman when I heard a loud *whack* and felt John's hands and arms go limp. The knife clattered to the linoleum at my feet and the floor shook as John went down behind me like a crashing blimp. I spun around to find myself looking at a cop with a wooden baton the size of a Louisville Slugger in his hand and a satisfied smile on his face. "Bingo," he said. "Nice of you to leave the back door unlocked." *Nice of Lauralee*, I thought.

I felt my knees turning to soft rubber. "Nice of you to get here before your partner let this guy cut off my head," I said. "Now, if you'll excuse me, I need to sit down." I staggered around John's motionless body and collapsed into the closest chair. The officer who'd been blocking the doorway followed me.

He held out his hand. "I'm Officer Burnham," he said. "I wasn't going to let him cut your throat. I was just stalling for time until Officer Wilson got close enough to take the bastard out."

I gripped Officer Burnham's hand with mine, which was still shaking of its own volition. "Nice to know," I said. "If you'd stalled him any longer, I wouldn't be talking to you." I wiped my other hand across my throat and it came away smeared with blood.

"Yeah, the timing got a little dicey," Burnham said. "Let me get somebody to look at that scratch on your neck." Scratch, hell, it felt like a canyon. Burnham went away and I cupped my hand over the wound, slumped back in the chair and looked up at the ceiling, which appeared to be whirling in circles. I was wondering how the ceiling could swirl like that when the entire room went dark.

The next thing I saw was the face of a female EMT whose hands were applying a disinfectant to my wound. The medication set my flesh on fire and I yelped. The EMT stepped back and laughed. "I told you this would sting a little but I guess you didn't hear me," she said. "You seemed to be kind of out of it for a minute or two."

"Obviously the guy didn't cut deep enough to get your vocal chords," said a familiar voice. I turned toward the sound and saw Alan Jeffrey looking down at me. "I was just thinking how peaceful that would be."

"No way. I'd get an artificial larynx and turn the volume all the way up," I said.

"Damn modern technology," Al said. "I guess it's just as well that he didn't peel your Adam's apple."

"He came close. He was rotten to the core."

"Well, this lady has something to stem the blood."

Al backed away and the EMT, who said her name was Jackie, pressed a square of gauze against the wound on my neck and stuck it down with two strips of white tape. "The wound is oozing a little, so you'll want to change that dressing in an hour or so," she said. "I'll leave you some gauze and a roll of tape."

"Oozing?" I said. "How much is that in pints?"

Jackie laughed again. "You won't be needing a transfusion. It's kind of like you cut yourself shaving."

"I can't stand the sight of blood, especially when it's my own," I said. "That's why I use an electric shaver and not a blade."

"Then stay away from big men with sharp knives. I'll be leaving now. If that wound doesn't heal the way it should, call your doctor. Bye." She dropped two packets of gauze and a roll of adhesive tape into my lap and departed with a flick of her hand.

Al returned to my field of vision. "You gonna be okay?" he asked. "You're not going to lose your head over this?"

"Seems like everything's still in place," I said. "Thanks for calling in the troops."

"Lucky I called you when I did."

"If you hadn't, I'd be on the way Duluth with Mr. Obachuma and his knife."

"Why Duluth?"

"I told him that was where Martha and Zhoumaya went. I'm a habitual liar when someone's throat is in danger of being cut."

"He had the knife to your throat before the cops came?"

"He had the knife to Lauralee's throat before you called."

"Who's Lauralee?"

"Hey, Mr. Mitchell," said Officer Burnham. "Didn't I see a woman in here when you first opened the door?"

"Yes, you did," I said.

"So where the hell is she?"

# Chapter Twenty-Seven

## Looking for Lauralee

Y ES, WHERE WAS LAURALEE? She had slipped away with as little sound as one hand clapping while John and I were haggling over the future condition of my throat with Officer Burnham.

A quick search of the apartment, including all the closets and both bathrooms, convinced us that she was not inside. Officer Wilson said he had not encountered her on the back deck during his surreptitious entrance. I wanted to get down on the floor and check under the bed but I was so shaky that I wouldn't have been able to get up, so I asked Al to do it.

"Nothing under there," he said. "Not even a dust bunny. Congratulate Martha on her housekeeping for me."

"How do you know that I'm not the one who busts the dust bunnies?" I said.

"Because the floors in your old apartment were hopping with dust bunnies before Martha moved in."

"That's a hare-brained accusation," I said, even though I knew he was right.

Two officers were assigned to search outside for Lauralee. Two others had the pleasure of handcuffing Robert "John" Obachuma, who had been revived by EMT Jackie and her partner, and were walking him to an ambulance that was double parked in front of the house for transportation to Regions Hospital. There he would be shackled and held under armed guard while being checked for a possible concussion. "Wouldn't want to be accused of police brutality by the nice man who was going to slash your throat," Officer Burnham said.

As the ambulance pulled away, it was followed immediately by a dark-colored Prius that had been parked at the curb beside it. I pointed to the departing Prius and said, "I'll bet there goes the woman we're looking for. She snuck out to her car but the ambulance had her parked in."

"Damn it, I'll bet you're right," Burnham said. "We didn't check the cars for occupants. We need to get a statement from her. Do you know where she lives?"

"I do," I said. "I have the address at my office. I'll e-mail it in the morning."

"You can bring it with you in the morning when you come in to give your statement. How about nine o'clock?"

"How about later in the day? I have an assignment to meet someone at seven thirty in Falcon Heights."

We agreed on 1:30 p.m. and Burnham departed, along with his troops, leaving Al and me alone.

"You really think you'll be up to meeting this John Doe guy in the morning?" Al said.

"Wouldn't miss it for all the knives in Liberia," I said.

Al said he'd be ready at 7:00 a.m. and departed, leaving me alone with Sherlock Holmes. I was about to sit down with the cat when I realized I had a story to report, even if it was my day off. I couldn't imagine facing Don O'Rourke the next day if his first knowledge of my visit from Robert Obachuma came from a TV news report.

I decided to do it by phone. Fred Donlin, the night city editor, expressed surprise and concern, and then transferred my call to a veteran reporter named John Boxwood. John expressed surprise and concern as well, and then said to tell him what happened and he'd put the story together. I'd been planning to dictate, but discovered that my mind was too messed up to think coherently in orderly sentences, so I agreed to this.

In a disjointed, back-and-forth way, I told Boxwood everything that had happened. I thought about leaving out the visit from Lauralee Baker, but decided to include it with the explanation that she was a source in the Marilee Anderson case who had come to give me some background information. I was afraid if I didn't mention Lauralee that the police report would include her presence and every other news report in the Twin Cities would pick up this tidbit. If Martha heard if first from Trish Valentine reporting live, she would assume that I was hiding something from her, which would have been correct.

When I finished my staggering report to Boxwood, I put down the phone and collapsed on the sofa with Sherlock beside me. It was then that the reality of what I'd just been through crashed into my brain. I was sweating, but I felt cold and started to shake. I'd been threatened by other killers, but never in such a close, physical manner. Both looking down a gun barrel and being pushed over the side of a boat into deep water had been terrifying. But being held in an iron grip and having a knife blade actually slicing through the skin of my neck had been beyond horrific.

For the first time in several years, I found myself feeling that I absolutely needed a drink. Only alcohol could steady my trembling body and soothe my racing, jumping brain. I told myself that this would be the most damn foolish thing an alcoholic could do and felt relieved that there wasn't any alcohol in the house.

Ah, but there was. The bottle of wine that Martha had shared with Zhoumaya had not been emptied. It had to be somewhere in a kitchen cupboard. I told myself, "Do not look for it."

I looked for it. And I found it. I held a one-third-full bottle of merlot in my quivering right hand. With the left hand, I pulled out the silver stopper that Martha had stuck into the bottle to keep the wine fresh. I told myself that just one sip wouldn't hurt me. I needed this to steady my nerves and let me relax after the terror and shock of being held at knifepoint by a madman. I wouldn't even pour the wine into a glass. I'd take one tiny, steadying sip, put the stopper back, and set the bottle back on the cupboard shelf where I'd found it.

I was staring at the bottle, preparing to bring it to my lips, when my cell phone, which was lying on the counter beside the kitchen sink, rang. The caller ID read MARTHA. I picked up the phone in my left hand and said, "Hi."

"Hi, lover, how are you?" Martha said.

"I'm just fine now," I said.

"Your voice sounds a little weak. Are you okay?"

My right hand was still trembling as I poured the contents of the wine bottle down the sink. "Let me tell you about my day," I said. I could apologize later for wasting the wine.

\* \* \*

I PICKED UP AL at his home in the Midway at 7:10 a.m. and continued driving north on Snelling Avenue to Falcon Heights. I was still wearing a patch of gauze taped to my throat, even though the oozing had stopped after the second change. I preferred to have people curious about the bright white dressing rather than getting nauseous looking at the deep red scab.

This John Doe, who we'd dubbed John Doe the First, lived on a side street near the Minnesota State Fairgrounds. As we passed the fairgrounds, I remembered trying to pry information out of an uncooperative Falcon Heights homicide detective after a murder there the previous summer. Al remembered her also, and reminded me that her initials were KGB, which fit both her tactics and personality to a T.

We were singing, "Doe, a deer, a female deer," when I parked in front of John Doe's number, which was attached to a one-story rambler probably built in the housing boom that followed World War II. It was painted white, with green shutters and trim, and surrounded by a neatly kept assortment of shrubs and flowers. The small lawn was mowed and the sidewalk was free of debris. John Doe the First obviously took meticulous care of both the house and its surroundings.

A two-foot-tall plastic gnome with a red hat and a silly grin stood on the top step beside the front door. Al patted it on the head and rang the bell. Nobody came to the door. He rang again. Still no response.

"Maybe he's deaf and doesn't hear the bell," Al said. He knocked hard on the metal screen door. When this brought no response, he opened the screen door and knocked on the wooden inner door. Same result.

"I don't like this," Al said. "He promised he'd be here to meet us if we got here by seven thirty." He knocked again, but no one answered. He tried to turn the knob and discovered that the door was locked.

We decided to try the back door. We walked around to the side of the attached single-car garage and peeked in a small window. There was a black pickup truck inside. We continued around the garage to the backyard, which was as neat and trim as the front, and found a small porch in back. Al went up the steps and knocked loud enough to be heard at the house next door.

Getting no response, Al tried turning the knob. "It's open," he said. "I'm going to stick my head in and yell." He stuck his head in and yelled. Nobody yelled back.

"I'm going to peek inside," Al said. "Something's wrong with this picture. His pickup is in the garage and the door is unlocked. He should be in the house."

Al went in the back door and I climbed the steps to the porch. I was just opening the door when Al yelled, "Holy shit! Come here."

I bolted through the door into a small room containing a washer and a dryer. A few quick steps took me into the kitchen doorway, where Al stood looking into the room at a balding man lying on the floor. The man, who was wearing pants but no shirt, lay on his back with his eyes wide open and his right hand resting on the left side of his naked belly just beneath his ribs. The entire front of his body was coated with blood and the proverbial pool of blood (a cliché we were forbidden to use in the *Daily Dispatch*) had spread across a wide expanse of the kitchen floor. There was no point in wading through the sea of red to check him for a pulse.

With my breakfast rising in my throat, I swallowed hard, tiptoed around the red sea and escaped into the dining room. Al followed, almost stepping on my heels. My call to 911 was answered by a business-like woman who took my information and assured me that emergency personnel would be on the way immediately.

"Do you need an ambulance?" she asked.

"Too late for that," I said. "The victim is ready for a hearse."

Four minutes later, two Falcon Heights squad cars with lights flashing pulled up in front. Al unlocked the front door from the inside and greeted the officers who got out. I followed Al into the living room and stood pointing toward the kitchen.

All four cops strode past me to the kitchen, and after a quick look, one of them returned to the living room. "Did either of you touch anything?" he asked.

"Nothing, Officer," I said. Then I thought about what we might have touched. "We both grabbed the back doorknob. When you dust for prints, you'll find ours there."

"Hope you haven't messed up any others that might be there," he said.

"Homicide is on the way," said another officer, who had called in as soon as he'd seen the body.

"Who is this man?" asked the first officer. He wore a badge that said Harrison.

"Don't know his name," Al said. "He invited us here for an interview under the name John Doe."

"You got some explaining to do," Harrison said. "Don't you two go anywhere until homicide gets here."

Al and I adjourned to the front steps, where we sat waiting for homicide to arrive while the officers inside were doing their thing. After about ten minutes, another Falcon Heights squad car pulled up and a tall, dark-haired woman in a black pantsuit emerged from the passenger side.

"Oh, no," I said.

"Oh, yes," Al said.

It was KGB.

# Chapter Twenty-Eight

## Facing KGB

THE EXPRESSION ON her face told us that KGB, whose official title was Detective K.G. Barnes, was no happier to see us than we were to see her. We rose to greet her and she ignored the opportunity to shake my outstretched hand.

"In the four years we've been on the Falcon Heights police force we've worked two homicides. Why is it that you two have been present at both of them?" KGB said. She had the damnable habit of using the royal "we" when referring to herself.

"Just lucky, I guess," I said, letting her wonder whether I meant lucky for us or for her.

"We weren't really present at this one," Al said. "This victim was already dead when we got here." In the previous case, the victim had performed a bizarre death routine before our eyes on a small State Fairgrounds stage.

"So who is the victim?" KGB asked.

"He gave his name as John Doe," I said. "We suspect that it might be an alias."

"Aren't you the bright ones? So what are you doing here, if you don't know the man's real name?"

We explained the reason for our presence, telling her that John Doe had offered to tell us where we could find a woman who looked like the missing person from a twenty-five-year-old cold case in St. Paul.

"Couldn't you have kept the investigation in St. Paul?" KGB asked.

"I actually invited him to meet us downtown but he insisted that we come here," Al said. "Sorry about getting you involved."

"Well, we've got work to do," KGB said. "We'll need statements from both of you." She looked at a large silver watch on her wrist. "One o'clock, our office. We're sure you know where it's located."

"I'm sorry but you'll have to get in line," I said. "I have a one thirty date at the St. Paul PD to give a statement from another crime scene."

"Jesus, what are you guys? Some kind of magnets for all kinds of criminals?"

"Sometimes it seems that way," I said. "This particular criminal was drawn to me by a desire to slit my throat."

I half expected KGB to say she wished he'd been successful, but she merely frowned and said, "Can you make it by three thirty?"

"I'm not sure," I said. "Maybe we'd better make it four o'clock to be on the safe side."

She agreed and hustled into the house. A young man who'd driven the car for KGB and stood behind her during our conversation followed her in. "Sounds like my partner isn't exactly in love with you guys," he said as he went past us on his way into the house.

"A detective that observant will go far," Al said. "Our afternoon with the KGB should really be fun."

"I'm looking forward to it with all the enthusiasm of a man facing a colonoscopy," I said.

"You don't face a colonoscopy, it goes up your ass."

"That's what I'm afraid KGB will do."

Meanwhile, we had a lot of work to do. I called Don O'Rourke and told him what we'd found and what was happening. He told us to stay on the scene, find out who the victim was, and how he was killed. That meant we'd be dealing with Detective K.G. Barnes all morning.

We went back into the house to ask some questions and were ordered to leave immediately unless we could identify the body. Already aware that KGB would not accept "John Doe" as a valid ID, we went back outside. I retrieved my laptop from the car and we resumed our seated position at the top of the front steps.

Going online, I learned from the city's reverse directory that the house was the residence of Henry L. Moustakas. Chasing the name through Google, I found a Henry Moustakas whose phone number matched the one that our John Doe the First had given to Al. This man was sixty-four years old and was employed by St. Adolphus Catholic Church in north Minneapolis as a maintenance man. At that age he could have been partially bald, and the church was within an easy commuting distance from this house.

Next I Googled the church, found its office phone number and called. A woman answered and I asked for Henry Moustakas. "Old Hank hasn't come in yet this morning," she said. "He's almost always here by now but he seems to be late today. May I take a message?"

I decided not to pass on the bad news about Old Hank. I told the woman that I'd try back later and thanked her.

"No problem," she said. Aargh! She must have been younger than she sounded.

I e-mailed what I'd learned to Don, and Al forwarded two photos of the house and a shot he'd taken of Detective K.G. Barnes as she was walking toward us from her car.

"How was he killed?" was Don's e-mail response.

"Looks like he was stabbed. I'll check with KGB," I replied.

I either had to wait for KGB to offer a statement or beard the lion in her den. Remembering how little information she'd offered the media in the previous case, my choice was obvious. I again entered the house and found KGB seated at the polished oak dining room table, talking on her cell phone. She glared at me and waved me back toward the door. I took a seat at the other end of the table and folded my hands in a prayerful pose on the tabletop.

KGB snapped off her phone and said, "You can't be in here. This is a crime scene."

"I'm aware of that," I said. "What I need to know is the probable cause of the victim's death. Looked very bloody. Was he shot or stabbed?"

"You'll have to wait for the M.E. on that. Now get out of here or we'll have you handcuffed and placed under arrest."

I stood up. "How long before the M.E. gets here?"

"He just left his office. Now out!"

"Can you confirm that the victim's name is Henry Moustakas?"

She looked surprised to hear that I had a name. "We're not releasing the victim's name until his family has been notified." She rose and took a step toward me. Thinking she might be carrying handcuffs, I turned and hustled out the front door.

"Any luck?" Al asked as I sat down beside him.

"She says we have to wait for the M.E."

"Story of my life, sit around and wait."

"We could take turns playing Solitaire on my laptop."

"I'd rather watch the grass grow in Henry's yard."

"With two of us, we can watch every solitary blade."

"A singularly exciting prospect. But while we've been sitting here with nothing to do, I started wondering something," Al said. "Do you think Henry Moustakas's murder had anything to do with his plan to tell us where to find that Marilee Anderson lookalike?"

I'd been wondering the same thing. Was Henry Moustakas murdered in an early-morning break-in gone bad? Or was it possible that Marilee Anderson was alive in the Twin Cities and that somebody who didn't want her to be found knew Henry was meeting with us? Had Marilee been held captive all these years? And, if so, who might her captor be?

The door behind us opened and one of the original cops on the scene came out carrying a roll of yellow police line tape. He asked us to move off the top step so he could begin stringing the tape around the house. We slid down one level and continued to monitor Old Hank's grass.

# Chapter Twenty-Nine

## Over Cooked

THE ARRIVAL OF Dr. Lyle Lundberg, the Ramsey County medical examiner, interrupted our perusal of the growing grass. He nodded a greeting as we rose from our seats on the steps and I said I'd like to have a statement on the probable cause of death when he'd finished examining the body. He said he'd talk to me then, ducked under the yellow tape, and went into the house. Al and I resumed our contemplation of the growth of the greensward.

"How much do you think it has grown since we started watching?" Al asked.

"About one-tenth of an imperceptible amount," I said.

"I see," he said.

This witty repartee was broken by a greeting from a new arrival. "Hi, guys," said Trish Valentine, who was coming up the walk followed by Tony, her faithful cameraman. Trish was wearing a baby blue skirt that stopped well above her knees and a silky white blouse with the top three buttons flying free. I didn't notice what Tony was wearing, if anything.

"About time you got here," Al said. "You're usually on the scene before the corpse is cold."

"Trish Valentine reporting live," she said. "Whose corpse is cooling?"

"Cops won't release a name until they notify the family," I said. "He's a white male, about sixty-something, and he's resting on his back in the kitchen. M.E. is looking at him as we speak."

"That's all you know?"

She'd have to read the rest in the *Daily Dispatch*. "That's all we've been told by the homicide investigator. You might remember her: Detective K.G. Barnes."

"Oh, God! Not KGB?"

"The one and only. Prepare to report live on a lot of no comments."

Trish seated herself beside me on the steps. Her skirt slid upward to within an inch of providing a view of whatever style panties she was wearing and her unbuttoned blouse revealed a tantalizing expanse of suntanned breasts. Unable to decide which part of Trish's anatomy to ogle, I turned my eyes back to the growing grass, but they wouldn't focus there. Trish's charms were too much of a diversion to resist after my lengthy observation of the dead man's lawn.

By the time Dr. Lundberg emerged from the house, crews from two other TV channels had arrived, along with a reporter-and-photographer team from the Minneapolis paper. The three of us got off our butts and joined the gathering at the foot of the front steps to hear the doctor's report.

"All I can tell you is that the victim has a stab wound in his abdomen that resulted in a great deal of blood loss," the M.E. said. "I can't say for certain if that was the actual cause of death until we've done an autopsy. As for time of death, I'd estimate that the victim died about twelve to fifteen hours ago." Using my incredible mathematical skills, I deduced that this would place Henry's demise at between 8:00 p.m. and 11:00 p.m. Thursday.

"Did the knife reach his heart?" Trish asked.

"I won't know that until we do the autopsy," Dr. Lundberg said. "But as I just said, the victim lost a great deal of blood."

"So it could have reached his heart?"

"I have no further comments, except to remind you that I haven't confirmed that the wound was caused by a knife," the doctor said. "You'll all be notified when the autopsy results are available. Have a good day, everyone." He came down the steps and the clump of media parted like the Red Sea opening before Moses to let him pass through to his car.

*   *   *

I WROTE A STORY that included the address of the house and the fact that the owner was listed as Henry L. Moustakas. As usual, Detective K.G. Barnes had answered "no comment at this time" to every question reporters asked at the scene. This left little for the TV reporters to report live, and gave the *Daily Dispatch* a big lead on the story. I wondered what Trish Valentine would say when she learned that Al and I had discovered the body upon arriving for an interview. The one thing I held back in my story was the purpose of the interview. Let the rest of the world wonder about that.

Friday afternoon turned into a blur of questions and answers. I sat with two interrogators at the St. Paul PD for an hour while they questioned me from every possible angle on my adventure with Robert Obachuma. When they were finished, I was told to remain seated. They left the room and were replaced by Special Agent Clarence Jordan of the FBI.

Jordan began our conversation by implying that I was a damn fool for letting Obachuma into my house. This was not necessary. I already knew I was a damn fool for letting Obachuma into my house. Then Jordan asked me the same questions the police had asked in several different ways. I was finally told I could leave the police station five minutes after Al was supposed to pick me up for our trip to Falcon Heights to meet with KGB. He was waiting for me, parked in front of a fire hydrant twenty feet from the front door of the police station.

"I hope KGB takes you first," I said as Al pulled away from the fire plug. "I need as much time as I can get to change gears

from rehashing my tussle with Mr. John Doe the Second to telling
how we found the late Mr. John Doe the First."

"They must have given you one hell of a grilling," Al said.

"If I was a steak, I'd be too overcooked to eat."

"With all that, did they get to the meat of the issue?"

"My answers left them nothing to beef about."

"Well done," Al said.

We arrived at the Falcon Heights police station at two minutes after four. In a loud, stern voice, Detective K.G. Barnes let us
know that this was not acceptable before leading me into the interrogation room. I was mentally exhausted from the session downtown and my slowness in responding to some of KGB's questions
increased her anger. At one point she practically accused Al and
me of committing the crime. When she finally finished, my head
felt like a punching bag that had been knocked around by the world
heavyweight champion, whoever that might be at the moment.

It was a few minutes after six when Al's session with KGB
ended. On the way to the car he said that Carol's orders were to
bring me to dinner at their house. Left on my own, I'd have gone
to bed without eating that night. I didn't have enough energy to
pick up a phone and call for delivery of a pizza.

*　*　*

IN AN IDEAL WORLD, I would have had Saturday off and could have
slept until noon. In the real world, I had to be at work at 8:00
a.m. and wouldn't be free to go home and crash until 1:00 p.m.
After two physically, emotionally, and mentally high-stress days,
I had the enthusiasm of a man going to the gallows as I slouched
past Eddy Gambrell, the assistant city editor who sat at Don
O'Rourke's desk on Saturdays. I was hoping to slip past him and
slump dumbly at my desk for a while before he realized I was
available for an assignment.

No such luck. Eddy spotted me, even though I was doing my best to look small. "Hey, Mitch, your buddy with the knife is being arraigned in fifteen minutes. Hustle up to the courthouse and see if he says anything worth quoting."

Hustle? I did my best. I hiked up the street to the courthouse and found the right courtroom just as two burly officers were bringing in my buddy "John." He was dressed in an orange jailhouse jumpsuit, his ankles were shackled, and his hands were cuffed behind his back. When he saw me, he drilled me with a look that drove deeper than his knife blade. I thought of the cliché "if looks could kill," and realized that if this were true, I would be lying lifeless on the courtroom floor.

The arraignment took all of three minutes. The prosecutor read the charges—assault with a deadly weapon, kidnapping, threatening to commit homicide, resisting arrest—and the judge asked for his plea. Obachuma snarled, "Not guilty," and the prosecutor asked that he be held on a million dollars bail until his next court appearance. Obachuma's court-appointed attorney requested that he be released on a much smaller bond. The prosecutor recited the obvious facts about the seriousness of the crime and the defendant's affinity for foreign travel. The judge set bail at $500,000 and impounded the defendant's passport, and Obachuma was trundled out by his two muscular escorts.

"Hi, Mitch," said Obachuma's lawyer as he walked past me on his way out. I recognized him as a member of the law firm where Martha worked. It made sense—Linda L. Lansing not only was noted for her work as a defense attorney but also employed a stable of high-powered defenders who were available for civic duty. Still, the irony of my wife's colleague defending the man who'd almost slit my throat was hard to swallow, even with an intact throat.

It didn't take much more than three minutes for me to write the story of the arraignment. I put it in context with some rehashing of Obachuma's visit to my apartment and sent it to Eddy.

"He didn't say anything else?" Eddy e-mailed back.

"I wanted to ask if he still had a headache but they dragged him out too fast," I replied. I heard Eddy laugh when he read it.

I was about to get up and go for a cup of coffee when my phone rang. It was Lauralee Baker.

"I'm just calling to see if you're okay," she said. "I'm sorry I ran out on you, but I wasn't thinking about anything but getting as far away from that awful man as I could. I took off my heels so they wouldn't make any noise and snuck out barefoot. I don't even remember getting into my car, but once I got there I saw that the ambulance had me parked in so I just ducked down and laid low. I didn't want to get dragged back in there, even by the cops."

"I don't blame you," I said. "Have the cops talked to you?"

"Oh, yes, I had to come down to the station and give them a statement. I'm downtown right now, in fact. Maybe you'd like to meet me for a drinky-poo somewhere."

"And then again, maybe I wouldn't. I think the less we get together the better it will be for my marriage vows. But I do want to hear from you if you get any more threatening calls."

"I wish you weren't such a goddamn old straight arrow," Lauralee said. "I could really use a good night in the sack with a stud like you."

"A couple of years ago I'd have been on you like an over-sexed rabbit," I said. "The way it is now, it ain't going to happen. But as I said, call me if you hear any more from the caller with the raspy voice."

"Oh, all right. I'll take no for an answer this time but the offer and my legs are always open for you."

"I appreciate your openness, but I'm afraid the subject is closed. Bye, Lauralee." I hung up, amazed at what a good boy I'd become. I needed Martha to be home soon.

# Chapter Thirty

## Getting Nowhere

SUNDAY AFTERNOON, I made my obligatory weekly call to my mother and her mother on the farm near Harmony. I always make these calls in mid-afternoon because Mom and Grandma Goodie often go out for lunch after being in the Methodist church from 10:30 a.m. until noon. During football season I wait until halftime of the Vikings game so that Grandma Goodie can walk away from the TV set without worrying about missing a crucial play.

Mom had read my Friday morning story about being held at knifepoint and had called that day to make sure that my head and my body were still all of a piece. This meant that Mom could pass the phone to Grandma Goodie quicker than usual because we had already had our customary discussion of the uncertainty of the weather, the state of the corn crop, and the foibles of Minnesota politicians.

My conversation with Grandma Goodie started as it always did, with her asking if I'd been to church and me saying I didn't make it this week.

"The way you stuck your neck out this week, I'd think you'd be in church thanking God you're still alive and begging for mercy on your soul," she said.

"I've thanked the police who rescued me, and I don't plan to stick my neck out in front of a knife again anytime soon," I said.

"I don't suppose you planned it this time, but there you were with the knife at your neck then, and where do you think your soul would've gone if he'd used it?"

"My point is that he didn't use it, and I'm still alive and kicking and planning to stay that way."

"Remember what Robert Burns said about the best laid plans of mice and men, Warnie Baby."

"Yes, they 'gang aft a-gley,'" I said. "But Burns actually said 'schemes,' not 'plans,' and I'm not scheming."

"Bosh. Schemes, plans, same thing," she said. "You should be planning or scheming or whatever you want to call it about getting right with God so the next time somebody cuts your throat your soul will be safe in heaven's hands."

"The next time somebody cuts my throat? Ever the optimist, aren't you?"

"You know what I mean, Warnie Baby. How many times has some lunatic attacked you in that crazy job of yours? How do you dare stay away from church?"

I didn't want to count the times. "I've always come out just fine, Grandma," I said. "Now suppose we talk about something pleasant, like baseball."

"Nothing pleasant about the Twins," Grandma Goodie said. "They're not anywhere near first place."

"But they're not in last place like they were last year," I said. I veered away from the Twins to less hackle-raising subjects, and eventually we ended the conversation with mutual expressions of love—and a final plea for me to take better care of my soul. Thinking again about the knife blade sliding across my throat, I had to admit that she had a point.

\* \* \*

MONDAY MORNING, I SAT down at my desk and looked at the mess in front of me. Unopened snail mail, unread newspapers, and unread memos to return phone calls were scattered all across the usual detritus that formed the base of the desktop clutter. My adventure at knifepoint and our day of discovery at the home of Al's would-be informant had taken control of my life. The stuff of my daily routine had been cast aside since Thursday, as had our search for the answer to Marilee Anderson's disappearance. We were no closer to learning Marilee's fate than we had been a week earlier. We knew why she'd disappeared, but we still had no idea where she'd gone after apparently escaping from the pimp who'd bought her from her father. Nor did we know why she'd never returned home.

Al arrived at my desk with coffee and we talked about getting nowhere on the Anderson case while I opened some press releases, put the past week's newspapers into the recycle basket beside my desk and sorted through some other junk left over from the previous week.

"Looks like our John Doe the First's murder leaves us at a dead end on the blue-eyed lady," Al said.

"Don't let a homicide kill your curiosity," I said. "I'll call Brownie. Maybe he's dug up something more alive than Skeleton X."

I called Brownie and, as requested, held the line for a minute that stretched into 410 seconds. When he finally returned, I asked if he had anything new on the Marilee Anderson case and he said he didn't. I told him why we had visited the late Henry Moustakas, and this inspired Brownie to deliver a lecture on why Al and I should have called him when Moustakas offered to lead us to the alleged Marilee lookalike. "Damn it, Mitch, you two always try to bypass the police and you always fuck it up," he said.

"Not always," I said.

"Okay, name one time that the suspect didn't either get away or damn near kill you when you and your buddy with the camera tried to tackle him without police backup."

He had me there. Al and I had a perfect record of providing incentives for confessed killers to flee, and invariably one or both of us got injured in the process. On the other hand, we always got a great story with pictures out of the events that led to the flight of the accused, and they'd all been caught eventually. Okay, sometimes they were captured more than a thousand miles away from St. Paul, but what the heck—they all ended up in jail.

I said as much to Brownie and his response could not be printed in a family newspaper. He offered to provide me with details of how much it had cost the taxpayers for police to pursue criminals that Al and I had spooked into long-distance flight, but I saw no news value in this so I did not accept the offer. I did point out that Henry Moustakas was a news source, not a suspected killer who would run away, and that police backup wouldn't have restored him to life when we found him Friday morning. Our conversation ended with Brownie grumbling his usual, "Have a good day, Mitch," and I went back to sorting out the layers of paper on my desk.

It was the kind of day I needed after the horror of having a knife at my throat and the shock of discovering a blood-covered corpse on a kitchen floor. I rewrote a couple of press releases, returned a couple of phone calls that resulted in itsy-bitsy stories and went out to the West Side to interview a woman who had been chased into her house by a fox that was probably rabid. Really a big news day in St. Paul.

When my phone rang shortly after two o'clock, I got a really bad feeling about the call. For no logical reason, I dreaded picking up the phone. My reporter's intuition told me it would be Morrie or some other lunatic I didn't want to talk to.

I desperately wanted the ringing to stop, but it continued. I had just decided to let it go to voicemail when I saw Corinne Ramey giving me a "what-the-hell's-wrong-with-you?" look. I gave up. I greeted the caller with a curt, *Daily Dispatch*, Warren Mitchell."

"Good morning, Mr. Mitchell," said a smooth male voice. "I'm calling you from Alaska."

"Alaska? Why are you calling the St. Paul paper from way out there?"

"I think you'll understand when I tell you who I am. My name is Jim Bjornquist."

So much for my reporter's intuition.

# Chapter Thirty-One

## Slick Situation

M Y RIGHT HAND scrabbled across my desk groping for a notepad and a useable ballpoint while my brain was trying to formulate a coherent response to this startling turn of events.

"Well, hello, Jim Bjornquist," I said after too long a pause. "Are you calling about Marilee Anderson?" Really dumb question. Why else would he be calling?

"That's right," he said. "I saw in the *National Enquirer* that her case has been reopened and that her dad shot himself."

"It was in the *National Enquirer*?"

"Oh, yah. Right on the front page. I saw St. Paul in the headline so I had to read it, and when I did I almost piss—uh, sorry . . . I almost peed in my pants right there in the checkout line. They even had a picture of Marilee's house."

"So how'd you know to call me in particular? My name wasn't in the *Enquirer* story, was it?" I had found both a pad and a pen and I was ready to write.

"Oh, no, nothing like that," he said. "After I got home I went online and Googled the *Daily Dispatch* and found your stories about the buried body and her old man's suicide."

This all seemed too easy. "And how do I know that you're really Jim Bjornquist and not some kook calling to play a prank on the paper?" I asked.

"Oh, yah, I suppose you get those, dontcha? Well, I can tell you some things about what happened that nobody else knows but me."

"If nobody else knows them, how can I confirm them?"

"Oh, jeez, I never thought of that. Maybe I can think of something you can check on. Or maybe *you* can. Maybe something you know that you haven't put in the paper."

I decided to take him at his word for the moment, and would try to trip him up somewhere along the way. "Okay, let's say you really are Jim Bjornquist. Tell me something you think I don't know."

"Well I don't think you know that the first name of the pimp who bought Marilee from her old man was Slick."

"You're right about that. Did he have a last name?"

"Oh, yah, he probably did, but I don't remember ever hearing it. I'll bet if you ask some of the cops who were on the vice squad back then they would remember Slick. He was around the neighborhood a lot looking for young girls and I'm pretty sure the cops ran him in a couple of times."

Good start. This was one item I could use for confirmation that my caller really was Jim Bjornquist. I drew a big asterisk by that note. "Tell me more," I said. "Tell me about you and Marilee. Were you two in love?"

"I ain't sure it was love," Jim said. "But we were getting together and doing it every chance we had—if you know what I mean."

"You mean you were having sex?"

"That's the nice way to put it. We were screwing like a couple of bunny rabbits all spring and summer. Then she got knocked up."

"Also like a bunny rabbit. You didn't use protection?"

"We usually did. I mean, we sold rubbers at the store so it was no problem to get them, but we just got going too far a couple of times without one and *wham*."

"I believe the expression is 'wham, bam, thank you, ma'am.'"

"Hey, you got that right," Jim said. "I'd forgot that old joke."

"Okay, now Marilee was pregnant. How did you feel about that?" I said.

"I was scared shitless. Uh, sorry. Anyway, I didn't want no baby. I was only nineteen and didn't have no money or nothing. So I said we should find a place to get an abortion. But Marilee, she said no way—that having an abortion was a bigger sin in the eyes of the lord than having a baby without being married."

"She was Catholic, right?"

"Oh, yah, you bet she was. Not that she went to church all that much, but when it come down to having an abortion she wouldn't go against her religion."

"So, then what was the plan? Or wasn't there one?" I said.

"Well, we knew her old man would beat the crap out of her if he found out she was pregnant, and probably come after me, too. So we decided to get out of town."

"If he'd really beaten her up it might have solved the abortion problem."

"Oh, yah, it might have, but there wasn't no way I was going let her get beat up by that mean old son of a bitch," Jim said. "I had an older cousin living out in Stockton, California, and I called her and told her what was going on. She said we could come out there and stay with her while Marilee was having the baby and I was looking for a job."

"So why were you two still in St. Paul the day Marilee disappeared?"

"The problem was we didn't have enough money to make the trip right away. We had to save up for three or four weeks—me from my paycheck and her from the scroungy little allowance she got from her mother. Please don't put this in the paper, but I even snuck a few bucks out of the cash drawer to go with what the store was paying me. We'd actually got to where we were going to buy bus tickets and bail out for California the next weekend. Then her old man sold her to Slick."

"You stole money from the store?"

"Oh, yah, but I paid them back years ago. I sent the money to Bert Love."

"He told me he's never heard from you," I said.

"I sent it anonymous, cash with no name," Jim said. "You could ask him if he ever got fifty dollars in an envelope with no name on it. Probably about two years after I left town."

Another point of confirmation. "I'll do that. We'll see if he remembers getting something like that more than twenty years ago." I drew another big asterisk by that note. "You left the day after Marilee vanished. Did you go to your cousin in Stockton?"

"No. After what happened with Slick, I didn't want to get her involved with me. I took a train to Seattle instead, and got a job on a fishing boat."

"Okay, so tell me: what did happen with Slick?"

There was a long silence before I heard Jim suck in a deep breath and blow it out into my earpiece. "It's hard to talk about it, Mr. Mitchell. But here goes." He took another deep breath before he started. "I was behind the counter in the store that morning and there weren't any customers, so I was just kind of staring half asleep out the front window when I saw Marilee coming on the other side of the street. That kind of woke me up, and I watched her come across and walk toward our front door.

"Then, I don't know where he came from, but all of a sudden Slick was beside her and he grabbed her arm and started yanking her away from the door. Marilee yelled something at him and tried to pull away, but he was way stronger than she was and he started hauling her up the street. Well, I knew who he was and what he was and I wasn't going let him take my girlfriend away and start selling her ass on the street. So I went around the counter and ran out the door and yelled at him to let Marilee go.

"Well, of course he didn't. He just said for me to fuck off and kept pulling Marilee along. She was screaming and fighting something fierce and I was running after them, and he all of a sudden smacked her across the face with the back of his free hand. That really pissed me off, and when I caught up to them I grabbed the arm he was holding her with and tried to yank it off of her." I noticed that Jimmy wasn't apologizing for his language any more.

"Well, he swung at me with his other hand but I ducked under it and I bit him in the arm he was holding Marilee with. I mean I really sank my teeth into that arm. It was hairy and sweaty, and I can still feel it and taste it now that I think about it. Anyhow, he was so surprised that he let go of Marilee and I quit biting him and yelled at her to run like hell and get away.

"She took off like a shot, and Slick started to chase her but I tackled him and we went down on the sidewalk. He must have hit his head because he was laying on his face for a minute without moving and I jumped up off of him. I was standing there, wondering what to do next, when he rolled over and sat up and pulled a big old knife out of his belt. I knew what to do then, and I took off running for the store. He took off after me, yelling that he was going to kill me, but I beat him to the door and slammed it in his face and snapped the lock.

"Slick stood outside, yanking away on the door and waving the knife and saying he'd be waiting for me and that he'd kill me when he caught me. I yelled back that I was going to call the cops and I went to the phone behind the counter to do that. Before I could punch in the number, Slick took off running, so I didn't make the call. Later, I wished that I would have."

He paused for breath and I asked, "Why is that?"

"Because then we might have found Marilee," he said. "I went back to the front window and looked all around but I didn't see her anywhere, so I figured she must have run home. Then a couple of hours later when her old man came in looking for her, I found out that she hadn't gone home. But I didn't have no clue where she went, and as the day went on and her old man didn't find her anywhere in the neighborhood, I didn't know where else to look for her."

"Didn't you tell her father and the police that you hadn't seen her at all?" I asked.

"Oh, yah, I sort of lied to him about that because I was scared that he was mad at her and that he'd give her a whipping for not coming home with whatever he'd sent her to the store to get. I didn't know that he'd actually sold her to Slick and was faking not knowing what had happened to her. The rotten bastard used to beat her on her bare ass, you know. Got off on it, I think. Anyhow I figured she must be hiding 'til it was safer to go home so I told him she hadn't come into the store, which actually was the truth because she hadn't. Then later when the cops asked me, I had to tell the same thing to them."

The whole story sounded weird to me. "So you didn't know for sure where Marilee was, but you packed up your stuff that night and took off for Seattle the next morning?" I said.

"I called their house that night and disguised my voice and asked for Marilee, and her mom said she wasn't there. I didn't know where to look for her. I mean, the neighbors and the cops had been looking all day. The only thing I knew for sure was that Slick would be coming after me with that knife as soon as he had a chance, so I threw some clothes together, went to the depot early in the morning and caught the first train heading west, which was going to Seattle. When I got there I called the Andersons' house again and asked for Marilee, and her mom said she'd disappeared. Then I figured either Slick had come back and caught her, or she'd taken the chance to get away from home and was hiding from her old man somewhere."

"But you never came back to St. Paul to look for her?" I said.

"I was scared to come back at first, because of Slick," Jim said. "I didn't know her old man had killed him. Then I met a girl in Seattle and we had a baby together before she left me for a guy with more money. By that time I'd forgotten all about Marilee and I decided to move to Alaska and look for a better job."

"Did you find one?"

"Don't I wish? I'm still working on a goddamn fishing boat, only at least this one's my own."

"Why haven't you ever contacted your family back here?"

"My folks died in a car crash when I was little so I was living with my grandma, who really didn't want me. I did call her from Seattle off and on. Then I called one day and a stranger answered and told me that Grandma had dropped dead in the kitchen of a massive heart attack. There wasn't nobody else there that I could talk to after that."

"No brothers or sisters? What about your cousin Roger?" I asked.

"Roger's wife said he was in the army in Afghanistan, and I'm an only child. Like Marilee. That's one of the things we had in common," Jim said.

"What were some of the others?"

He was silent for a moment before he said, "We both hated our home lives and we both really liked to screw."

"She was underage. You could have done jail time if her parents had found out."

"I know. I never thought about that at the time."

"Would you be willing to tell all this to the St. Paul police? Maybe leaving out the part about having sex with a fifteen-year-old?"

"Oh, yah, I suppose so. Everything except the sex and maybe the part about taking the fifty dollars."

"I won't mention either one if you don't."

"You don't think they'll come after me for lying to them way back then, do you?"

"I'm sure the statute of limitations on lying to an officer is long past. Now, give me a number where I can reach you after I check out what you've told me. I'm not writing a story until I'm convinced that you're who you say you are."

"I can give you what my parents' first names were and what my grandma's name was, along with her address and her birthday. You can check those things out. I wouldn't know that kind of stuff if I was just some wingnut calling in to make you look foolish, would I?"

"Probably not," I said. He recited that information, and I wrote it down and drew a really big asterisk next to it. He followed up by giving me his phone number, his e-mail address, and his street address in Ketchikan.

"I'm on Facebook, too," he said. "If you want to, you can 'like' my page."

"I like you very much," I said. "And you'll soon be hearing from a detective named Brown who will like you even more."

# Chapter Thirty-Two

## Fact Checking

JIMMY BJORNQUIST!" Don O'Rourke shouted it so loud that every head in the newsroom turned his way. "You just talked to Jimmy Bjornquist?"

"He claimed to be Jimmy Bjornquist and he sounded authentic," I said.

"What did he say? Can we get his picture? Where is he?" Don said.

"In Ketchikan, Alaska. Want to send Al up there for pix?"

"Buy me a plane ticket and I'm on the way," said Al, who had come running out of the photo department when he heard Don yell out Bjornquist's name.

"Don't you wish?" Don said. "Damn, I was hoping he was right here in town."

"Has he got a cell phone up there?" Al asked.

"I don't know," I said. "He's got e-mail."

"If he's got a cell phone, you could ask him to shoot a selfie and e-mail it to us," Al said.

"Great idea," Don said.

"I'm not so sure he'd be up for that," I said.

"All you can do is ask," Don said.

"Okay, I'll try," I said. "But first I need to check out some things to make sure it really was Jimmy and not some smartass playing games with the paper."

"Well, get busy checking," Don said. "Then call him and ask him for a selfie and get started writing that story."

I decided to begin by finding out if anybody in the police department remembered a pimp named Slick. I called Brownie and got the usual, "Homicidebrown."

"*Dailydispatch*mitchell," I said. "I bet you'll never guess who I just talked to on the phone."

"How should I know? Was it Mickey Mouse? The Tooth Fairy? The ghost of Skeleton X?"

"Even better than Exie's ghost. The living, breathing body of Jimmy Bjornquist."

A moment of silence, and then, "Are you shittin' me?"

"Have I ever done that?

"Yes, lots of times."

"Okay, but this time I'm not. The guy said he was Jim Bjornquist and he sounded very authentic. I need to check some things to verify that it was him, and one of them involves the police department. I need you to ask around and see if anybody who was working vice when Marilee disappeared remembers a pimp named Slick operating in that part of town."

"Slick? Slick what?"

"Jimmy never knew the guy's last name, but he says that Skeleton X is a pimp named Slick."

"Okay, I'll ask around. Anything else? Do you have this guy's phone number so that I can talk to him?"

"I do, and I'll give it to you on the condition that you won't talk about this to any other reporter until my story—assuming there'll be one—hits the paper."

"Fair enough. I'll call you back if I find out anything about Slick. And I want a rundown on what Bjornquist told you before your story hits the paper."

"Fair enough. Happy hunting for Slick. And here's the phone number."

Brownie copied the number and said, "Thanks."

"You're welcome," I said.

"I'm glad you said that. I hate it when I thank somebody and they say 'no problem.' Have a good day, Mitch." How about that? An unexpected comrade in etiquette arms.

I was smiling when I put down the phone, which prompted Corinne Ramey to ask what I was so pleased about.

"You wouldn't understand," I said. "It's an inside issue."

"Okay, no problem," she said. Apparently nothing was a problem for this woman.

The information the caller had given me about Jimmy Bjornquist's parents and grandmother checked out. I even found a news clip about the accident in which his parents were killed—a head-on with a pickup truck on an ice-slicked road in freezing rain. The date was appropriate; Jimmy would have been three years old. I also found an obit for his grandmother. Again, the date was appropriate. Jimmy would have been living in Seattle when she died.

The only asterisk left to check out was my note about fifty dollars being sent to Adelbert Love. I hoped I could do this one by phone rather than make another trip to the senior care center. I called the number, identified myself, and asked the woman who answered if it would be possible to speak with Mr. Love. She put me on hold and I listened to some music from the fifties while she was away. When she returned, she said she would transfer my call to a phone that Mr. Love was holding in his hand.

"Hey, sonny, what's up?" said Adelbert Love's cheerful voice. "You're cuttin' into my card game, you know."

"Are you playing Solitaire?" I asked.

"Heck no. Cribbage. And Ellie's beatin' my butt again."

"You're still playing Cribbage with Mrs. Miller?"

"That's right. Ellie and me have been playin' every day since you told me about her. Sometimes I have to introduce myself again because she forgot who I am overnight, but she ain't forgot how to play a wicked game of Cribbage. So what can I do for you?"

"I need you to think back about twenty-three years," I said. "Do you remember ever getting an envelope in the mail with fifty dollars in it and no return address or note?

After a silence so prolonged that I was afraid the connection had been broken, Love said, "Yeah, now that I think about it, there was a piece of mail like that way back, about that time. I wondered about where that fifty bucks came from for a long time. How'd you find out about it?"

"I talked to the sender this morning. It was Jim Bjornquist. He told me that he'd anonymously returned fifty bucks that he'd taken from the store."

"Well, I'll be dipped," Love said. "So that was from Jimmy. And you say you talked to him today? Where the hell is he?"

I told him where Jimmy had gone originally, where he was currently, and what he was doing in Ketchikan.

"He was a good boy," Love said. "Kind of lazy, but all kids that age were. Never realized he'd swiped fifty bucks from the till. He could've kept it and I'd never have known the difference. Anything else I can tell you?"

"No, sir, you've helped verify that the man who called me really was Jim Bjornquist. I'll let you get back to losing your card game. Thanks for your help."

"You're welcome," he said. Ah, yes, a true gentleman.

I had enough verification to start on my story without waiting on word from the police department. I was on about the tenth graf when that word came on a call from Brownie, who'd found a veteran vice squad officer who remembered a pimp called Slick.

"Slick Jackson was his full name," Brownie said. "Operated kind of as a team with a loan shark named Moneybags Mahoney. Eddie says they were a couple of really vicious bastards. Says Jack Anderson did society a favor by cutting Slick's throat."

"Great," I said. "Everything else checks out. I'm going to call Jim right now and ask him if he'll send us a selfie. After that I guess you can call him any time. Thanks for your help."

"You're welcome." How I love to hear those words.

To my amazement, Jim Bjornquist agreed to send us a selfie. When it arrived, we compared it to a picture in the *Daily Dispatch* files that had been acquired from Jim Bjornquist's grandmother a day after Marilee Anderson vanished. The two faces were similar enough to give us another point of verification. Bjornquist's cheeks had fattened and his hairline had retreated a bit in the ensuing twenty-five years, but there was no doubt about who he was.

I went back to my computer and finished my story, which I then sent to Don O'Rourke. I called Brownie and gave him a nutshell version of what Bjornquist had told me, omitting the underage sex and the borrowed fifty dollars.

It was after six o'clock when I sat back in my chair, feeling incredibly pleased and satisfied with myself.

"You look like the cat that ate a whole cage full of canaries," Al said as he came by my desk to say good night.

I grinned like a carved Halloween pumpkin. "I haven't felt this good about a story in years," I said.

"I don't blame you. It's a great story. It's only missing one thing."

I couldn't imagine what I'd left out. I stopped grinning and asked, "What's missing?"

"Where did Marilee Anderson go after she got away from Slick?"

# Chapter Thirty-Three

## Getting Warmer?

NORMALLY I DO VERY little talking at my Monday night Alcoholics Anonymous meetings. But many in the group had read the story of my encounter with Robert Obachuma, so on this Monday night I was asked question after question about those awful minutes. Without realizing what I was doing, I eventually rambled from a description of the feel of a knife at my throat to a confession of my desperate desire for a drink. This led to more intense questioning, and in excruciating detail, I poured out the whole episode of the wine bottle and my rescue by Martha's just-in-time phone call. When I finished, my face was running with sweat, my armpits were drenched, and my body felt like it had followed the wine down the sink drain.

My face was still moist when the session ended, which caused Jayne Halvorson to ask if I had enough energy to indulge in our usual post-meeting ginger ale at Herbie's Bar. I thought a jolt of sugary drink would help me get home safely, so I made the trek to Herbie's on slightly elastic knees.

After a couple of swigs of ginger ale, I found the strength to speak. "I don't know which hit me harder, remembering the knife at my throat or telling the group about my close call with the wine."

"They were both pretty traumatic," Jayne said. "But I'm betting it was harder to talk about the wine."

"I think you win that bet. I never meant to mention the wine at all. I just sort of slid into it, and then everybody was asking questions and there was no going back."

"Did you tell Martha that her call saved you from drinking yourself into God knows what kind of a mess?"

"I haven't told her yet. I know she'll feel guilty about having left the wine in the house, so I'm waiting until she gets home and I have to explain the missing bottle."

"Just be sure you remember to tell her," Jayne said. "She might not want to leave alcohol around the house next time she's gone."

"I might not want to have another crazy bastard put me into a condition that calls for alcohol."

We sipped ginger ale in silence for a couple of minutes before she said, "Didn't I read that you had another strange experience the day after the knife at your throat?"

"I did," I said. "Al and I did. We found a body in a veritable Lake Superior of blood when we went to interview a guy who claimed to know something about our cold case girl, Marilee Anderson."

"Do you think the murder of that man had anything to do with the case?"

"I don't know. It could be that or it could have been a break-in that went really down the toilet."

"What do the police think?"

"Who knows? The investigator is our old friend K.G. Barnes of the Falcon Heights Police Department."

"The woman who wouldn't talk to the media after the State Fair killing?"

"The very one."

"Did you ever try my suggestion?" Jayne had advised me to try softening up KGB by inviting her to a non-business, off-the-record lunch.

"We eventually had lunch together but it didn't work out," I said. "She just has a crazy hatred of the press."

"More likely it's fear—the fear of saying too much or making a mistake. If lunch didn't work, maybe you can play on the fear. Try raising the possibility of something bad happening if she's too close-mouthed."

"What would that be?"

"I don't know. Try to come up with something. You're the reporter. I can't do all your thinking for you." She opened her purse, took out a small notebook and a pen, and wrote on a page. She tore out the page and handed it to me. "Here's something I can do for you. Here's my phone number."

"I already have your number in my cell phone," I said.

"This is written in nice big numbers. Put it up where you can see it, and remember to call it the next time you're all alone and drooling for a drink."

"You're assuming that something extremely traumatic will happen to me again."

"Your history tells me that the odds in favor of that are pretty good."

She had me there.

\* \* \*

WHEN I BOOTED UP my computer Tuesday morning I found an e-mail informing the media that the Ramsey County medical examiner would discuss the results of the autopsy on Henry L. Moustakas at 10:30 a.m. I relayed this information to Don O'Rourke, who promptly assigned Al and me to cover it.

"You look kind of limp this morning," Al said as we sat in the cafeteria drinking coffee prior to our departure. "And the bags under your eyes would hold a pound of potato chips."

"Tough night at AA," I said. "Everybody wanted to hear about that goon holding the knife to my throat. I got the shakes all over again just telling about it and I didn't sleep all that well when I got home."

"I guess it was neck and neck whether the cops would get there before he cut your throat." Leave it to Al to find a one-liner to brighten my day.

"Even after the cops arrived it was touch and almost go," I said. I had stopped covering the scab with gauze and I caressed it between my thumb and forefinger as I spoke. It was hard and rough and blessedly dry.

Al saw the move. "Don't worry, nothing's leaking out," he said. "Not even cider from your Adam's apple."

"I'll drink to that," I said. I finished my coffee with two big gulps and we went to listen to Dr. Lyle Lundberg discuss some serious bloodshed.

The usual crowd was on hand for the medical examiner's report. I took my customary position behind Trish Valentine, who was clad as skimpily as Channel Four's dress code would allow because the temperature outdoors was ninety-two degrees. I knew her translucent, low-cut blouse would draw Dr. Lundberg's attention, which would put me in his line of vision if I raised my hand to ask a question.

At precisely 10:30 a.m., Dr. Lundberg entered the meeting room, followed by KGB and her boss, Falcon Heights Police Chief Victoria Tubb. The good doctor looked first in our direction and began to swivel his head leftward to scan the audience. His head stopped in mid-swivel and jerked back our way for a second look at Trish's generously exposed cleavage before it turned away again for a complete scan of the assemblage. The white-haired M.E. was in his middle sixties, but his male instincts were still in their prime.

"Our autopsy has shown that Henry L. Moustakas died from a massive loss of blood caused by a stab wound that pierced a major artery," Dr. Lundberg said. "The wound did not result in immediate death. The victim's heart continued to beat for several moments, all but emptying his body of blood." Okay, that explained the expanse of red that covered most of the kitchen floor.

"The wound was inflicted by a long, narrow blade, which entered just below the rib cage on the victim's left side. The victim was found lying on his back with his right hand covering the wound, as if he had attempted to stop the flow of blood. The time of death is estimated at approximately six o'clock on the morning of July twenty-fourth. That's all I have unless you have questions."

True to form, Dr. Lundberg was looking at Trish, and her hand shot up. "What was the victim wearing?" she asked. "Was he dressed for the day or was he in pajamas?"

The doctor smiled. "I'd say he was partially dressed for the day. He was wearing trousers but no shirt. The killer had a bare upper torso to aim at."

He was still staring down Trish's blouse at her upper torso when I asked, "Would you say the killer was right-handed?"

Raising his eyes far enough to look at me, Dr. Lundberg said, "The positioning of the wound toward the victim's left side would indicate that the blow was struck by a right-handed person facing him." Exactly as I'd imagined.

"Are there any clues as to the killer's motive?" asked a man behind me. "Was it a robbery gone bad, or what?"

"That's out of my area of expertise," Dr. Lundberg said. "Perhaps Chief Tubb would respond to that."

Chief Tubb stepped forward. "We have no evidence that would lead to a motive at this time," she said.

"How about suspects?" asked Barry Ziebart of Channel Five. "Did the neighbors see or hear anything?"

"We have no suspects and Detective Barnes has received no information from any of the neighbors at this time," Chief Tubb said. I made a note to question some of Old Hank's neighbors for my next story.

"What about family?" Trish asked. "Who are the victim's survivors?"

"The victim lived alone and had never been married," the chief said. "We found a contact number for a brother in Minot, North Dakota, who will be coming to claim the victim's remains as soon as we release it. The brother is older—I believe he said he's sixty-eight. He has a wife and two adult children, but both of the parents are deceased, as are all of their aunts and uncles."

I asked for the brother's name and the answer was Herbert. How about that? Old Hank and Old Herb.

After a couple of more questions, Chief Tubb indicated that the session was over and the trio left the room. Before turning to follow the two officers, Dr. Lundberg took a last look at Trish Valentine. All he saw was her back, because she was facing the camera and reporting live.

* * *

MY E-MAIL CONTAINED a message from St. Adolphus Catholic Church, which reminded me that I had left a voicemail message there on Saturday asking for a comment on the maintenance man they called Old Hank. The call had not been returned, and this e-mail was a canned statement from the pastor, Father Joseph, expressing deep sorrow over the loss of their longtime employee and friend, Henry Moustaskas.

Seeking something more personal, I called the church again and asked the woman who answered if I could speak with Father Joseph. She wasn't sure that he was available, but after several minutes of waiting on hold a man with a hearty bass voice greeted me and identified himself as Father Joseph.

I explained my mission and noted that during a previous call, the secretary had referred to the departed as Old Hank.

206

"Well, yes, I guess some folks here called him that," Father Joseph said. "He's worked in the church, the rectory, and the convent here for quite a number of years so the ladies, in particular, got quite familiar with him. He was a bachelor and he would flirt with the ladies a little, don't you know."

"He flirted with nuns?" I said.

"Oh, more with our lay people than with our nuns, but all the ladies loved him. It's a sad day here, Mr. Mitchell, a sad day indeed." He spoke with an Irish lilt that I hadn't expected from a priest at a church named St. Adolphus.

"I'm sorry for your loss. Tell me, Father, was there anyone you know of who might not have loved him?"

"Oh, no, I can't think of anyone. If you're asking if anybody here might have killed him I can give you a flat no, Mr. Mitchell. There's nobody here at St. Adolphus capable of such a thing, and certainly not when it's Henry."

"Did I hear you say you have a convent there in addition to the church?"

"Oh, yes, a small one. We have about half a dozen nuns and a few lay people living here on the grounds. I'm sure as you're born that none of them had any quarrel with Henry, either."

"How about outside-of-the-church staff and the people in the convent? Anybody you can think of who might have had a gripe against Henry?"

"In the congregation, you mean? Again, I've got to say a flat-out no, Mr. Mitchell. Henry always did his job real well and went out of his way to help fix anybody's problems. I can't imagine why anybody would want to hurt a man like Henry. It must have been some sneaking house-breaker that got caught in the act and stabbed poor Henry in order to get away. I do hope the police catch the man who did this awful thing."

"I do, too," I said. "Have the police talked to you and your staff?"

"Oh, yes," he said. "A woman detective came by and questioned us all one by one in my office. Very intense young lady. Not a very pleasant bedside manner, if you know what I mean. I think her name was Barnes."

"I'm sure it was. Detective Barnes is not noted for either her personality or her tactfulness. Anyhow, I'll let you get back to work now and I thank you for your help."

"Oh, you're very welcome, Mr. Mitchell, and blessings on you." *And blessings on you, Father Joseph, for knowing the proper response,* I thought.

I caught Don O'Rourke just as he was leaving for the day and suggested that Al and I start the next day knocking on doors and quizzing people in Henry Moustakas's neighborhood. Don agreed that it might be worthwhile, so I passed the word to Al and said I'd pick him up in the morning.

"You're thinking Old Hank's killing has some connection to our cold case, aren't you?" Al said.

"Think about it," I said. "I've talked to a woman who saw a woman that looked like Marilee Anderson at a Catholic church in north Minneapolis. And Old Hank Moustakis, who worked at a Catholic church in north Minneapolis, wanted to tell us about knowing where we could find Marilee Anderson. Is it pure coincidence? Or are we getting warm?"

"Could be that," Al said. "Or we could just be feeling the July weather."

# Chapter Thirty-Four

## Old Hank's Neighborhood

W
E HAD DECIDED to get an early start Wednesday in an effort to catch some of Old Hank's working neighbors before they left home. The first one we encountered, at 6:35 a.m., was a muscular middle-aged man in jeans and a T-shirt who was about to get into a well-used Chevy sedan. He lived three houses south of Henry Moustakas.

He told us his name was Jim and that he didn't want either his name or his picture in the paper. "I didn't see nothin' and I didn't hear nothin' that mornin'," he said. "Now, I'm kinda in a hurry to get to the job, so if you'll excuse me, I'll be goin'."

"What is the job?" I asked.

"Roofin' a house in Shoreview. So long, guys." He slid into the driver's seat of the Chevy, slammed the door, and drove away.

"A roofer," Al said. "High-level work."

"We should have wished him top of the morning," I said.

We moved one house closer to Old Hank's and rang the doorbell. The inner door was opened about twelve inches by a barrel-shaped woman with hair that looked like it hadn't been combed yet that morning. She was wearing a fuzzy pink bathrobe and floppy black slippers. She squinted at us through the screen door and said, "Yeah?"

I explained who we were and asked if she or anyone else in the house had seen or heard anything unusual around six o'clock last Friday morning. "No," she said and slammed the door. I heard her click the lock into place.

"Real sweetie pie," Al said.

"I admire a woman who doesn't mince words," I said.

We received a less frigid reception at the house next door to Henry's. After showing our *Daily Dispatch* ID cards, we were actually invited in by the slender gray-haired man who answered the bell. "My wife's still sleeping, so I can let you in, but talk quiet. She's been scared stiff to open the door for anybody ever since poor Hank got killed. I tell her, hell's bells, with all the cops that've been around here, the killer ain't coming back."

He said his name was Arthur Sommers and that he and his wife Hazel had lived next door to Hank for more than twenty years. "I miss the guy already," Sommers said. "Two or three times a week we'd have a beer together on my back porch after he got home from work. I been retired for five years so it was good to have somebody to talk to besides the wife. In the winter he'd come over and play gin rummy."

"Did he ever talk about having any trouble with people at work?" I asked.

"Never. He talked about the people there like they was family. Never heard him say a bad word about anybody there. You think somebody there might have killed him?"

"Anything is possible," I said. "How about you? Did you see or hear anything unusual outside the morning Hank was killed?"

"You know, of all days, that was the one morning I slept in," he said. "Usually I'm up and around before six, like I was this morning, but I got to bed late Thursday night because we watched a movie on TV and I didn't wake up 'til after seven, when the cops came roaring up."

"How about your wife? Was she awake early?"

"Never happen. She's famous in our family for not being a morning person. You don't dare call her on the phone before ten o'clock in the morning."

We turned down an offer of coffee, Al took a mug shot of Arthur Sommers, and I thanked him as we went out the door.

"I didn't give you much, but you're welcome," he said. Just the response I'd expected from a man his age.

"Are we wasting our time here?" Al asked as we walked past Henry's house. "Chief Tubb said that none of the neighbors had told good old KGB anything."

"Experience tells me that it's wise to double-check anything that involves good old KGB," I said.

At the house on the other side of Henry's, I was able to prove my point.

The bell was answered by a young woman prepared to go to an office job. She wore a navy pantsuit with a pale blue blouse set off at the throat by a red-and-white striped dress scarf. Her brown hair was curled into a bun without a strand straying from its designated place and her makeup had been applied with the skill of a theatre artist. She was, in a word, gorgeous.

She didn't open the inner door more than a crack until both of us had shown her our ID cards through the screen. Even after she invited us in, she stayed out of range of a handshake. I wondered if the black handbag slung over her shoulder contained a gun.

"You'll pardon me if I'm super careful about who I let in," she said. "After what happened next door, my husband didn't want to leave the house for work before I did, but he had to because he's got a much longer commute."

"I'm grateful that you let us in at all," I said. "I can understand your husband's concern about leaving you alone."

"You know, you somehow look familiar. Are you the reporter who had a knife stuck in his throat?" she said. My mug shot had run with the story about my adventure with Robert Obachuma.

"You've got a good eye," I said. "It was me." I pointed to the scab on my throat and she gave a little gasp.

"Oh, my God," she said. "He really did stab you."

"Just a nick with the edge of the blade," I said with the throwaway tone of a self-effacing hero.

"Oh, go ahead and tell her you blacked out from the sight of your own blood," Al said. Great backup from a buddy.

"I'd have fainted on the spot at the sight of the knife without it having to cut me," the woman said. "Oh, my name is Naomi Jacobsen, in case you're wondering."

I had been. I wrote it in my notebook and asked the question about seeing or hearing anything unusual. I was pleasantly surprised by Naomi's answer.

"I was in the kitchen poaching an egg when I heard tires screeching, and I ran and looked out and saw a black car taking off like a shot from in front of Henry's house," she said. "It went racing past here, kind of weaving back and forth across the center line, and then I lost sight of it."

"Do you know what kind of car it was?" I asked.

"It was a black sedan, a small one, but it went by so fast I didn't see what make it was. They all look so much alike now that you have to see the logo to tell whether it's a Ford or a Toyota."

"Ain't that the truth?" Al said. "Did you see the driver?"

"Not really. I saw a dark shape but not any features. Couldn't tell if it was a man or a woman."

"Only one person in the car?" he said.

"That's all I saw, just the driver," Naomi said.

"You said the car was weaving?" I said.

"Yeah, it looked kind of like the driver was having trouble controlling it at that speed."

"Have you told the police about this?" I asked.

"Oh, yes. I talked to a woman detective by the name of Barnes. I'll never forget her, because she had an attitude." Ah, yes, nothing from the neighbors, according to Detective K.G. Barnes.

"She's sort of known for her attitude," Al said.

"What he means is that she's known to be a bitch," I said.

"As I woman, I don't like to hear that word, but I'd say that in Detective Barnes's case it could be accurate. Now, if you gentlemen are through with me, I really have to get on my way to work."

"We'd like a quick photo and then you can be on your way," Al said. "Where do you work?"

"At the *Minneapolis Globe*," she said. "But I read the St. Paul paper every day."

As we left, I thanked Naomi for her help.

"No problem," she said. Aargh! Young people.

"Imagine that," Al said as we left. "Interviewing someone who works at the *Globe*."

"Small world," I said.

We questioned two more people before calling it quits, and got a partial corroboration of Naomi's statement from a seventy-something woman dog walker, who had been walking her Shih Tzu—yet another one—a little after 6:00 a.m. on the Friday of Henry's death.

"I heard this awful screeching of tires, and when I looked around, here comes this big black sedan tearing up the street like a rocket," Ann McDermott said, pointing in the direction of Henry's house. "I grabbed Cuddles and held her while that monster went ripping by."

"You say it was a big black car?" I said.

"Looked as big as a frickin' tank coming at us," she said.

"You didn't see what kind it was?"

"I didn't care what kind it was, I just wanted to be sure Cuddles was safe. The car wasn't going in a straight line and I was scared it might zoom over to the sidewalk."

"Good idea to hold the dog," Al said. "Did you see the driver?"

"Not really. I was too busy grabbing Cuddles and ducking out of the way to look for any driver."

"Well, thank you for your time and your help," I said as Al took Ann's picture cuddling Cuddles.

"Oh, that's okay," she said. Disappointing. She was of the generation that should give the proper response.

We returned to the office with a couple of new facts I could put in a story. Two women had seen a black car, either small or as big as a frickin' tank, leaving from in front of Henry's house, weaving at high speed with screeching tires at the estimated time of Henry's death. With Al's pix of the people interviewed, it made a tolerable follow story on the Falcon Heights murder case. It was so tolerable, in fact, that it brought me a phone call in response the next morning—at home on my day off, no less.

# Chapter Thirty-Five

## Day Off

"WHO GAVE YOU permission to talk to those people about the murder of Henry Moustakas?" asked Detective K.G. Barnes.

"The Founding Fathers," I said. "Surely you've heard of the First Amendment."

"You and your photographer buddy are poking your noses into police business," she said. "That's going beyond your First Amendment rights."

I wanted to tell her she was full of crap, but I said, "So sue me. Sue the paper. Sue the corporation that owns us. But be aware that Al and I might be snooping around out there in your little police kingdom again before the case is solved. *If* it's solved." I couldn't resist that final dig.

"Oh, don't worry, Mr. First Amendment, the case will be solved," KGB said. "We have a perfect record in solving homicides."

"That's right," I said. "You're one-for-one in that category. But as I recall, you had help from a certain reporter-photographer team who figured it out first."

There was a moment of silence, and I could imagine steam whistling out of KGB's ears as she remembered how we'd one-upped her. "Just take this as a warning," she said at last. "You two stay out of Falcon Heights or we promise to find a way to put you behind bars for something." Her voice rose in a crescendo as she spoke.

"Thanks for the warning," I said.

"No problem," she said at top volume as she broke off the call. I knew she would give that uncouth response.

The next call I received was far more encouraging. It came just before noon from Martha Todd, who said that the case in Moorhead had been settled and that she was in her car and about to leave the motel parking lot. "See you about five o'clock," she said.

I greeted this news with a whoop of joy and asked if she wanted me to try to make something for dinner.

"Yes, reservations at the nearest restaurant," she said. "That's the one thing you know how to make without burning something or creating a hellacious mess in the kitchen." I couldn't argue with that. My lack of culinary skills was unmatched and undeniable.

Shortly after lunch, my doorbell rang. I peeked out the window and ascertained that the caller was friendly. When I opened the door, Zhoumaya Jones rolled through in her wheelchair. "I just got home from hiding out with my friend and the first thing I need to do is apologize and thank you," she said.

"You're welcome for whatever you're thanking me for, but you've got no reason to apologize," I said.

"No reason to apologize? I run away and hide from a lunatic killer and leave you to get your throat cut and I've got no reason to apologize? I'm just thanking the Lord that you're alive to apologize to."

"Well, we're both still alive and safe from John or Robert or whatever the hell his name is now. Let's leave it at that."

"Mitch, when I read your story about that bastard holding a knife to your throat I felt so ashamed of myself for running away that I couldn't even pick up the phone and call you. It's taken me this long to work up the nerve to face you."

"You did the right thing," I said. "I did the stupid thing by opening the door without making sure that it was Clarence from the FBI. If I'd used half a brain, the guy never would have gotten inside and my neck would never have been nicked."

I poured us both some iced tea and we sat and talked for nearly an hour. As Zhoumaya was leaving, I invited her to join Martha and me for dinner.

"Oh, no, Mitch, I can't do that," she said. "You and Martha have got a whole week's worth of talk to talk, and whole week's worth of something else to do when you get home from dinner. I'm not going to get in the way of any of that."

I couldn't argue with that, either. Zhoumaya's forecast was right on the mark. Martha and I did a week's worth of talking over our dinner in the restaurant, and then we did our best to catch up on a week's worth of loving when we got back to our bedroom. When we reached a state of exhaustion, sometime past midnight, we agreed to continue our catch-up efforts on the following night.

"We've still got several nights worth of catching up to do," I said.

"And after we catch up, there's no harm in getting a few nights ahead," Martha said. Once again, I couldn't argue with that.

\* \* \*

"YOU LOOK LIKE something the cat dragged in," Al said as he handed me a cup of coffee at my desk Friday morning.

"Martha got home last night," I said. "We sat up half the night talking about everything that happened while she was gone."

"Oh, I'm sure all you did half the night was talk. But please spare me the details. Anything interesting happening here in the world of news reporting today?"

"Not yet. Right now there's nothing new on either the cold case or the current hot case. I'll check with both Brownie and our buddy KGB later this morning, after I do a story that Don gave me at City Hall." I told Al about the previous day's tele-phone encounter with Detective Barnes and he suggested going back to Falcon Heights to nail a copy of the Constitution on the front door of the police station.

"We'd better use tape instead of a nail or she'll charge us with vandalism," I said.

"How tacky of her," Al said.

My call to Brownie netted me a grumpy "good morning," a five-minute canned music concert on hold, and a "have a good day, Mitch." Alaska resident James Bjornquist had not re-sponded to a message Brownie had left on his phone, and the St. Paul PD was no closer to determining the fate of Marilee An-derson than it had been the previous day.

My call to KGB netted me the information that she was in a meeting and wouldn't be discussing the Moustakas murder case with the media on this day. What a surprise.

Thus frustrated in my pursuit of both cold and hot case news, I put on the navy blue blazer I had slung over a corner of my desk and walked up to City Hall to cover a developer's presen-tation to the City Planning Board. The boredom actually felt good after all the action I'd been swept up in during the last few days.

After lunch, I had little to do except shuffle papers and try to look busy when Don glanced my way. I was seriously consid-ering another trip to Falcon Heights just to piss off Detective K.G. Barnes when my phone rang.

The high-pitched voice was so raspy and heavily distorted that I couldn't tell if it was male or female. "I have a tip for you," it said.

"What about?" I asked. I had the awful feeling that this could be another nut like Morrie calling about Russian radar peek-ing into his bathroom, so I wasn't all that interested in the reply.

"Marilee Anderson," said the voice.

Now I was interested.

# Chapter Thirty-Six

## Getting Warm?

W HAT CAN YOU tell me about Marilee Anderson?" I asked. Again, my right hand began searching the desktop for note-taking materials.

"I can tell you where she went," the voice said.

I had pulled a blank sheet of paper out of the pile and was picking up a ballpoint when I said, "Okay, where did she go?"

"Not on the phone."

"She didn't go on the phone?" I hoped my flip response would encourage the caller to keep talking so I could get a better clue to his or her gender.

"Don't act stupid. We need to meet in person."

I thought about Old Hank. "The last person I was supposed to meet in person met up with a sharp knife instead," I said.

"I know," said the voice. The rasp was softening and I had a sense that the caller was female. "I'm not worried about that."

"So where do you want me to meet you?"

"St. Adolphus Church in Minneapolis." The church where Old Hank worked and probably where Helen Hammersley had seen a woman she thought looked like Al's updated photo of Marilee Anderson. "You know where that is?"

"I can find it," I said.

"Come to the small cottage behind the church, on the left side, next to the convent," the voice said in a hoarse whisper. Now I wasn't so sure it was a woman.

"When?" I asked.

"How about today? In two hours?"

I looked at my watch. It was 1:28 p.m. "I can do that. Who do I ask for?"

"You won't have to ask. Just knock on the door at three thirty."

"I'm bringing along my photographer friend."

The caller was silent for a moment before responding. "Okay, bring him. But no pictures." The line went dead.

My feet barely touched the floor as I raced to the city desk to tell Don O'Rourke about this amazing turn of events. Don was as excited as I was to think that the solution to the puzzle he'd tried to solve twenty-five years ago could be only a couple of hours away. He sent me to the photo department to get Al for a planning session and we both returned almost drooling in anticipation.

"You've got to be careful with this," Don said. "Think about what happened to the guy in Falcon Heights. If this case is connected to his murder, the same killer might go after this caller and you might arrive at a very bad time. You should for once do what Detective Brown wants and arrange for a police backup."

"I'll call Brownie and ask him to set up something with the Minneapolis cops," I said. "He might even take a trip across the city line himself to get a first-hand report on what the raspy fake voice tells us."

"You couldn't tell if the raspy fake voice was male or female?" Al asked.

"Not really. I was thinking it was a woman and then it got more masculine."

"Maybe it was the ghost of Old Hank Moustakas. He called me using a raspy fake voice to set up our meeting."

"I don't think Old Hank had a twin," I said. "But come to think of it, Marilee's cousin Lauralee got her death threat from a caller with a raspy fake voice."

"You make damn sure you've got police backup," Don said. "You don't know what you're walking into." I repeated my pledge to set up things with Brownie.

Our next problem was how to get a picture without upsetting our caller. Al decided that the best way was for him to receive a call on his cell phone and take a quick shot as he ended the phone conversation.

"Won't the flash spook him . . . or her?" Don asked.

"I'll turn off the flash," Al said. "We'll have to count on the room having enough light to give us a decent image."

"Who's going to make the call?" I asked.

"I'll make the call," Don said. "We should set up an exact time."

"If the person figures out what Al is doing, he or she might get pissed and throw us out," I said. "Give me enough time to ask some questions before making the phone call." We decided that Don would call at 3:47 p.m., giving us seventeen minutes to get in, get settled, and get some serious answers.

When our skull session ended, I went to my desk and dug my pocket-size tape recorder out of the middle drawer. I loaded it with a fresh tape and put it in my shirt pocket. Next I called Detective Lieutenant Curtis Brown's number. I got his voicemail, telling me to leave a message and he would get back to me.

"That's no good," I said out loud.

"What's no good?" asked Corinne Ramey, whose sensitive ears seemed to pick up everything I said.

"Nothing," I said. "Just muttering to myself."

"Sounded like you were arguing," she said.

"That's debatable," I said.

I called the St. Paul Police Department and asked to speak with any homicide detective but Mike Reilly, knowing I'd get no cooperation from him. After a short wait I heard a click and a voice said, "This is Detective Townsend, how can I help you?"

Perfect. I had previously worked with Terry Townsend, who was a young detective with a bright future, and he had been as helpful as a detective was allowed to be when dealing with the media. I told him I was trying to reach Detective Brown and explained the possibility of our cold case caller in Minneapolis also being connected to the murder in Falcon Heights.

"Detective Brown is away from the office on personal business and won't be back today," Townsend said. "This sounds like you definitely should have a backup and I think I can arrange it. I'll call Minneapolis and request a backup for you at St. Adolphus Church, beginning a few minutes before three thirty. Give me your number and I'll call you when the backup is arranged."

I gave him my cell number and suggested he call that in case we were already on our way to the church before the arrangements were complete.

"You really should wait until we're sure of backup before you leave St. Paul," Townsend said.

"Our appointment is for 3:30 p.m., and believe me, we're not going to be even one minute late," I said.

"I'll work as fast as I can, but do not go into that building until you're absolutely positive that the police have your back."

"Just please get it done before three thirty."

"I'll start the minute that we end this call."

"In that case, goodbye," I said. "And thank you."

"No problem," Townsend said. Aargh! They should make young cops take an etiquette course.

*   *   *

WE HAD NOT received confirmation of a police backup when Al parked the staff car in front of St. Adolphus Church at 3:12 p.m. We scanned the area around us and saw nothing that looked like a police car or a police officer. I checked my cell phone and made sure it was turned on and that the battery was charged. The answer was yes to both.

"Let's look around while we wait for the call," Al said. We got out and walked to the foot of the concrete steps at the front of the church. The stone building was at least sixty feet tall with a gold-colored cross rising from the peak of a pointed dome. The gray construction stone had darkened in splotches over the decades, but the front wall was brightened by a round, twelve-foot-diameter stained-glass window that glowed in the sunshine above massive double doors made of polished oak.

"Impressive," Al said as he photographed the church with his cell phone.

"Imposing," I said as I scribbled a few descriptive words into my notebook.

"Impervious," he said.

"Implausible," I said.

"What do you mean by that?"

"I mean that being this close to an actual solution to the Marilee Anderson case is implausible."

I suggested further exploration, so we turned left, walked past the church, and followed a flagstone path toward the rear of the building. At the end of the path we saw a small cottage that we assumed was our destination. My watch said 3:23 p.m. and we still hadn't received confirmation of a police backup.

"It's getting close," Al said. "Are we knocking on the door at three thirty if we don't have a call about backup?"

"That would be improvident and might prove importune," I said.

"I assume that means we're improvising."

"Your assumption is impeccable. I will knock on the cottage door at three thirty, come hell or high impossibility."

The cottage was a narrow one-story wooden structure painted dark brown, with an even darker brown door and two small milk-chocolate-brown-trimmed windows facing us. Behind the cottage was a patch of grass, with a sidewalk that led to a blacktopped alley. Parked in the alley was a small black Toyota sedan.

I pointed toward the Toyota. "Think that could look as big as a frickin' tank coming toward you?"

"Maybe, if it was going fast enough," Al said.

My watch dial read 3:28 p.m. Still no backup confirmation, and no officers in sight.

"Looks like we're on our own," I said.

"Think we're imperiled?" Al said.

"I know I'm impatient," I said.

"Let's be impetuous," he said.

I turned on the tape recorder in my shirt pocket and we walked to the cottage, where we stood on the doorstep looking at my watch. On the stroke of 3:30 I took a deep breath, seized the brass knocker, and rapped on the door.

The door opened wide enough to reveal the face of a woman with close-clipped blonde hair, and I found myself looking into the most intense pair of blue eyes I had ever seen.

"Marilee Anderson, I presume," I said.

# Chapter Thirty-Seven

## Cold Case Warmed

ITHOUT REPLYING to my Stanleyesque greeting, the woman backed up and opened the door wide enough for us pass through. She closed the door behind us and slid the locking bolt into place.

We were in a small entryway, and our hostess gestured silently toward an archway that led into a living room with windows on two sides, an opening to a hall on the far side, and a narrow open doorway to a combination kitchen-dining area on the other side. The floor was bare pine boards and the furniture consisted of a threadbare beige loveseat, two unpadded straight-backed wooden chairs, a dark wooden coffee table with assorted nicks and scratches, and two tired-looking metal floor lamps. All of the furnishings appeared to be of pre-World War II vintage. No newspapers or magazines cluttered the table and no TV set was in sight. "Spartan" would be a generous adjective to describe the comfort rating of the room.

"Please sit down," the woman said, gesturing toward the love seat. Her natural voice was higher in pitch and much more pleasant than the fake one she'd used on the phone. We sat and waited for further word. She was short, about five-foot-two and slender. Her blonde hair was clipped to a virtual crew cut, with flecks of gray visible at the temples. Her face, with its intense blue eyes, was strikingly similar to the advanced-age picture of Marilee Anderson that Al's friend had created. She was dressed like a scarecrow in a baggy dark blue T-shirt and sloppy khaki slacks that concealed any feminine curves her body might have had.

She seated herself in a wooden chair, facing us across the coffee table before she spoke. "Your assumption is partially correct. My name was Marilee Anderson when I left my parents' home. Now I'm simply called Mary."

"Pleased to meet you, whatever you're called now," I said. "I'm called Mitch; he's called Al."

"I've seen your picture, Mr. Mitchell," Marilee said. "I've been reading your paper with a great deal of interest every day for the past couple of weeks."

"I can imagine that you have," I said. "And I've been writing about your disappearance with a great deal of interest for the past couple of weeks."

"And you've been creating a great deal of public interest in my disappearance. What prompted you to pursue this story in such detail?"

"I have—I mean we—Al and I—have always taken great interest in cases that baffle the police. We like to try to solve them before the police do."

"I'm sure that's very commendable in your line of work," Marilee said. "However, the memories your stories have brought back aren't very pleasant for the subject of this particular unsolved case."

"I'm sorry to have dredged up an unhappy past, but when this all started I assumed, along with everyone else, that you were no longer living. I still pretty much thought that until you opened the door just now."

"You weren't expecting to see me?"

"Not really."

"Who were you expecting to see?"

"I don't really know. Possibly the person who'd given information about you to Henry Moustakas, or maybe the person who killed Henry Moustakas."

"Poor Old Hank," she said. "I feel so sorry for him."

"Do you have any idea who killed him? Or why?"

"No, to both. But I don't think it had anything to do with me. I certainly hope it didn't. I assume you must have other questions on your mind."

"Hundreds," I said. "Let's start with the day your father sent you to the store and you never came back. How about a play-by-play of that day's events?"

"So you can solve the case of the missing East Side teenager before the St. Paul police do?"

"I'd like very much to do that."

"Me, too," Al said.

"Very commendable. All right, I'll tell you about that day, but after that I'm going to ask a big favor of you."

"What's that?" I said.

"You'll find out soon enough," Marilee said. "Anyhow, here goes." She paused to gather her thoughts before she began and I snuck a peek at my watch. It read 3:35 p.m. Twelve minutes until Al's phone would ring and the interview might come to an unpleasant end.

Two of those precious minutes went by as Marilee excused herself to get a drink of water. She offered us drinks as well but we both said we were fine. When she returned from the kitchen she began walking in tight circles in the center of room, head down, looking at the floor as she talked.

"I didn't want to go to the store that morning, but I could see that Papa was very uptight about something and I didn't dare tell him I wouldn't go. My only hope was that Jimmy would be working, and that we could sneak a couple of kisses and play a little touchy-feely if there weren't any people in the store.

"When I was almost at the door of the store, I looked through the glass and saw Jimmy behind the counter. It looked like he was alone and I was just reaching for the door handle when a man I detested, a slimy creep that people called Slick, came around the corner of the store and grabbed me around the waist and pulled me away from the door. I let out a scream and he put one stinking, dirty hand over my mouth and began hauling me up the street. It looked like we were heading toward a big black car that was parked by the fire hydrant a little ways up the block on Arcade Street.

"I was fighting like everything to get away but Slick was really strong. He kept towing me along with one hand clamped over my mouth and I couldn't get loose. He told me to shut up, said that I was his girl from now on, that my father had given me to him to keep. Then all of a sudden Jimmy was there, trying to pull me away, and Slick had to take the hand off my mouth to fight with Jimmy. I starting screaming like crazy and fighting with Slick until Slick swung his fist and hit me right in the face, just below my eye, and I fell on the sidewalk with him still holding me with the other hand.

"I didn't know what was happening except Slick finally let go of me and I rolled away and got up. That must have been when Jimmy bit him, like he told you in your story. Jimmy yelled at me to run and I took off across Arcade Street as fast as I could go. I looked back once and saw Slick running after Jimmy waving a knife, and that scared me more so I ran even faster. I ran until I saw the church where Mama took me to Mass whenever she could make me go. I went up the front steps and tried the front door and it was open. I went in and ran down the center aisle looking for a place to hide. I went all the way around past the altar and ducked into one of the confessionals.

"I sat in there and caught my breath and started crying and wondering what to do. I didn't know if Slick had killed Jimmy and was looking for me or what. All I could think of was what he'd said about me being his to keep because Papa had given me to him. That meant I couldn't go home or Papa would give me back to him, and I'd heard about what Slick did with his girls. I was bawling my eyes out and Father Paul must have heard me because he knocked on the confessional door and asked if I needed help. Oh, Lord in heaven, did I ever need help.

"I came flying out of the confessional and just threw myself at Father Paul. He wrapped his arms around me and held me and told me everything would be okay and finally I stopped crying. He asked me what had happened and I told him that Papa had given me to Slick and that I got away and that I couldn't go home, and then I started bawling again. I just wanted to crawl in a hole somewhere where nobody could find me, not Slick or Papa or even Jimmy."

Marilee stopped walking and looked up. I saw tears glistening in the corners of those intense blue eyes. "I need another drink. Sorry," she said, and she walked briskly to the kitchen. When she returned, she resumed her head-down circling and her narrative.

"Father Paul managed to calm me down again, and when I'd stopped crying, he walked me into a little room in the back of the church and had me sit in a chair. He said he knew of a place where I might be able to go for a day or so to be safe from my father and from Slick. He got on the phone and talked for a long time with somebody, and then when he finished he said he could take me to a safe place in Minneapolis. He said they'd let me stay there for as long as I needed to hide from Papa and Slick, and that nobody would tell anybody where I was unless I said it was okay.

"We got in his car and he drove me over here, to St. Adolphus. There's a convent next to this cottage—you maybe saw it before you knocked—and Father Paul took me in there and we were met by a nun named Sister Cecilia. She hugged me and said they had an empty room that I could use for the night, and longer if I thought I needed it. I said I thought I would need it longer, because I couldn't go back where Slick or my father could get hold of me. She said I could stay until we could work out some safe place for me to go, to some relative or something.

"The only relatives I had were Uncle Eddie and Aunt Rose. Uncle Eddie lived right next door to us so I couldn't go there, and anyway I didn't like him because he was always putting his hands where they didn't belong. I was afraid to go to Aunt Rose because I knew that she'd call my mother or that Lauralee would open her big mouth and blab to some of her friends that I was hiding at their house. So I was pretty much stuck, and they let me stay here even after the cops and my parents stopped hunting for me. I didn't know that Papa had killed Slick so I was still afraid of him, too. After I'd been here awhile, some of the nuns started taking turns home-schooling me so I wouldn't be a dummy all my life. I just stayed and stayed and the nuns took care of getting me clothes and books and anything else that I needed.

"When I was eighteen, they gave me a job in the office working for Father Joseph. I've worked with him ever since, and I love my job and I love the people here. Father Joseph has been really good and loving to me all these years. And don't get any wrong ideas. When I said loving, I didn't mean anything sexual. Father Joseph is gay. When I was—"

Al's cell phone rang. "Oh, sorry," he said. He took the phone out of his pocket, answered it and talked for about thirty seconds before saying goodbye. He was facing Marilee when he ended the call and the way he held the phone I was sure he'd taken a picture. Marilee didn't seem to notice.

"I'm awfully sorry to interrupt you like that," Al said. "I'll turn this thing off so it doesn't ring again." He held the phone up toward Marilee as he turned it off and I suspected he had snuck another picture.

"That's all right," Marilee said. "I was almost done. All I was going to say was that when I was a little older, they moved me into this cottage with a retired nun who was ninety-some years old. I took care of her for a couple of years until she died, and I've stayed here in the cottage ever since." She let out a sigh of exhaustion and sat down in one of the wooden chairs.

"Don't you ever get out into the world?" I asked.

"Sometimes I go for walks or do some shopping close by, but not very often. And when I do, I always wear dark glasses and a big hat or a hood so nobody really sees my face. I was leaving the church to come back here when that woman in one of your stories saw me. She saw my eyes because I was barely out the church door and hadn't put the dark glasses on yet."

Another question popped into my mind. "Jimmy and Lauralee both said you were pregnant when you left. You haven't said anything about the baby. What happened to that baby?"

Marilee sighed again. "The baby never made it. I had a miscarriage a few days after I got here. The poor baby probably got hurt while I was fighting with Slick. I intentionally left that part out of what I told you. Please don't put it in your story." The intense blue eyes stared unblinking into mine.

"I guess I can skip that detail. But tell me, after all these years of hiding, what caused you to meet with us now?" I asked.

"When I saw your story about talking to Jimmy, it seemed like you were getting so close that you would eventually find me. It looked like you would never give up until you did. So I called you to tell you my story in return for the favor I mentioned before."

"And what is the favor?"

"I don't ever want to be found. I want you both to promise never to tell anybody where I am, where this conversation took place. I love my life here and I don't want to be dragged back to St. Paul to see my old mush-mouth mother who let Papa scream at me and whip my ass while he got his rocks off with me laying naked across his lap."

"I understand your feelings, but keeping your whereabouts secret might not be so easy," I said. "The St. Paul detective who's been hunting for you for twenty-five years will do everything he can to make me talk."

"Isn't there some short of shield law that says reporters can't be forced to reveal their sources?" she said.

"I don't know if that would apply here. This would be a matter of where you are, not who you are."

"So you won't keep my secret?"

"I'll try to, but I can't guarantee it."

Marilee turned to Al. "What about you?"

"Same thing," he said. "I won't tell anybody, but if it goes to court and it comes down to a choice of telling or going to jail, I'm certainly not going to choose jail."

"I guess all we can say is that we'll do our very best," I said.

Marilee bowed her head and was silent for a moment before she said, "I should have known better than to call you. I should have taken my chances on not being found, but first Old Hank called you and then Jimmy. I got really scared."

That puzzled me. "How does Old Hank fit into this?"

"Old Hank was the church janitor and he saw me almost every day for the Lord knows how many years. When he called Mr. Jeffrey to set up a meeting, he used a phone in the church office. I overhead him talking and realized that he had pegged me from that picture you ran showing what I look like now. That really got me worried; I didn't want the old fart to rat on me."

"Oh, my God!" Al said. "Did you kill Old Hank?"

"No, I did," said a female voice behind us.

# Chapter Thirty-Eight

## Sister Jonathan

ARILEE'S EYES WIDENED and her mouth fell open in surprise as she shot up from her chair. I snapped my head around so fast I heard my neck bones crack. Or maybe it was Al's neck bones that I heard, as his head had whipped around just as snappily.

The words that astonished us had come from a short, stocky woman with tinges of gray in her close-cropped black hair. She had an oval face ending with a squared-off chin, a prominent nose, and dark eyes that flashed as menacingly as Jack Nicholson's in *The Shining.* She was dressed all in black—a short-sleeved pullover top that hung outside loose-fitting, ankle-length slacks that brushed the tops of leather running shoes.

"Sister Jonathan!" Marilee said. Her tone indicated that she was as stunned as Al and I were.

*Oh, my God, a Jonathan Doe,* I thought. Funny how the mind works in a moment of surprise. I got up from the love seat, Al rose beside me, and we turned to face the newcomer.

"Missy Mary, I've been listening to you babbling away, spilling out your whole life story to these two, and I decided it was time to step in," Sister Jonathan said. "Didn't I tell you that you were a fool to invite them here? Now they're going to expose you to the whole world, and this place will be swarming with cops and TV cameras and reporters from all over hell and gone."

Marilee was still staring slack-jawed and wide-eyed, as if she'd been struck by lightning. She regained control of her jaw and said, "Did you . . . did you just say that you killed Old Hank?"

"That's what I said," Sister Jonathan said. "It was the only way to shut him up."

To me, Marilee said. "I begged him and begged him to cancel the meeting with you, and he finally promised to call it off."

"But he didn't keep his promise," Sister Jonathan said. "He didn't intend to shut up like her cousin did after I called her. I went to his house that morning to make sure that he'd canceled the meeting, and he laughed at me. He said there was a reward for information about her and that I'd have to cut his throat to keep him from talking to the press. Well, I wasn't tall enough to reach his throat, but I still had the last laugh."

I finally found my voice. "Wait a minute. You're a nun and you went out and killed a man?"

"She's not really a sister," Marilee said. "She's Father Joseph's housekeeper. Her last name is Jonathan and we all call her Sister because she's been living in the convent with the nuns for so long."

"Twenty-six years," Sister Jonathan said. "I was here when this one came in as a green, ignorant, teenage dolly, and I've taught her all about the pleasures of life."

"Meaning what?" Al asked.

"Meaning that I've been her lover for twenty-five years," Sister Jonathan said. "She told me she had a boyfriend back in St. Paul, but I taught her about real happiness—being a woman with another woman."

"Whoa, that's way more information than we need," I said. "On the other hand, you've just confessed to a cold-blooded killing, which is something we definitely can't keep secret."

"I know you can't," she said. "That's another reason why the two of you are going to be the ones who disappear this time."

"You're going to try to stab both of us?" Al said. He shuffled sideways, creating six feet of space between us.

"No, I'm going to shoot both of you." She reached behind her back and pulled a shiny handgun out of her waistband. Naturally, the gun was also black.

Marilee screamed.

"Shut up, you silly goose," Sister Jonathan said. "We can't let these two worthless hacks tear our lives apart." She waggled the gun back and forth. It was a revolver with a barrel opening that looked as big around as a bagel.

"No, no, you can't kill them," Marilee said. Tears began streaming down her cheeks. "I can't believe you want to kill them. Old Hank's death was bad enough. You can't—"

Sister Jonathan cut her off. "Shut your face, I said. It's the only way to save what we've had all these years."

"I don't want to save it that way," Marilee said. I was definitely on her side.

"We have no choice. They know we killed Old Hank. Or that I killed him for your sake." She turned toward me. "I killed him to keep our secret and because I love Missy Mary and I need her love."

"No," Marilee said. "I can't love you anymore if you kill these men. I'll give up my secret. I'll tell everyone the truth. Let these men go and get yourself away somewhere. I'll hate you if you kill them." Again, I was on her side.

"You don't know what you're saying," Sister Jonathan said. "We'll talk about it when I'm done with them. You'll see how much you need me, how you can't live without my warm body on yours and my—"

"I'll never let you touch me again," Marilee shouted. "Never, never, never."

"We'll see about that, Missy Mary," Sister Jonathan said. "Now, gentlemen, if you'll turn and face the back door, we're going for a little ride. One of you will even get to drive so I can keep Little Remmy here pointed at the other one's head."

"Little Remmy?" Al said. "You call your gun Little Remmy?"

"It's a Remington Special," she said. "Because it's so special, I gave it a special name. Now, both of you get your butts in gear to the back door. Don't make me mess up the cottage with a lot of blood."

"Might be hard to talk your way out of committing a mass murder in here," I said.

"Oh, I've got a great story cooked up in case you make me shoot you here. All about how you two apes were assaulting poor helpless Missy Mary here, and I had to save her from a gang rape."

"Missy Mary" still stood in front of her chair, sobbing. She bent at the waist, her head hanging down and her hands covering her face. Between sobs she was saying the word "stop" over and over again.

Al and I walked toward the back door, with Sister Jonathan keeping a careful distance behind us. As we reached the door, I felt my silenced cell phone vibrate in my pocket. I wondered who could be calling but I didn't think it was a good time to reach into my pocket. I didn't want to do anything that might startle Sister Jonathan and cause her left index finger to jerk tight on the trigger.

I opened the door and stepped out onto a blacktop path, followed by Al and then by Sister Jonathan. At Sister Jonathan's command, Al moved up beside me. I was looking for a chance to grab Little Remmy, but its holder was staying just far enough away to make such a move suicidal.

We were facing the black sedan parked in the alley. "Go to the car," Sister Jonathan said. "Mitchell, you drive. You with the cell phone camera, get in the front passenger seat. I'll be in the backseat with the gun pointed at your head, and I'll take that cell phone once we're in the car. I saw you sneaking pictures of my Missy Mary, even if she was too dumb to catch you."

We'd taken about three steps when a uniformed police officer appeared in the alley, stepping from behind the car. He looked startled to see us, but he quickly snapped to attention and yelled, "Hold it right there."

The cop's hand was moving toward his weapon when a gunshot exploded beside my left ear. The officer crashed to the ground, landing on his back in front of the car. I turned my head and saw the gun barrel only inches away. I was starting to reach for it when a flying body hit Sister Jonathan from behind and knocked her down onto her knees. The attacker, who I realized was Marilee Anderson, clung to the fallen woman's back, and Al and I piled on beside her.

Another gunshot went off in front of my face but I could see that the barrel was pointed toward the sky. Nobody hit with that shot. I reached out, grabbed the barrel, and started pulling and twisting it. Either Al or Marilee slammed Sister Jonathan's face into the blacktop and the gun finally came out of her hand. I flung Little Remmy as far as I could and the four of us wrestled on the blacktop for a minute.

A large body appeared above us, and then another. Both were wearing blue uniforms. I rolled out of the pile and yelled to them that their officer was down. One of them ran to the cop on the ground while the other separated Al and Sister Jonathan. Marilee was no longer in the pile—or in sight.

Sister Jonathan's nose was bleeding and her lips were bruised and bloody. She and Al both started to get up, but the officer ordered them to stay on the ground and drew his weapon as a persuasion. I was already standing and he ordered me to my knees.

"Al and I are the good guys, Officer," I said as I complied. "She shot your man."

"Just everybody stay where you are 'til we sort this out," the cop said. He spoke into the radio on his shoulder and a fourth officer soon came running up.

"Jerry's down," said the first officer, pointing toward the fallen cop. "Tom's with him, calling for an ambulance. This guy claims the woman shot Jerry. I don't really know what the hell's going on."

"I can tell you what's going on," I said. "Let me show you my ID. Al and I are the people you were sent here to protect. The woman was taking us away at gunpoint when your man appeared. She shot him, and we were able to jump her in the confusion. I got the gun away and threw it over there somewhere. You'll find her fingerprints on the butt and the trigger, and mine on the barrel."

While the cop's attention was on me, Sister Jonathan started to crawl away. She had risen to one knee when Al lunged after her and grabbed her right foot. The sound of the scrabble turned the officer's attention back to them and he yelled, "Hold it right there, lady, you ain't going nowhere. All of you, on your knees with your hands on your head."

Sister Jonathan stopped, Al released her ankle, and we all became quiet, waiting for the ambulance. With the officer's permission, I slowly reached into my pocket and took out my cell phone to see who had called as we were leaving the cottage with Little Remmy at our backs. I found a voice message from Detective Terry Townsend. "Hi, Mitch," he said. "This is to inform you that the police backup is in place. It's safe for you to enter the cottage now."

# Chapter Thirty-Nine

## Missing Person

A S LONG AS WE'VE lived together, Martha and I have been dining with Al and Carol Jeffrey and their kids, Kevin and Kristin, on Friday nights. We normally start the party with snacks at about 5:30 p.m., but on this Friday Al and I didn't get there until everyone else was finishing their slices of Carol's fresh-baked apple pie.

It took the rest of the afternoon for the police officers at the scene to get the situation resolved to their satisfaction. First priority, of course, was taking care of the wounded officer. Everything else was put on hold until Jerry, who was officially described as "alert and responding," had been loaded into an ambulance and sent on his way to the hospital. The flesh wound in the inner part of Jerry's upper right thigh was described by one of the attending EMTs as "not life threatening, but awful damn close to his right nut."

Once Jerry was on his way, an officer named Adam Olsen, who seemed to be in command, had Sister Jonathan, Al, and me escorted into the cottage. We were allowed to sit down while Olsen looked at our *Daily Dispatch* IDs and questioned us about the events that led up to the backyard shooting and wrestling match.

When Olsen was satisfied with our description of the pre-shooting activity, he called for Sister Jonathan to be handcuffed and taken to the police station. She complained loudly, insisted that I had done the shooting, and put up a momentary struggle when the handcuffs were being snapped on. Little Remmy had been retrieved and placed in an evidence bag, and it was taken away by the officers escorting Sister Jonathan.

"We'll be needing statements from you two, along with a statement from this Marilee Anderson you said you were interviewing," Olsen said. "Where is she?"

Where, indeed? We hadn't seen Marilee since the battle with Sister Jonathan had been broken up by the cops.

"She lives in this cottage," I said. "Maybe she's hiding in the bedroom."

Two police officers searched the bedroom, the bathroom, the kitchen, and the perimeter of the cottage with negative results. Next they searched the convent, to no avail. That left the church, which they combed completely under the guidance of a very distraught Father Joseph. Still no Marilee.

"Ain't that the shits?" Al said. "After twenty-five years we find her, and bam! She vanishes again right before our eyes."

"The foot is faster than the eye," I said.

"At least I got two pictures to prove we actually saw her. Unless she's like a vampire and the images aren't there." He took out his cell phone and checked. "Not a vampire. We got her."

"Don O'Rourke will be happy, anyway," I said. "I'm not so sure about Brownie. He'll probably accuse us of letting her get away."

"Maybe she'll hide in another Catholic church. If we check around, we might find her in one."

"I'd rather let the case go cold again. What's the point of dragging Marilee back for a media spectacular?"

"I'll go along with that. Let the frost begin to form right after our story and pix run in the *Daily Dispatch*."

We followed Olsen's squad car to the police station, where we were separated and interrogated all over again. When the questions were finished and our statements were printed and signed, we took the staff car back to the *Daily Dispatch* garage.

Al went to the photo department to do his thing while I told Fred Donlin, the night city editor, what we had. An hour later, I had finished writing the story and it was posted in the on-line edition along with Al's pix of Marilee and a couple of shots of the scene in the backyard at St. Adolphus.

I had called Martha during the ride to the Minneapolis police station and told her it would take us until well after dinner-time to wrap up our cold case coverage. She promised to keep our dinner warm, and when Al and I finally got to our place on Lexington Avenue, we received a warm greeting as well.

"What's with your ear?" Martha asked as our lips parted from her long, luscious welcoming kiss.

"It's finally stopped ringing and I can hear with it again," I said.

"I mean, what's the brown spot on the edge?" She grasped my left ear with her thumb and forefinger and examined it closely. "It looks like a burn." She sniffed. "And it smells like gunpowder."

"My God, was it that close when she fired?" I said.

"Who fired?" Martha said. "What fired? Who's she?"

"It's a long story. Al and I will give you all the details about how hot our cold case got after we've finished that food you've been keeping warm."

*   *   *

THE NEXT MORNING, I was putting the final touches on a follow story about Friday's fracas when my phone rang. It was Brownie.

"I see you let another one get away," he said.

"I told Al that you'd say that," I said. "But you can't blame us for this one. There were at least eight Minneapolis cops on the scene when Marilee did her disappearing act. She vanished right under the long nose of the law."

"Is the long nose of the press going to go looking for her?"

"As far as I'm concerned, the case can go cold again. We know what happened twenty-five years ago, and we know where she went and where she's been all this time. I don't need to know anything else."

"I thought you reporters kept going until the end of the story," Brownie said.

"In my book, yesterday was the end of the story," I said. "What about you?"

"This time her disappearance isn't in my jurisdiction. Let Minneapolis hunt for her if they want to. I'm out of it."

"I can't see them putting much effort into finding her. They've got Sister Jonathan in custody and they've got a copy of my tape of her telling us that she killed Henry Moustakas. They really don't need Marilee's statement. If they do look for her I'll write about the search, but I'm not going to try to find her on my own."

"I guess it's over, then," Brownie said. "Case closed after twenty-five years."

"Case closed after twenty-five years and three dead bodies," I said. "Slick the pimp, Jack Anderson the desperate daddy, and poor Old Hank the greedy janitor."

"May they all rest in peace. Have a good day, Mitch," said Brownie.

I was stacking things up on my desk, getting ready to go home, when Al appeared beside my desk. "So is the Marilee Anderson cold case officially wrapped up and put away?" he asked.

"Looks that way," I said. "There is one little thing that kind of leaves me wondering, though."

"What's that?"

"The M.E. said he was sure that Old Hank was stabbed by a right-handed person, didn't he?"

"Yeah, I think so."

"Well, what bothers me is that Sister Jonathan carried her gun and fired it with her left hand."

"That's right." I could almost see the wheels turning in Al's brain for a moment before he said, "Oh, God, you don't think she was covering up for . . ."

"I don't know. I'm only saying . . ."

Al shook his head. "Are you going to follow up and talk to the cops about it?"

"No, I'm done chasing Marilee Anderson. But I definitely will follow Sister Jonathan's case and watch her trial."

"Could be very interesting."

"Could be."

Al turned and walked away. Before I could follow him, my phone rang again.

"Hello, Mr. Mitchell, this is Andrew Miller," the caller said.

I couldn't place him. "Who?" I asked.

"Andrew Miller. I live next door to the Andersons. Or just Jill now, I guess."

"Oh, sure, now I remember. Your grandmother helped me find the Andersons when they went up north to the lake."

"That's right. And it's my grandmother that I'm calling about."

I remembered that she was ninety-one and frail. "I hope she's all right," I said.

"Oh, she's great," Miller said. "In fact, she's getting married to the card player you introduced her to."

"Married? Those two are getting married? In the nursing home?" Here was a great story for Monday: Eleanor Miller, ninety-one, to wed Adelbert Love, ninety-five.

"He has to remind her about it every day, but by God, they're getting officially hitched tomorrow," Miller said. "Grandma's like a teenage kid every time they talk about it. I'm just calling to invite you and your photographer buddy to the wedding, and to say thank you for getting them together."

"You're welcome," I said. I like to set a good example.

THE END

243

## Acknowledgements

My thanks to forensics expert Dr. E.P. Lyle for advice on the probable condition of a buried body in an unusual location after a certain number of years.